THE GREAT ESCAPE

Recent Titles by Leo Kessler from Severn House

Writing as Leo Kessler

S.S.Wotan Series

Battle for Hitler's Eagle's Nest
The Bormann Mission
Breakout from Stalingrad
Death's Eagles
Death from the Arctic Sky
Flight from Berlin
Operation Fury
Operation Glenn Miller
The Hitler Werewolf Murders
Stalag Assault
Wotan Missions

The Churchill Papers
Patton's Wall
The Screaming Eagles

Writing as Duncan Harding

Assault on St Nazaire
Attack New York!
Operation Judgement

Sink the Ark Royal
Sink the Bismarck
Sink the Cossack
Sink the Graf Spee
Sink the Prince of Wales
Sink the Tirpitz
The Tobruk Rescue

THE GREAT ESCAPE

Leo Kessler

This first world edition published in Great Britain 2002 by
SEVERN HOUSE PUBLISHERS LTD of
9-15 High Street, Sutton, Surrey SM1 1DF.
This first world edition published in the USA 2002 by
SEVERN HOUSE PUBLISHERS INC of
595 Madison Avenue, New York, N.Y. 10022.

British Library Cataloguing in Publication Data

Kessler, Leo, 1926-
   The great escape
   1. World War, 1939-1945 – Campaigns – Fiction
   2. War stories
   I. Title
   823.9'14 [F]

ISBN 0-7278-5665-0

Except where actual historical events and characters are being
described for the storyline of this novel, all situations in this
publication are fictitious and any resemblance to living persons
is purely coincidental.

Typeset by Hewer Text Ltd.,
Edinburgh, Scotland.
Printed and bound in Great Britain by
MPG Books Ltd., Bodmin, Cornwall.

No escape story of the Second World War was more daring in concept, more fantastic, more ambitious, more hopelessly fanatical than that of prisoners of D . . . It began with a bold master plan for a mass breakout of German POWs from prison camps in wartime Britain.

Col. Scotland, Head of British POW Interrogation Service, 1945

Another aspect of the Germans' thorough plans was the amazing scheme, somehow transmitted to Britain, for a breakout of German prisoners of war . . . It has still not been explained. We *do* know that the German prisoners began organizing for a mass breakout. They actually plotted to seize arsenals, obtain tanks and actually prepare for German landings in England.

Capt. Robert Merriam, Intelligence Officer, US 9th Army, 1947

Today only an ageing few remember all their effort and suffering. By and large the young fanatics who sought to stem the tide of Germany's defeat moulder in English soil, forgotten by history.

Charles Whiting: The March on London

PRELUDE:

MURDER FOR A CAUSE

'*A* CHTUNG!' Black One hissed, as they heard the crisp sound of bootnails on the gravel path outside. 'The warm brother is coming . . . Ready you Greys?'

The Greys, nervous, tense and unsure of themselves, raised their home-made clubs. They were all boys, captured in the summer in Normandy. Most of them had never fired a shot in anger. Black One, standing well into the shadows cast by the low tin ceiling of the big latrine, thought it was high time they were 'blooded'. After all, time was running out fast.

The footsteps came closer. Black One peered carefully over the low partitition. As was the Warm Brother's habit, the digusting pervert, he'd head for the six-man crapper at the far end of the big latrine. There he could play his disgusting, treacherous little games more safely. 'Remember,' he warned the Greys, 'you all strike *together*! That way you're all guilty and no one can point the finger at anyone else.' He gave a harsh little laugh; it wasn't a pleasant sound. 'That way no one can turn traitor against the others. Clear?'

'Clear, *Scharführer*,' the Greys echoed nervously.

Soon it would be 'lights out' and Black One knew they and their victim didn't have much time left before they were banged up for the night at Devizes POW camp. But the 'Warm Brother' and they had picked this time specifically when there'd be few POWs about and their Tommy guards would be preparing to finish for the day. Still it would be nip-and-tuck. The Greys would have to act fast. There was no time for nerves now. He fingered the home-made knife in the back pocket of his dyed-blue British battledress. If there was any hesitation, he'd strike

3

the first blow and then the rest of them could finish the treacherous bastard off.

Again he peered above the partition. The victim had definitely slowed. Perhaps he sensed something? Black One dismissed that alarming thought from his mind almost as soon as it had come. Of course, the Warm Brother hadn't; he couldn't. No, the Warm Brother was probably looking for his contact: that cunning old Tommy bastard, Old Tin Leg.

Now the victim was almost at the door of the main latrine. Here he'd pause, as they all did, unless they had the 'thin shits' and were in a great hurry. The stink from the privy always struck him across the face like a blow from a wet smelly palm and made him gasp.

The lookout in the main privy gave his poor imitation of a loud, juicy, satisfying fart. It was the signal. At the same time it was aimed at making the Warm Brother feel safe and not totally alone in the dark smelly surroundings of the camp latrine.

Black One grunted. His Greys tensed. He couldn't see their faces in the gloom, but he *could* feel their tension. 'Remember,' he hissed as the Warm Brother commenced making his way to the smaller crapper, 'this is an act of war. You are doing this for Folk, Fatherland and Führer.'

There was a subdued murmur of '*Jawohl, Scharführer*'. Then absolute silence, save for the sound of their own tense breathing. It was now or never.

'Come on, come on, you perverted banana-sucker,' Black One urged to himself, his big fists clasped white-knuckled together with pent-up tension. The Greys didn't know the real reason for what they were going to do. They thought they were going to kill a homosexual queer who was selling information to the Tommies for the goodies with which he could buy the sexual favours he craved. But there was more to it.

He broke off. The lookout had given another of his juicy, not unmusical farts. It was the signal that the Warm Brother had passed. Now it was his turn to act. The big SS non-com, code-named 'Black One', stepped into the narrow aisle between the thunderboxes, 'Corporal Hardt!' he snapped.

Hardt jumped as if he had been shot. Even in the growing gloom, Black One could see how he turned ashen with fear. Contemptuously the SS non-com told himself the traitor and queer had creamed his drawers even before he had seated himself on the thunderbox. 'Yes,' he quavered, trying to penetrate the gloom. '*Was ist los?*'

'*Der Teufel ist los!*'* Black One growled back. 'Grab him men!'

Before Hardt had time to run, the Greys had come out of the sides and grabbed him. In the same instant Black One emerged from his hiding place and, without the slightest hesitation, slapped the shocked corporal right across the face so that his glasses tumbled from his short-sighted eyes and fell to the ground. Deliberately the SS non-com ground them to bits under the heel of his steel-shod, highly polished jackboot.

Black One wasted no time. Already he could hear the guard marching up outside, approaching the main gate to the German camp, with the guard commander snapping in that strange Tommy fashion of giving orders, 'Bags o' swank now . . . Show them Jerry bastards what real soldiers are like . . . Remember who yer are . . . bags o'swank!'

His face contorted in disdain momentarily. Then he remembered the job at hand. He stared hard at the prisoner. 'Well Mr Warm Brother,' he said in a jaunty mocking tone, 'how does it feel now? To be a prisoner of the people you have constantly betrayed?'

Around Hardt, the Greys growled menacingly. The former, however, tried to bluster it out. 'What do you mean, *Scharführer?*' he protested. 'I have never betrayed anyone. I might be a White, but I can swear on my mother's head—' His protest ended in a howl of pain, as Black One punched him in the guts with a fist like a small pile-driver.

'Don't lie to me, you slime-shitter,' the SS non-com snarled. 'We know all about those cosy little meetings with that cunning Tommy swine, Old Tin Leg.'

* 'What's up . . . The devil's up!' *Transl.*

'I never—' Hardt's protest was stopped once again when Black One punched him. Now his body slumped forward suddenly, as if all the fight had gone from him. Big sad tears started to roll down his wan cheeks. 'What are you going to do with me?' he asked in a choked voice.

For a moment or two Black One didn't answer. He was listening. Not only to the Tommy guard commander who was screeching in that English fashion, '*H'order arms . . . stand at ease . . . stand easy*', but also to the sound the lookout made as he removed the wooden top from the crapper.

'Do with you?' he echoed after a moment. 'Nothing much.' He forced a smile, but there was no warmth in the smile and his steely blue eyes remained as hard and arrogant as ever. 'Just ask you a few questions. That's all . . . If you answer them truthfully and then promise to keep your trap shut to the Tommies about them afterwards, you can go back to your hut.'

The relief on Hardt's ashen face was obvious, but those of the Greys looked as tense and hate-filled as ever. Black One was pleased. He had put some stiffener into their backs, that was for sure. From now onwards, they'd do whatever he said, especially after . . . But he didn't think that particular overwhelming thought to its logical conclusion. Instead he snapped, very businesslike now, 'All right, what did you tell that cunning old Tommy bastard?'

Hardt seemed to hesitate and Black One snarled, 'We haven't all the time in the world. Piss or get off the pot. It'll be all the worse for you, Hardt, if you don't come clean at once.'

Hardt swallowed hard, his Adam's apple going up and down his scrawny throat like an express lift. 'Just answered a few questions about the . . . er . . . morale in the camp, that's all,' he admitted reluctantly.

'*Morale!*' Black One couldn't resist the sneer. 'You mean you told him who the camp's ringleaders are, didn't you, you treacherous bastard!'

'No, I didn't—' the corporal's protest ended in a yelp of pain, as Black One reached out and slapped him across the cheek hard. Up in his stall, the lookout had finished removing the crapper's seat; the privy was ready and waiting. Beyond, the guard commander was detailing off his men: 'You Jones 75, you'll lock up Hut One . . . Privates Earl and Whiting – Whiting, are you listening to me, you pregnant penguin? – you'll take two. Watch them Jerry bastards haven't concealed somebody under the frigging floorboards agen. Them Blacks are real pains in the arse.'

Black One told himself they had three or four minutes at the most before the guard commander turned his men loose on the huts; he couldn't waste much more time on the traitor. He'd have to get to the core of the problem worrying him straight away.

'All right, Hardt, here's your last chance. Answer this one honestly and you can make yourself out of the dust.'* He grinned at the tense Greys. They knew what kind of dust the traitor was going to make soon.

'Anything . . . just let me go, *Scharführer*.' The corporal's voice was near to breaking now.

'*Schon gut*.' Now Black One wasted no more time. 'What do they know about our plan?'

'Your plan—'

The SS non-com hit him across the face. He would have fallen, but for the Greys holding Hardt. 'Don't play games with me, you damned pervert. Answer the question,' Black One snapped. 'What do the Tommies know?' His face was full of menace now and all the others were growling threateningly, as if they were realising for the first time just what a swine the terrified prisoner was: betraying his own comrades like this.

Hardt swallowed the copper-tasting blood which had flooded his cut mouth. Thickly he said, 'Nothing. I swear to you, the English know nothing. I didn't know much about –' he lowered his gaze momentarily, unable to meet Black One's fervent, menacing look – 'about it myself. I just indicated that something funny was going on here – and Tin-Leg already knew that.'

* In German: *Aus dem Staub machen* – to go away. Transl.

7

'Did you – or he – name names?'

Out of the gloom to the rear of the tense little group, the lookout had appeared noiselessly. He raised his thumb in the English gesture. Everything was ready.

'No . . . no . . . I swear it. No names, *Scharführer*,' the prisoner quavered. 'I wouldn't do that . . . for anything . . . not betray the names of my comrades—' He broke off suddenly and Black One looked at his battledress trousers in disgust. Hardt had pissed himself with fear.

'Are you sure?'

'Yes . . . yes . . . I swear I didn't name anyone, *Scharführer*.'

The latter flashed a look at the green-glowing dial of his Wehrmacht wristwatch, which he had been able to smuggle through the various searches after he was shot and captured with the *Hitlerjugend* at Caen, back in July. One minute to go before they were banged up. He nodded to the Greys. They had been well briefed, greenhorns with their spoons still wet that they were. They shoved the prisoner forward, two of them twisting his arms behind his skinny back cruelly. 'What—'

Black One hit him again and he fell silent. They pushed him down the stinking aisle. Suddenly his eyes opened very wide with absolute horror. He saw for the first time the open privy and the loathsome yellow mess below writhing with white maggots. 'No,' he screamed, realising what was going to happen, eyes bulging from his head like those of a man demented. '*NO!*'

With a grunt Black One pushed him forward. The others tensed with their clubs. The lookout seized the long squeegee used to clean the floor of the latrine. Desperately the prisoner grabbed for the hessian sacking between the cubicles. It ripped in his hands. Then the pack of Greys were upon him, thrusting and beating, grunting like wild animals in at the kill.

Eyes wide and wild with horror, the prisoner started back into the open privy. The lookout thrust forward the heavy squeegee. It caught Hardt in his skinny chest. He staggered back, desperately trying to save himself. To no avail. He fell over the side. The yellow filth shot upwards. With a muffled curse the SS non-com jumped back. The prisoner went under, while the Greys stood poised with the clubs raised, chests heaving as if they were running a great race.

Hardt came up again. He was covered with ordure. When he gasped for breath, his mouth bubbled an obscene yellow, his teeth abruptly a brilliant white. Feverishly he tried to claw his way out. He didn't have a chance. Crazed with rage and fear, the Greys started to hammer him with their clubs. The lookout joined in with his squeegee. Farting continually for some unknown reason, he brought the heavy instrument down on the corporal's hands as they clasped the side of the dripping privy which he tried to pull himself out. He screamed and disappeared under once more, bubbles belching to the surface as the air escaped from his lungs.

He came up again, with an obscene squelching noise. Meaningless noises came from his bright red lips. It was like a fish appearing on the surface before it died.

Black One nodded to the lookout. He needed no urging. His eyes sparkled fanatically. He slammed the instrument down once more. It smacked against Hardt's skull. There was the sound of bone crunching and cracking. Hardt's head shot to one side. His eyes rolled till only the whites showed. He was dying and unconscious. His head slumped forward, chin first. The obscene liquid reached to his mouth. Still he did nothing to fight it, as the gasping Greys ceased their terrible beating. Awed and frightened, they watched as he let it flow into his gaping mouth. Someone started to retch. A moment later he was vomiting violently.

The head sank below the surface. For a few moments bubbles of trapped air exploded there. A pale weak hand surfaced, its fingers jerked convulsively. The lookout raised his squeegee. There was no need. The hand disappeared the next instant. A moment or two later, the yellow surface of that terrible pit was completely without movement. Wordlessly the Greys began to replace the boards.

BOOK ONE:

A WHITE MAN'S ARMY

One

A dolf Hitler looked up at the scar-faced giant and his pallid features softened. All around, his general staff officers were filing out of the briefing hut to set about the morning's duties. Outside, the heavily armed SS guards, who were everywhere these days since the attempted assassination of the Führer the previous July, were clicking to attention. But their eyes were still suspicious. At the 'Wolf's Lair' no one trusted anyone these days, even the Führer's top generals. Anyone and everyone, whatever his rank, could be a traitor.

As Colonel-General Jodl, Hitler's chief of operations, went out, Hitler clasped the giant's hands in both of his in the Austrian fashion (for they both stemmed from that country). His smile grew and he said in a shaky voice, 'Stay a while, my dear Skorzeny,' indicating the two easy chairs in the corner of the spartan wooden room. 'I'd like to talk to you under four eyes.' He meant alone, without witnesses.

SS Obersturmbannführer Otto Skorzeny, head of the SS's 'Hunting Commando', clicked his heels together and a little uneasily followed the Führer's directions. It was a great honour to be alone with the Führer, but it was unnerving. Adolf Hitler, he knew from past experience, was unpredictable. What had prompted the Führer to ask him to sit down like this privately? Still, he knew better than to look even curious. He set his scarred face that looked like the work of a butcher who had gone mad, wielding one of his cleavers, in the look of an obedient, disciplined soldier about to be given his orders, and waited.

Hitler let his trembling, crippled arm fall down to his side, where it hung helplessly, as if it didn't belong to his body, and

13

commenced; and for once he didn't lecture or digress. He got down to business at once, as if he had rediscovered his old dynamic sense of urgency. 'Skorzeny,' he declared, 'I am going to give you the most important job of your life.' He paused melodramatically like the actor he really was and then said, 'In December, Germany will start a great offensive in the West . . . This offensive could well decide the fate and future of our beloved Germany.' He paused and waited for the giant's reaction.

He got it. Skorzeny's mouth dropped open like that of some village yokel. 'Germany . . . going over to the offensive . . . in the West', the words ran through his agile brain crazily. It was unbelievable. Even iron-clad patriots like himself, who owed everything to Hitler and the National Socialist cause, knew Germany had virtually lost the war. In the West, the Anglo-Americans had already crossed the German frontier and were battering at the country's last defensive line, the *Westwall*. In the East, the Russians were already crossing the Vistula in Poland and driving for East Prussia and there seemed nothing to stop them. Even Hitler's generals had turned against him and had tried to murder him in this very place three months before. Now the Führer talked of offensives!

Hitler's smile broadened. He could obviously read Skorzeny's thoughts, for he said pleasantly, his Austrian accent broadening as he spoke to his compatriot, 'Yes, you heard correctly, *mein lieber Skorzeny*, offensive. I have been preparing for it for nearly two months now. Indeed since the day those damned Jewish gangsters, the Americans, ventured on to our holy German soil, I was determined to throw them back. What do you say to that now?'

Skorzeny had nothing to say really; his brain was racing electrically, wondering what Hitler expected of him. But he mumbled something, which satisfied the Führer, who continued with: 'They, the Allies, expect to find a stinking corpse once they attack us in earnest. But they will be surprised greatly. We are being rejuvenated. Scores of new divisions are being formed. Our factories are turning out tanks by the hundreds.

Indeed I expect two thousand of the new jets to be flying by the time we march westwards once more as we did in the great days of 1940.' Now his face was flushed hectically like that of an overexcited consumptive, Skorzeny couldn't help thinking. All the same his enthusiasm was contagious and Skorzeny was already reeling with these figures that Hitler seemed to be able to produce out of a hat like a magician does a rabbit at a children's party to the amazed gasps of joy of his audience. Still, at the back of his bullet head, a small voice was asking, *'But Otto, what has all this got to do with you, a lowly SS Colonel? Why is the Führer of the Greater German Reich, master of two hundred million people, telling YOU all this, eh?'*

Again Hitler seemed able to read his mind, for, gasping a little with the effort of so much talking, Hitler said, 'I have told you so much so that you will realise that everything has been considered and weighed very carefully . . . Every detail of our attack west has been considered.' He paused and looked hard at Skorzeny with eyes that were no longer vague and watery, but were hard and magnetic as they had been in the old days when Skorzeny had first met Hitler and the latter had asked him to rescue his old comrade, Mussolini, the Italian dictator, from his mountain fastness prison in Italy. 'Now you, my dear Skorzeny, and your Hunting Commando will play an important role – a very important one – in this new offensive in the West.'

'Yes, *mein Führer?*' Skorzeny managed to say.

'*Jawohl, ja*! As an advance guard for the drive of the 6th SS Panzer Army westwards, you will capture one or more bridges over the River Meuse and hold them till the SS arrive. You will carry out this operation – ' he paused and stared hard at his fellow Austrian, as if he expected an objection to come the next moment – 'in British or American uniform.'

Surprisingly the scar-faced giant didn't object. Perhaps he was too surprised, or awed by Hitler's confidence, so the latter went on hastly, 'The enemy has already used this trick, which is contrary to the rules of war. Only a couple of days ago, my Intelligence informed me that there were Americans dressed in

15

Leo Kessler

German uniform used in the capture of our old imperial city of Aachen on the border with Holland.'

'I understand, sir,' Skorzeny answered, for he guessed the Führer expected some kind of comment, though he didn't dare mention that anyone caught at the front in enemy uniform would undoubtedly be shot as a spy.

'In order to conceal your preparations, Skorzeny,' Hitler continued, '*not* only from the enemy, but also from your own troops, tell them we are expecting a full-scale enemy attack between Cologne and Bonn. They are preparing to meet that attack.'

Skorzeny nodded his understanding. 'Time is short, *mein Führer*. I can think of other tasks to aid this new offensive you have planned so well,' he added the bit of flattery of the kind Hitler liked. He always believed *he* could plan operations much better than his staff-trained senior officers.

'I know . . . I know. But you must do your best.' He looked curious. 'But you mentioned other things, Skorzeny?'

'Well, sir, we have already planned – even before I knew of your plans – to take the war by clandestine means to the enemy's own homeland.'

'The Americans?'

'*Jawohl, mein Führer*. I have been working together with Admiral Doenitz, head of the Submarine Service. He is working on a feasibility plan to deliver one of the new V-2s currently being employed against London, by submarine and to be aimed at New York.'

Hitler's face lit up. He clapped his two weak hands together feebly like a delighted child. 'Excellent . . . excellent, my dear fellow! Only you could have thought of something like that. That will teach those Jewish air gangsters – to have a ton of high explosive drop into their own backyard. *Kolossal*, Skorzeny'. Anything else?'

The scar-faced SS man hesitated.

'*Los, Skorzeny*,' Hitler urged him in a jovial manner that the SS man had not experienced these many months, '*raus mit der Sprache* . . . get it off your chest.'

16

'Well, sir, it's difficult and I certainly haven't worked out all the details yet. But it's this. You mentioned the new divisions you have formed from young men weeded out from industry, other branches of the service, Air Force, Navy etc. etc.'

'Yes . . . yes.'

'Well, *mein Führer*, there is only one source of manpower that, if I may say so, you seem to have overlooked.'

Hitler's jovial look vanished. 'Pray tell me which, Skorzeny,' he commanded.

Skorzeny licked his lips, which were suddenly dry for some reason he couldn't fathom. 'We are talking, *mein Führer*,' he began hesitantly, 'about some quarter of a million fit young German soldiers, who have been well fed and nourished over the last months and even years, far away from the stresses and strains of the battlefield.'

Hitler looked at his fellow Austrian as if he had suddenly gone mad. 'I don't understand, Skorzeny,' he said.

'Yes, *mein Führer*, I can understand why. But let me explain, please. No one has remarked about this so far as I know, sir, but I have been considering the possibility for some time—'

'Please hurry it, Skorzeny,' Hitler urged excitedly, eager to find out the details of a large number of German soldiers, the equivalent of several army corps, who weren't being used in combat when Germany was scraping the barrel for manpower, with men as old as fifty-five being called to the colours.

'It is like this, *mein Führer* . . .' Hurriedly Skorzeny explained his bold, imaginative plan to Hitler, while the latter listened intently, his face showing his ever-growing excitement as the details sank in.

When the big SS officer was finished, Hitler looked at him in frank admiration. 'My God, Skorzeny, what a thought! A kind of gigantic Trojan Horse.' His faded eyes sparkled. 'But how could you pull it off?'

'It will take weeks yet, *mein Führer*. But I have my agents in place. They are in contact with us over secret radios. If, with a bit of luck, everything goes well, as I have planned, the operation will start to coincide with your great new offensive in the West.'

'In three devils' name, Skorzeny!' Hitler exclaimed. 'Think of it. An army to the enemy's rear, able to block his resupply ports, cut off reinforcements, new armour, supplies. Without his ports, Skorzeny, believe you me, *Obersturmbannführer*, those Anglo-American swine have already half lost the battle to come. Skorzeny, there'll be general's stars in this for you, if you pull it off.'

Skorzeny attempted to look modest, though it was difficult for him. By nature he wasn't a modest man. 'I do it for our holy cause, *mein Führer*, not for personal gain or glory.'

'Well said, old friend,' Hitler responded. Then he was solemn once more. 'Skorzeny, I ask you for permission to give this bold operation of yours its code-name.'

Skorzeny flushed. 'It is a great honour, sir.' He waited.

Hitler didn't even hesitate. Immediately he announced, as if he were addressing one of his great pre-war rallies at Nuremberg, 'I shall call the op its obvious name.'

'And that is, *mein Führer*?'

'Operation Trojan Horse.'

Five minutes later *Obersturmbannführer* Skorzeny was on his way again on the long journey from Rastenburg to his headquarters at Friedensthal, his mind buzzing electrically with ideas and plans. Behind him he left Adolf Hitler, the one-time master of Europe, slumped at the table, head supported by his good hand. He looked like a man at the end of his tether who had made an irrevocable decision: one which would make or break him. For the man who had terrorised and dominated the Old Continent for nearly six years now knew that, if he failed, it would be the end of him and his vaunted 'Thousand-Year Reich'.

Two

A thousand miles away Lt Washington Lee of the US Corps of Counter-Intelligence drifted with apparent casualness into the Ace o' Spades. It was a typical GI bar, of which there were a score or so in the ancient French garrison town of Verdun, save for one difference. All the sweating happy faces in the tightly packed room around the bar and tiny dance floor were black.

The long narrow *estaminet* with the raised platform at the end for '*Le Dancing*', as the French called it, had been broken into a series of little alcoves like some provincial drugstore back home, the handsome young officer couldn't help thinking. But instead of the usual bobby-socks high-school girls, the women here were sluttish drunken blondes, with whore written all over their venial faces, who were busy promoting the fragile French economy by plying their trade with their hands under the table on sweating, brilliantined GIs; naturally for the good ole Yankee dollar, the young officer couldn't help thinking a little cynically.

He paused at the zinc bar, soaked with beer suds, and said in fluent French, learned at the Sorbonne in 1939, '*Une biere, Jo-Jo . . . pression.*'

The cock-eyed barman, with the cigarette seemingly glued to his bottom lip, grinned. He always did. It amused him that the young officer with the keen alert gaze spoke better Parisian French than he did, and he had been born out at Versailles.

Slowly and carefully, making it last, the young officer sipped the weak frothy French beer while he surveyed the room, as he had done these many nights ever since he had been posted to SHAEF in early fall. As usual the noise was terrific. The French

19

assumed that '*les Americains*', especially if they were '*les singes*', the monkeys, as they called the US coloured men, liked their music very loud. Thus on the little platform, the three-piece band of French Senegalese, giants of men, the sweat pouring down their brown, ritually scarred faces, were playing *bal musette* with much clashing of cymbals and slamming of the big drum. No one was dancing. But that didn't matter. The '*singes*' had already filled their red fezes with nickels and dimes and the free beer paid for by the GIs kept coming and coming.

Washington Lee stiffled a yawn. The place was the same as it had been every other night he had visited it as part of his duties; and once more he wondered if he needed a Harvard-Sorbonne education to carry out this kind of work. He hadn't volunteered for the US Army to 'shovel shit in Louisiana' as he had told the recruiting officer. He wanted to 'fight against fascism'. The white officer had been sympathetic, but he had laid it on the line before recommending the Corps of Counter-Intelligence: 'Mr Lee, you must remember this is a segregated Army. We have a few coloured guys in the artillery and armour. But the rest of your folk are limited to the supply service, you know, what we call the Quartermaster Branch.'

Back in 1943 he had been inclined to protest, but had thought better of it. If he had, the Army might well have assigned him to one of those black 'shit-shovelling' outfits. If he kept his lip buttoned and played the 'good nigger', they'd allow him to use his knowledge of languages and education in the Intelligence outfit the decent white officer had recommended.

Now, a year later, he wondered. He looked at himself in the fly-blown mirror behind the bar and saw a face that some would say Nature had played a dirty trick on. It was the kind of face that had stared back at him from a dozen recruiting posters, stating '*Uncle Sam Wants You!*' It was heavy-jawed, with gleaming white teeth, keen and tough: that ideal all-American face that movie stars and top soldiers were supposed to have, save for one thing. The goddam skin was *black*!

Lt Lee sighed once again at the thought. It was a tough row to hoe. Still he was as determined as ever to get into the shooting war. Naturally he had a duty to his fellow black Americans of the COM Z.* They had it tough in a prejudiced US Army, filled, it seemed, with southern rednecks. They did all the dirty work and were recompensed with hatred from many of their white comrades and contempt from those civilians who accepted the scurrilous stories the whites spread about the blacks. Why, the rednecks had even convinced a lot of French folk that blacks had tails curled up inside their pants like goddam apes. Why else would the former call the black GIs *'singes'*?

'M'sieu,' Jo-Jo interrupted his gloomy reverie. With a nod he indicated the heavy felt blackout curtain which covered the door to the little GI bar. 'Problem?'

Lt Lee put down his glass. Three white GIs, obviously drunk, had pushed their way in, and were hanging about with weapons, as if they were going to fight the rest of World War Two single-handed; and all bore the American Eagle patch of the 101st Airborne Division: an outfit which was notorious for being trouble, Lee told himself, trouble with a capital 'T'.

In essence, it was no job of his to concern himself with the discipline – or the lack of it – of the ordinary GI, he was concerned with counter-intelligence. All the same he noted the sudden hush that had descended upon the bar now that the three drunken, swaggering paratroopers had made their appearance. White GIs of their type only turned up in bars restricted – unofficially – to coloured troops by mistake, and when they were looking for trouble; and it was clear that these three were out for just that. Slowly, Lt Lee eased the leather holster of his Colt .45 to his front and pulled the holster flap. With the men of the Screaming Eagles, it was no use trying to use common sense and reason; all the veterans of Normandy and Holland understood when they were drunk was the snub nose of a Colt pointing in the direction of their hearts. Opposite him Jo-Jo brought out his 'pacifier', as he called his rubber club, and laid it underneath the dirty napkin on the bar. He winked. Lt Lee winked back. They understood each other.

* Communication Zone, from which supplies were shipped to the front.

'There's the stink of dinge in here,' the tallest of the three said in a Texan accent. 'No mistaking it. Real black dinge and that's worse than the stink of a wetback greaser.'

The other two laughed and looked provocatively around the bar, as if hoping that someone might challenge their comrade's statement. No one did. Even the thickest coloured man present knew the reputation of the 'Screaming Eagles'. Already Eisenhower, the Supreme Commander, had threatened to have one of them hanged publicly in order to restore the division's discipline, which had gone totally to pieces during the fierce fighting in Holland in the early fall.

'Let's belly up to the bar . . . might get rid of the stink, Jake,' a blond one with a nasty fresh scar on his right cheek said. 'Wonders never cease, they say.'

Together the three of them pushed their way through the whores and their partners, elbowing hard those who were too slow. There were sudden angry murmurs. Jo-Jo looked alarmed. His fingers stole to the napkin. Lt Lee frowned. The matter might yet fizzle away to nothing. The Quartermaster coloured boys were usually a tame bunch except on pay days. All the same they had to submit to the whims and prejudices of their white bosses during the day. At night they wanted to be among their own kind and live their own lives.

The three men ordered beer and a shot of cognac. Lee started to relax. The coloured men at their tables did, too. Perhaps the paratroopers would simply down their drinks, realise that this was not the place for them, make a crack about the smell of the company, something of that kind, and then swagger out in those jumpboots of which they were inordinately proud. Lee told himself they'd certainly not make a pass at the 'nigger whores'. For that matter he wouldn't himself; he'd be scared of the kind of 'souvenirs' their kind usually passed out to the unfortunate guys who paid for their services.

It seemed that the whores thought the danger posed by the paratroopers was about over, too. For now a big-bosomed, dyed blonde in high, wooden, platform-heeled shoes, tight black skirt that emphasised her ample curves and dirty white blouse from which her breasts bulged and threatened to bounce out at any moment, staggered on to the little round stage. She shouted something to the permanently grinning Senegalese. That was followed by a handful of coins.

The Senegalese, probably all deserters from the French Colonial Army, obliged. They gave her a roll on the drums and a whack at the cymbals. She grinned and started to sway back and forth from the ample hips drunkenly, but sexually provocatively. The move met with her audience's sudden approval. There was a burst of catcalls and whistles.

'Shake it, baby!' the coloured soldiers yelled in delight.

The whore needed no urging. She indulged in some sort of drunken, private, erotic fancy. The Senegalese joined in the best they could. The blonde began revolving her broad hips in time to the rhythm. The sweat started to roll down her powder-raddled face. Her mouth fell open. She gasped. Her gaze turned upwards, as if she were now completely enveloped in some personal sexual passion, for there was no mistaking that grinding movement of her loins – and the GIs loved it, save for the biggest of the airborne troopers.

Now, without stopping her lascivious grinding, the blonde ripped open her blouse. She revealed a black crêpe-de-Chine slip under which her big breasts jiggled and wobbled, as if they had an independent life of their own.

Now the GIs were stumbling to their feet, shoving each other in order to get a better view of the whore in the throes of her self-induced sexual passion. 'Goddamit,' the big paratrooper yelled in disgust, 'how can a white woman, even if she's a whore, perform for a bunch o' spades like that?' He spat on to the sawdust floor. 'It's downright wrong.'

The coloured soldiers didn't seem to notice. They were too excited by the display of naked raw sex. 'Hubba-hubba-hubba!' they cried in delight. 'Take 'em off, babe . . . Sock it to me, sugar!'

The drums thudded faster. The cymbals clashed. The Senegalese were sweating. Their broad, normally good-humoured faces were set in a look of naked rapacity. They, too, were seized by the raw lechery of the whore's performance. The blonde, lips parted, nostrils flared, lifted up one ample hip and ripped open the buttons of her skirt. She stopped momentarily and let it slip to the floor.

The GIs whistled and clapped with delight. She was naked below the waist, save for a pair of black silk stockings, rolled up at her plump, dimpled white knees. Here and there the coloured soldiers began to rub the front of their bulging pants suggestively. At the bar the big paratrooper grew progressively angrier, muttering to himself in impotent fury.

Again the blonde commenced her dance. Her whole body began to shake. Frantically her plump belly moved in and out. Her breasts shuddered. Sweat poured from her. Now she began to mime the sex act in explicit detail. The audience loved it.

Suddenly, startlingly, the blonde broke into great shuddering jerks. She was reaching a climax. She thrust her clenched fists cruelly back and forth, hitting her stomach. Harsh obscenities escaped her wet, slack lips. Her legs straddled, the muscles of her thighs clenched hard, her hips gyrating in a wild circle. Meaningless words and groans came tumbling from her harsh gaping mouth.

The tall paratrooper had had enough. He downed the rest of his beer. 'Shoot, you're like a goddam bunch o' hogs in a trough of mash!' he yelled and threw his glass at the woman. It missed. But the shattering glass brought the woman to her senses. She stopped in mid-dance. The Senegalese faltered. The music died away. Suddenly a heavy hush descended upon the crowded bar, as the steam went out of the act and the coloured soldiers stood there, the animation disappearing from their sweating black faces to be replaced by a look of bewilderment.

'Why you do that, soldier?' someone broke the silence, a note of reproach in his deep Southern voice. 'You no right to spoil it, whitey.'

A colt appeared in the paratrooper's hand as if by magic. He crouched, his eyes red and dangerous. 'Don't you dare talk to me like that, nigger,' he threatened through gritted teeth. 'I'm a combat soldier . . . not a frigging black bastard, who's behind the line, abusing our women.'

Under other circumstances, Lt Lee would have smiled at that 'abusing our women'. The big half-naked whore looked as if she were the one who'd be doing the abusing. But he did not smile. The situation was too serious. It was obvious that the paratroopers had come here looking specifically for trouble. What was he to do? In essence it was none of his concern. But the black GIs were a hopeless bunch. They didn't stand a chance against the combat-wise armed paratroopers; and besides, in France in the fall of 1944, justice was on the side of the combat soldier, who was virtually always white. Lee bit his bottom lip and decided, for the time being at least, he'd stay and try to cool the situation if it became necessary.

The soldier who had spoken was not afraid. He stood up so that the paratrooper could see him. He was a big overweight corporal, whose belly testified to his fondness for the good life. But now the good life was forgotten. He was sore and his broad, gleaming black face showed it. Indignantly he said in that barely intelligible southern accent of his, 'What you come in here for, man? This place is for niggers . . . We don't want no white trash in *our* place.'

'Shut your mush mouth, nigger,' the paratrooper retorted calmly and jerked up the muzzle of his big pistol dangerously, 'or I'll blow it frigging off.'

The corporal hesitated, but Lt Lee didn't give either of the two a chance to escalate the little drama. Calmly, in that cool New England voice of his, he commanded, 'All right, that's enough. The fun's over. Let's settle down now – and that's an order.'

As if shot, the paratrooper spun round, pistol still levelled. Just in time he caught the gasp, as he recognised that the big tough-looking young man in an officer's uniform was black. Lee looked back at him calmly. Then, after allowing the man to take in the fact that he was speaking to a black officer, he snapped, 'All right, put that pistol back in your holster and then the three of you finish your drinks and be on your way.'

Behind the bar, hand still gripping the pipe beneath the

teatowel, Jo-Jo forced a smile and said in his fractured English, 'Free drinks . . . You go . . . See you later, alligator.'

The paratrooper looked at him and said, 'Shut ya frigging mouth, frog.' Then he looked Lee up and down, as if he were some drill instructor back in basic training eyeing a new recruit and not liking what he saw one bit. Out of the side of his mouth he said to his buddies, 'Get a load o' that. A nigger dressed up as an officer. What will the Army dream up next?' He feigned a great horse laugh, but his red eyes remained cold and lethal.

Lee caught hold of himself. He was used to insults on account of his colour. But as he had grown older and learned just what physical strength, plus a powerful right hook, could do, he had grown ever less inclined to accept them. 'Enough of that kind of talk, soldier,' he answered. 'Now do as you're told and haul ass. Got it?'

'Fuck you, *lootenant.*'

'I won't tell you again, soldier.'

Now the GI bar had gone deadly silent. Jo-Jo behind the zinc counter prepared to strike. The soldiers gawped. The half-naked blonde whore stared stupidly. It was like the end of the first act in some cheap play when there was about to be the explosion that the audience expected now to come. It came. 'Holster that pistol,' Lee snapped. 'No bullshit. That's an order.'

Deliberately the paratrooper spat on the floor once more and growled, a cynical grin on his face, 'Make me, black boy—'

He never finished. Lee lashed out. His fist caught the paratrooper completely by surprise. It landed on the point of his chin. His head clicked back audibly. His knees started to crumble like those of a newborn foal. The pistol dropped from his abruptly nerveless fingers in the same instant that the French bartender leaned over and neatly tapped the second para over the back of the head. He pitched forward, unconscious before he hit the floor.

That did it. The third one, the smallest, put up his hands in front of his body protectively, crying, 'Kay . . . kay . . . I won't cause no trouble . . . Honest Injun.'

His broad chest heaving slightly, Lt Lee considered for a moment before he lowered his fist to say, 'All right, get yourself outa here while you've got the chance, soldier . . . I'm gonna have to call the paddy wagon for these other two beauts. They're out like a light.'

'Gee, thanks, Lieutenant,' the third man said gratefully, 'Thanks. I'm off.'

A moment later he had fled, leaving Lt Lee with the two unconscious paratroopers, realising for the first time that he was in trouble – big trouble.

Three

'At ease,' Major Malloy commanded and then his big Irish face, slab-like and mottled by a red spider's web of ruptured veins, the result of nearly three decades of hard drinking, relaxed. 'Kay,' he added, 'take the weight off your feet, Lee, and sit down for Jasus' sake . . . Relax.'

Lee did as he was commanded, though he had never felt less like relaxing. The last week had been murder. He had been back and forth to SHAEF HQ in Versailles twice, reported to the commanding general of the 101st Airborne Division and had been threatened with everything from execution to castration, or so it seemed to his poor confused mind. Now he knew his CO, Malloy, the old-time ex-Chicago cop, was going to give him the Top Brass's verdict – and he wasn't looking forward to it, one little bit.

Malloy swung his size elevens on to the desk in front of him, loosened his belt to make himself more comfortable and said, 'The ordure has well and truly hit the ventilator, as you well know, Lee.'

The handsome black officer nodded miserably. 'I know, sir . . . I know.'

Malloy grinned, but without any apparent sympathy for his predicament. 'Yeah, son, they've really got your black dong in the meat grinder – ' he made an explicit churning motion with his big ham fist and Lee shuddered involuntarily – 'and a lot of them fancy pants at SHAEF like it. The natives are getting restless.'

Under other circumstances, Lee might have protested at the references to his colour, but he never quite knew with Malloy what his position on the black question was. As Malloy often proclaimed to anyone prepared to listen in the officesr' club, 'Let's get this crystal clear. I hate everybody – fags, dykes, rednecks, moxies, niggers . . . Why, there's even a few Micks who get up my big fish-eater's Catholic nose.' So Lee kept quiet and listened miserably, waiting to hear the verdict. Perhaps he'd join the other coloured 'shit shovellers from Louisiana' after all. 'Taylor, the commanding general of the 101st, really blew his top. You put a couple of his heroes into hospital and he needs the bodies for the next drop. And Taylor, you'd better believe it, has plenty of clout at SHAEF. All those West Pointers stick together in a crisis. Lucky for you, Lee, however, Eleanor – ' he meant President Roosevelt's wife – 'has been informed about your case in Washington and Ike daren't offend *her*. So, for the time being, Taylor don't count. One thing, however – you can't stay in France. Everybody and his goddam brother wants you out! Is that understood?'

Washington Lee nodded and waited, as if he already knew that Major Malloy, the arch wheeler-and-dealer, had somehow settled his fate. Surprisingly enough for a man who wasn't often given to philosophising or digressions, Malloy didn't get to the point straight away. Instead he said in an unusually conversational manner for him, 'You see, Washington – God, your ma and pa did you no favour when they gave you that name, Lee.'

'I know, sir, but they thought it was the right kind of patriotic name for a black kid.'

Malloy nodded. 'Well, as I was saying, you're a bright guy with the right instincts doing the right thing at that bar. But it just happens you're on the scene fifty years too early.' He laughed, voice thickened by decades of cheap cigars and even cheaper whiskey.

'How do you mean, sir?'

'Like this. One day blacks, or at least some of them like educated ones like yourself, will have the same rights and privileges as us white guys. When my folks came over from the Old Country last century, they were treated like dirt in Boston. Catholic, Irish and didn't know how to use a knife and fork. It took twenty or thirty years till we Micks got our noses in the trough with your upper class WASPs. With you blacks it's gonna take a lot longer. Look at that commie Paul Robson – Harvard, All American, movie star, and what has it got him. I'll tell ya – file a foot long in Mr Hoover's FBI main office.' He noted the bewilderment on the handsome young officer's face and said, 'So you're asking yourself, what's the old Mick fart rambling on about? What is all this crap to me? I'll tell you, Washington.' He puffed out a ring of blue smoke from the cheap cigar he was smoking like a man who was well satisfied with his world, but was willing to pass on the secret of his personal success to anyone who was prepared to listen.

Lt Lee waited. Outside, the sky was becoming leaden and threatening. A cold wind was whipping up the scraps of paper in the courtyard below. It looked as if it might well snow before the day was out. Snow was forecast early for Europe this year. The boys in the foxholes up at the front on the German border were going to have a hard time this winter. All the same, Lee told himself, he would dearly have loved to have been up there with them instead of here, fighting to keep clear of all the damned US Army's rearline politics.

'As I said, you're ahead of your time and unless you want to be a fall guy for your race, you've just gotta accept that fact.'

'I take your point, sir. I know what you mean about fighting the big battle for my race. But for the time being, all I'm concerned with is fighting the battle against the Nazis.'

'Well said, Washington,' Malloy responded and pulled a face, as if the name 'Washington' had again touched a sore spot. 'So this is what I've done for you.' He leaned forward in the manner of the old-time cop about to pass on an illegal tip – or threat – and said, 'They want you out of France for the time being. Kay, I've taken care of that.' He chuckled suddenly. 'I'm having you transferred to England.'

'*England?*' Lee echoed. 'But that's even further away from the fighting front, sir.'

'It might be for the moment, Washington. But it's not going to remain that way for long, at least for you.'

'How do you mean, sir?'

'Well, the grapevine tells me that there are currently three US divisions there at the moment, training: that means getting drunk on warm Limey beer and fucking their dames.'

Lee told himself his boss was a cynic, as all good cops should be, but he didn't mind, for suddenly he realised that tough old Malloy, who always boasted he'd 'seen everything and done everything – and then some', had his best interests at heart. So he held his peace, though he was dying to ask what all this had to do with him.

Now Malloy answered his unspoken question. He tapped his broken-knuckled big fist on the paper-littered desk in front of him. 'Yesterday I got a request through channels for an officer to build up a small CIC team for one of those three divisions in England. It's the 11th Armored, as green as the corn, but scheduled to leave for the Continent here and frontline training in two months' time. I've recommended you for that particular slot, Washington, though I didn't tell 'em that goddamned given name of yourn – it'd have been a dead giveaway.'

Lee's heart skipped a beat. 'You mean a combat mission?' he gasped, his young face gleaming with renewed hope and sudden enthusiasm, as he realised that his position had been abruptly reversed. Malloy had succeeded in getting him off SHAEF's shit list. More, he had gotten him a combat mission, as far as the CIC could be said to go into combat. At least he'd be at the fighting front.

Malloy saw the enthusiasm and said warningly, 'Hold ya horses, young man. It ain't gonna be that easy, remember. They don't know your colour – yet. It's up to you to convince them that you know your job and get the show on the road before they can start objecting and trying to get you transferred out.' Malloy grinned abruptly and held out his hand. 'After all, Lee, you are a way-out, awkward, black son-of-a-bitch.'

As Lee took the big hand, for once he didn't mind that old, 'black son-of-a-bitch'; for he knew he had a friend.

Thus it was that Lieutenant Washington Lee was virtually smuggled out of the old French garrison town, where a quarter of a century before on those grim heights, which overshadowed

Verdun and where nothing grew, the German and French armies had bled almost to death. With his orders cut, all he possessed packed in a duffle bag, he passed down the lines of communication, heading for what the movie comic Bob Hope was now calling 'Old Jolly'.

A day later he was in Cherbourg and waiting for an empty landing craft or the like to take him across the Channel to the unknown country, where he would – with a bit of luck – be at long last accepted as a full paid-up member of the United States of America.

But the sole port in American hands on the Atlantic-North Sea coast was packed with troops coming and going, reinforcements for the front pouring in by their thousand, cannon fodder to be wasted away on the Siegfried Line, serious casualties being evacuated to the packed military hospitals across the water in England, and the hundreds of dirty, dishevelled field-greys waiting to be taken first to Britain for processing and then to the United States, safely away from the fighting front.

As the well-nourished port officers, virtually all black, save for their commanders – and all, black and white, growing richer and richer from Cherbourg's flourishing black market – told Washington time and time again when he requested transportation over the water to his new posting, 'Lootenant, do what everybody else does, sell your Class Six ration – a carton of Luckies is enough – and get yourself shacked up with some frog whore. They're coming from all over France to shake down the GIs here. Because, you'd better believe it, no one's interested in getting you across that water over to the Limeys. Enjoy yourself – hang loose!'

It didn't matter that he didn't want to 'hang loose', but wanted to get into the shooting war. There seemed no way that he'd get across that stretch of grey-green water, unless he was prepared to swim it.

Thus it was that he spent his days, glad to get out of the stifling confines of the 'ripple-dipple', Cherbourg's reinforcement depot, which housed young 'sixty-day wonders', callow boys who had passed officers' school back in the States in sixty short days (hence the name), and where fearful young men who lost their nerve committed suicide every day when they were ordered to the front and the sudden death waiting for them there.

A couple of times he had casual sex (paid) with one or two of the better-looking whores, who looked, as far as he could judge, as if they might be donating a small 'souvenir' to him after the act of love. But if the experiences were necessary, they weren't very enjoyable, but mechanical, and ended in the usual procedure of money changing hands and his 'own true love' (as Washington called them cynically to himself) departing to find yet another partner. Still, they kept his nerves (impatient as he was to reach the 11th Armored Division) under control and gave him food for thought – after all, in the Year of Our Lord, 1944, it was not very commonplace for a young negro of no great means to bed two white women who were prepared – naturally for money – to cater for his every sexual desire.

All the same, he kept that somewhat heady knowledge to himself, although it contrasted with his first sexual experiences with a white woman in Harvard as a freshman back in the late 1930s when one of the white maids had allowed him to play with her drooping tits for five dollars a throw. A couple of times he had laughed to himself somewhat bitterly at the thought and considered, remembering Malloy's words: 'In fifty years' time when I come to write my autobiography, I'll even be able to write about *that*.' Unfortunately Lt Washington Lee would never live that long to write his autobiography or anything else for that matter; what he would learn worth writing about for the general public would die with him . . .

It was nearly a week after he had arrived in Cherbourg, still impatient to get to his new posting, but realising by now he'd have to wait just like the rest, especially as the wounded were pouring into the port from the new front in what the *Stars & Stripes** called 'the Green Hell of the Hurtgen', that he met

* The US Army news paper.

Marie-Claire – the young Parisienne, who spoke English like a New England graduate of Smith or Berkeley, who wasn't a prostitute and who didn't seem to notice that he was black, and who actually fell in love with him.

It seemed as if Major Malloy was wrong after all. For the chic young Parisienne wasn't one bit ashamed to be seen walking with him, a black American soldier, in the centre of Cherbourg, even when senior American officers appeared about to have a heart attack at this shocking and unusual sight. It wasn't going to take Malloy's fifty years after all.

Four

The pathologist had gone to work on the dead body with a will. He had come blustering in, a big man with a crimson face and hands like hams, who looked more like a farmer than a doctor, singing 'Fee, fie, foo, fum, I smell the blood of an Englishman', until the Major had slapped his tin leg with his cane impatiently and corrected him with "Fraid you're wrong there, Doc. He's a Hun as it happens to be.'

'Never mind,' the pathologist had retorted happily. 'Body after all and he's worth thirty bob to me.' With that he had started to examine the naked corpse laid out on the metal slab, declaiming as he did so:

Ah lovely appearance of Death,
What sight upon earth is so fair?
Not all the gay pageants that breathe
Can with a dead body compare.

'Doolally!' Sergeant Hawkins had murmured to the Major and the latter could only nod his head in agreement and add for his own private consideration, 'And the whole bloody universe is in the same state.'

'Found him last night when the Huns were cleaning out the privies,' Major Clapton, the camp's Security Officer, known as 'Old Tin Leg' behind his back, said aloud for the pathologist's benefit. 'Cleaned him up a bit, identified him as one of ours, missing for a couple of weeks now, and called you in to give us whatever information you can.'

'Good show. Pleased you cleaned him up a bit. Though he

still pongs,' the big burly doctor said in his breezy manner, 'but then I suppose all Huns pong a bit, what?'

'What?' Clapton echoed and again looked at Sergeant Hawkins, as if to say 'This one is really loopy'. But then, he told himself, doctors were hard to find in the winter of 1944. All the young and healthy ones were in the Services. The general public, including POW camp staff, were left with the dregs, ill or insane, or both.

Still, the pathologist went to work professionally enough. He gazed and felt the length of the naked corpse, occasionally bending forward and, almost touching the dead body with his long nose, he peering hard at it through his glasses. Tin Leg waited, his gaze moving from the corpse to the window. Outside, camp life was going on as normal, despite the biting cold wind that seemed to be coming straight from Siberia.

To Tin Leg, the camp and its occupants seemed no different than Holzminden* back in 1917 after the Huns had shot off his leg and captured him, save that prisoners wore field grey instead of khaki. There were the 'hearties', indulging in physical jerks or jogging round the 'track', just inside the wire parallel to the 'death zone' into which any sentry was entitled to fire if a prisoner entered it. There were the 'funnies', who were either mad or feigned madness in an attempt to be repatriated. They were engaged in a multitude of strange activities from practising yoga half-naked like Gandhi, despite the cold, to playing the same damned tune maddeningly over and over again on the flute. There were discussion groups, wandering across the compound in an attempt to keep warm, discussing everything from Goethe to the Gold Standard. As Tin Leg waited for the pathologist to make his first pronouncement he told himself that there was only one difference between this English camp in Devizes and the Holzminden one, and that was the 'Blacks'.

* A notorious First World War German POW camp at the place of that name.

The Great Escape

There weren't many of them, but the few there were were definitely cocks of the walk. Mostly ex-SS, paratroopers and a handful of U-boat sailors, they swaggered about, menacing, arrogant looks on their faces, throwing 'Heil Hitler' salutes at one another as if they were still free in their own damned homeland, knowing that the general run of prisoners were deadly scared of them. It was for that reason that he and Sergeant Hawkins were here in the Medical Hut this freezingly cold winter's morning.

The pathologist took his time. Cynically Tin Leg told himself that perhaps he might be paid overtime. All the same, he was thorough, working on the corpse with his magnifying glass and pincers in a close manner that Tin Leg couldn't have tolerated. A couple of times, he even touched the dead man's cold yellow flesh and rubbed it before examing whatever had come off on the thumb and forefinger of his surgical glove. Once he said, almost as if to himself, 'Well the shit did one thing, Major, it did preserve the corpse better.' But before Tin Leg could ask a question, the doctor had gone to examine another part of the body.

For a while he seemed to be very concerned with the corpse's genitals, taking a pencil and turning the limp, useless organ to left and right and staring hard at whatever was disclosed. 'Wasn't a Jew then,' he muttered, again as if to himself, 'But then as a Nazi Hun he wouldn't be circumsised, would he?'

Hawkins, the old sweat, shook his head in mock wonder, exclaiming under his breath, 'Medical officers – I've shat 'em before breakfast.' It was a sentiment with which an increasingly impatient Tin Leg was inclined to agree.

A moment or two later the pathologist turned the corpse over on to its face and now he seemed to speed up his examination, nodding his big head and grunting 'yes . . . yes', as if he had found something of significance which confirmed what he had already discovered.

Finally he turned and faced the two soldiers. 'Well, I'll open him up in half a mo. But this is what I can tell you now.' He beamed at them, as if they were congenital idiots with whom one had to speak clearly and slowly so that they might conceivably understand what he was saying to them. 'The dead man was a homosexual. There is clear evidence of that from his rectum and, to a certain degree, his genitals, if you follow me?' He frowned.

Sergeant Hawkins, nobody's fool, couldn't resist the opportunity. 'You mean he was a nancy boy, sir, a Mary Ann, Queen of All the Fairies?' he enquired, an innocent look on his wrinkled nutbrown face, the product of years in the far-flung regions of the British Empire.

'Yes, something like that, Sergeant, though the terms are not quite familiar—'

'Was he murdered?' Tin Leg cut in impatiently; he felt he had wasted enough time in this place. 'Any clue how . . . and,' he added a little helplessly, '*who* did it?'

'*How* is quite easy, Major.'

'Yes?'

'He was beaten about the body and especially about the head with several hard objects. Look.' He held up his gloved hand. 'Splinters . . . from some sort of wooden object . . . and this.' He turned and riffled the body's long hair until the deathly pale scalp was visible. Gently he pressed the skull. The bone gave. 'Heavy impact bruising around the area of the wound and as you can see the skull is cracked. Four of his injuries are set together and there is deep bruising of the neck muscles. This suggests to me that the victim was already incapable of resisting or he was held by the neck – strongly by a left hand – when he was struck about the head.'

Sergeant Hawkins, for all his innate cynicism, was impressed. 'Crikey, like ruddy Sherlock Holmes.'

'Better,' the pathologist said and looked modestly at his shit-stained rubber gloves. 'And he was alive still, I'll be bound – I'll confirm that in his lungs when I open him up in half a mo – at the time he was pushed into the sewage.'

Tin Leg's always dicey stomach churned momentarily at the thought. Hurriedly he asked, 'No clue, Doc, about who might have done the dirty deed, I suppose?'

Surprisingly enough the pathologist grinned and answered,

'Yes, there is. Well, enough to get someone started on the murderer. For,' his face grew serious, 'we are dealing with murder. Funny, what, a murder inside a prison. Never attended that kind of death before, I admit.'

The Major let him finish, but by now his mind was racing. Had the medic really come up with a clue that might lead him to the murderer and to what was going on in the POW camp? For he had known for weeks now that something was happening here among the Huns. As he had said to his second-in-command, Sergeant Hawkins, more than once, 'Hawkins, I can feel it in my bones. Once you've been behind the wire – ' he meant the barbed wire of a prisoner-of-war camp – 'you never lose the feeling . . . that there's something afoot.'

'Rather you than me, sir,' was always Hawkins' standard reply. 'It's knowledge dearly bought, sir. I mean, what a frigging life, if you can't have yer pint o' wallop of an evening and get a bit of the other every Saturday night. No sir, you can have yer ruddy POW camps.'

'Now,' Tin Leg said somewhat hesitantly, as if he were afraid that the doctor would disappoint him with whatever evidence of a murderer he might have found during his examination of the dead Hun, 'what is it?'

'This.' The pathologist opened the palm of his left glove. There in the middle of the rubber there was the dull glint of silver.

For a moment the Major was too startled to identify it aloud.

Not Sergeant Hawkins. He exclaimed immediately, 'Well, I frigging live and breathe, sir . . . it's . . . the collar dog of the SS!'

For a moment a heavy silence hung over the little Nissen hut, which stank of ether and human faeces, as the two soldiers stared fixedly at the crooked runes of that organisation which had held the whole of Europe in fear and trembling these last five years or so – Himmler's Armed SS: the badge of those black-clad blond giants who had blazed the trail of the 'New Order' across three continents and a dozen different countries.

Seemingly the pathologist didn't notice their astonishment; or if he did, he didn't remark upon it. Instead, holding the badge up to the naked bulb so that they could see it better in the

weak yellow light, he said, 'If you look more closely, you can
see the threads of material here . . . and here.' He pointed at the
crooked cross of the pagan Nordics.' Under the lense, you can
see those bits of cloth are ragged, indicating that the badge had
been pulled off the material forcibly.'

'From the assailant's collar?' Tin Leg said, helping the medic.

'Yes.' He looked at the middle-aged major and undersized
sergeant, also middle-aged, as if seeing them for the first time.
'Does it help you?'

The NCO looked up at his superior. He mouthed the word
'Blacks'.

The pathologist caught the word. He said, 'Black . . . what
does that mean?'

The Major hesitated and then told himself that within a
couple of hours or so the civilian doctor would be back in his
Southampton hospital, the PM here in the remote POW camp
at Devizes already half-forgotten. No harm could be done by
appeasing his curiosity now. So he said, 'Black is a category for
the the Huns we – er – look after here. That's all.'

The pathologist looked interested. 'Black,' he began, 'why,
that's a strange categorisation, Major. Why—'

Major Clapton didn't give him a chance to continue. He said,
slapping his tin leg with his swagger cane, as if he were in a great
hurry to get away, 'Got to see a dog about a bone, Doc. Thanks
for your assistance. The chief clerk will see you get your fee –
the orderly room opposite the gate. We've got a staff car
waiting for you when you're finished. But if you're not in a
great hurry, why not come over to the Mess? There'll be a jar or
two and we've got Spam on the menu today.' And with that
promise of great culinary delights in store, he put on his cap,
saluted and limped out, his tin leg squeaking noisily.

The pathologist watched them go. Then he picked up his
scalpel and, whistling through his teeth happily, he began his
incision just above the genitals. The dead man's guts started to
spill out in a nice neat orderly fashion. He wouldn't need the
slops bucket, after all . . .

Outside, Tin Leg pulled up his collar against the biting cold of the compound. Sergeant Hawkins frowned. He was a regular, having been in the Army since he'd enlisted as a drummer boy just at the end of the First World War. He was a stickler for proper dress; he never would have turned up the collar of his battledress blouse, however cold it was. All the same he forgave the Major. The Old Man might not observe all the rules, but he *was* a good fighting soldier. He'd seen more battles than some of his senior officers had had good frigging dinners. Now he said, as he tried to keep in step with Major and his tin leg, 'What do you think, sir? Something to do with our problem?'

The Major nodded, taking in the group of 'Blacks' at the far end of the compound, huddled together and murmuring under their breath; and as always that arrogant bastard, *Scharführer* Heidreich in their centre, running the show. He was a handsome, perfect physical specimen in the Hun fashion – blond, bold and blue-eyed, his teeth gleaming like polished ivory when he smiled, which was often. All the same, Major Clapton wouldn't trust him as far as he could throw him – and that was not at all. 'Yes, I think, Sergeant – ' he frowned with frustration – 'The buggers are too full of themselves. They have been for weeks now. It's almost as if they're getting orders and information from outside which is encouraging them. It's certain that the Greys and Whites are scared of 'em. But how are they getting that info? Bugger it, tell me that, Sergeant Hawkins.'

Hawkins had his answer ready; he had had for several days now. 'They've got a secret radio, sir,' he snapped without hesitation. 'They call it "Radio Loens". Twice I've overheard 'em mention it – not the BBC Forces Radio or anything like that which we listen to in the camp. Radio Loens.'

'Radio Loens?' the Major echoed and now there was no mistaking the look of excitement on his old, lined, weary face. 'Did you say Loens?'

'I did, sir, and I looked it up in a German dictionary and there isn't such a word.'

'I'm not surprised, Hawkins. Loens is not the name of a thing . . . it's that of a man.'

'A man?'

'Yes, did you hear this ever?' Suddenly Tin Leg started – to Hawkins's amazement – to whistle. Even the POWs close by were surprised. They looked as amazed as Hawkins. But here and there a couple with malicious smiles on their faces began to applaud and join in – admittedly in low voices, as if they were half afraid to be heard – '*Kommt die Kunde, du bist gefallen . . . Denn wir fahren . . . fahren gegen Eng-geland Engeland.*'

Abruptly Major Clapton flushed red and shouted in German, then in English, 'Any man who doesn't stop singing immediately is heading straight into the cooler for fifteen days! *Nun wirds bald?*'

The singing ceased as abruptly as it had started, though the group of Blacks around *Scharführer* Heidreich continued to grin maliciously. He shouted across boldly, '*Bravo Herr Major! Gut gemacht!*'

'Cheeky bugger.' Clapton swore as Hawkins said, 'Yes, now I know. I heard it last month when we got that batch of U-boat men. Glad they whipped them off smartish to the Yanks and America. They were singing that song.'

'Yes,' Clapton responded, 'and do you know who wrote it back in the last show?'

Hawkins shook his head.

'I'll tell you, Sergeant. It was a Jerry named Loens – *Hermann* Loens, if I'm not mistaken. He hated the British, although he was supposed to be a bit of a poet.'

'And didn't know it,' Hawkins chimed.

Clapton ignored the comment. 'So we have a murder on our hands, obviously carried out by those bloody Blacks over there – ' he indicated the Heidreich group with his cane – 'or on their orders. We have a radio, code-named "Loens". And Loens was the name of that dead poet who hated the British and wrote a virulent anti-British marching song which was adopted by Kaiser Bill's navy in the last war and which today they still sing, though since 1940 and cancellation by Hitler of 'Operation Sealion'* there has not been much of a chance that

* The German plan to invade Britain in the summer of that year.

the Huns would ever "march against England", as the song has it.' He shook his greying head in bewilderment. 'Now what do you make of all that, Sergeant Hawkins?'

Hawkins shook his head and said in a voice filled with exasperation, 'Search me, sir . . . but I'm buggered – pardon my French – if I can make head nor tail of it.'

Opposite them, *Scharführer* Heidreich continued to grin in that so German, malicious fashion of his, as if *he* knew all right.

Five

T he big US Army 2½-ton truck came rumbling along the
dead-straight, cobbled French road fringed with winter-
naked poplars. In the back half a dozen shabby German POWs
in their ankle-length greatcoats stood shivering, as if they were
in the throes of a fever, the ends of their pinched noses red and
dripping.

Enviously, as they swayed back and forth with the road's
potholes, they stared at the well-fed GI guard. He was wrapped
in a thick, real-wool coat, his hands clad in a pair of thick
woollen khaki gloves. In his turn the young soldier, his jaws
moving back and forth as he chewed gum like a contented cow
does its cud, stared back at them watchfully. It was still a way to
the Cherbourg POW cage and he wasn't about to lose his
prisoners. That would mean a swift posting to a rifle company
in the line and sudden death.

Now the deuce-and-a-half slowed. They were approaching a
major crossroads and the usual check. The guard relaxed a
little. The coloured driver braked. The guard poked his head
around the canvas, his eyes watering immediately in the icy
wind. A black MP stood there from the 'Red Ball Express'.* At
his side there was a shabby French gendarme in a cape. The
guard ducked back under cover while the MP checked the
driver's trip ticket. While he did so, the French policeman
nodded imperceptibly to the German POWs. The guard didn't
notice. He was too busy sticking another piece of gum in his
mouth. They rolled on, heading west.

* A supply route from Cherbourg to the front, manned by coloured drivers.

44

The Great Escape

The miles passed in leaden, freezing boredom. The French countryside on both sides of the road lay dead and seemingly empty. Perhaps it was too cold and the soil too winter-barren for the farmers. Perhaps they were in their parlours, nestled around their blazing iron stoves, reading farmer papers, while their wives knitted or sewed at their side. The guard, a farm boy himself, wished he was with them, however boring, rather than being trapped here with half a dozen hulking kraut soldiers. They slowed down to enter a tumbledown village. It was nearly as empty as the desolate countryside. However, near the Café des Sports opposite the washing troughs and church, there were a few twisted, sour-faced men in suits and *sabots* smoking pipes. They stared at the American truck. The black driver waved cheerfully. They did not respond. They stared back at their 'liberators' sourly with a kind of dogged peasant defiance. One of them actually took his little white pipe out of his mouth and spat a stream of yellow tobacco juice into the gutter.

'Happy bastards,' the GI guard commented.

The freezing prisoners didn't respond. Probably they didn't speak English.

It was about then, as the truck started to leave the tumble-down village, that a little girl with spindle-like legs ran out of the baker's. She took the long white loaf she was carrying and threw it into the back of the truck. It struck the guard and fell to his feet on the muddy steel floor. 'Well I'll be fucked!' he exclaimed and, raising his voice, was about to shout at the girl, but she'd already disappeared into the next stairwell. 'The little French bitch,' he said and stared down at the dirty loaf. It looked warm, but he daren't eat it. He'd been warned about the dangers of, not only French dames, but also their food and water; a guy could get more diseases than you could shake a stick at in France, according to the medics. With his foot, he edged the loaf towards the surprised German POWs. 'Here,' he said, 'some chow.' He made a gesture as if he was shoving food into his mouth, saying, '*du versten . . . essen.*'

They did.

One of them seized the loaf eagerly, a look of delight at the treat to come in his eyes. Next moment the light faded. He made a cutting gesture with his dirty right hand and said, '*Messer?*'

The GI understood. He wanted to divide the bread fairly and needed a knife to do so. He shook his head firmly. 'Hell no,' he snapped. '*Nix Messer*. I'm not having you Krauts sticking a knife in my ribs. I'm not that kind of a jerk. Hey, gimme the loaf, I'll do it for you with my sidearm.' He held out his free hand.

The German smiled and handed him the loaf with a polite '*bitte schön*'.

Carefully he took it, not removing his gaze from the prisoners for a moment. Now he placed his M-1 rifle between his knees, pulled out his bayonet and prepared to slice the still-warm loaf. He never managed it. In that same instant the first German dived forward. The startled GI caught a glimpse of the silver SS runes on the German's collar. It was about the last thing he did see.

Next moment a body came hurtling through the air. He gasped with shock. He went down on to the wet floor. His bayonet rattled after him. A heavy nailed boot slammed into his jaw. His head clicked back. A handful of teeth shot into the mud like white pearls. Next minute everything went black . . .

Five minutes later, the guard, stripped to his long johns, was bundled up in the back of the truck, with the SS man who had attacked him dressed now in his GI uniform, happily smoking one of his looted Chesterfields and seated on the tailgate like a man who hadn't a care in the world. The truck rumbled on into the growing darkness . . .

Doktor, Doktor Josef-Maria Pettinger, once known to the *Abwehr*, the German Secret Service, as 'the little Doctor' (which he was, twice over), had come a long way for this 'appointment with destiny', as he called it to himself, whenever he thought of the operation's long-term potential – a whole lifetime to be exact. Indeed, his life, since he was conceived by a father he had never seen, had been one long training for an operation which in this dire winter of 1944 might change the whole future of his Fatherland, the Greater German Reich.

Back in 1915 his father had marched away. *Oberleutnant der Reserve*, School Inspector Ignaz Pettinger had marched away with his Swabian Infantry Regiment heading for the slaughter of the Western Front, never to return (at least during Josef-Maria's baby years). The average life of an infantry officer in the trenches that year of 1915 had been some six weeks. Surprisingly enough the ex-Imperial school inspector had survived three years. Perhaps he had just been lucky. In the end, however, Ignaz Pettinger was transferred to the divisional staff, which should have meant he would survive the war. But that wasn't to be. On the afternoon of 11 November 1918, four hours after the armistice had been declared and the guns had ceased firing, his father had crossed the no man's land between the trenches in the Metz area to discuss the terms of his division's withdrawal from the French front. He had never reached the lines of the US 1st Army.

As his father's shocked comrades had told his mother when the division had marched back into their garrison at a flag-bedecked Stuttgart, with the bands playing and crowds cheering as if they had won the war and not lost it, the *Oberleutnant* had been shot in cold blood in broad daylight by a drunken Yankee officer who had missed all the fighting and had cried, 'I'm gonna get me a Heinie before I goddam go home!' He had.

All he remembered of that disclosure was the bands playing and his mother declaring, 'On the first day of peace, shot by the Yankee murderers!'

Pettinger looked around the faces of his comrades in the back of the truck, still driven by the unsuspecting Negro of the 'Red Ball Express'. Their hangdog looks had vanished now. Those who had managed to hide their 'flatmen' when they had been first searched by the *Amis* were raising the little bottles to their lips and gratefully guzzling the hot, fiery schnapps. Others were looting the GI guard's and driver's packs for C-rations and anything else edible they could find.

Pettinger was pleased. They had reverted to being the tough, swaggering devil-may-care Skorzeny troopers that they were. What was it they always boasted, 'Roll on death and let's have a fuck at the angels?' It was a sentiment that the little double-doctor approved of . . .

During his boyhood his hatred of the *Amis* had been nurtured by his widowed mother who had attempted to eke out a living in the midst of terrible inflation and the collapse of the Mark on a worthless pension paid by the Weimar socialist government. For the lonely, disturbed, intelligent boy, the *Amis* had always been 'terrorists', 'gangsters', 'degenerate cowboys'.

Surprisingly enough, however, when the only chance he had of continuing his studies was to go to Yale in 1938 for a year on an American scholarship, he found he liked the Americans.

They were open, hospitable and kind. For the poor provincial student, whose life had been hitherto centred on his widowed mother and his books, he had found America an eye-opener. For the first time in his poverty-stricken life, Pettinger had begun to enjoy himself. He went to fraterniy clambakes and 'bull sessions' over endless glasses of weak beer. He actually started to date girls and 'scored', now and again, as his 'frat brothers' phrased it enviously. It seemed, in the United States, life was all sunshine, internationally respected professors and, above all, *fun*!

In 1939 when Germany had gone to war, he had hurried back on the *Bremen* to volunteer. He hadn't the slightest interest in politics and the whys and wherefores of this new war. But he was a patriot like all his family. He knew he had to sacrifice the goodlife for the sake of his country. But, in one respect, he was different from that father he had never known. Instead of volunteering for the infantry, he had applied to join the German Secret Service, *die Abwehr*, for he had already guessed from his year at Yale that America would join in the war on the side of the 'English cousins' and he had no intention *then* of shooting his former US buddies.

Admiral Canaris, the head of the *Abwehr*, had welcomed the 'double-doctor' – for by now he had obtained an American doctorate to go with his German *Doc.Phil.* – with open arms. After all, *he* was a brilliant linguist, together with all his other talents, and, snob that he was, Admiral Canaris always considered his *Abwehr* as a 'service of gentlemen'. A *Herr Doktor* was most welcome.

Between 1939 and 1941, Pettinger served secretly on many fronts under many different guises. He was a bricklayer's labourer working on Maginot Line constructions in French Alsace. A year later he had been transformed into a Baltic German horse-trader in Lithuania, spying on the Russians. Thereafter he was transferred to the Middle East to become a Maltese merchant in Alexandria, working with Egyptian nationalists against the British . . .

In 1942, when the enemy raids on Germany had started in earnest after the first RAF 'Thousand Bomber Raid' on Cologne that May, he had been urgently summoned back to Stuttgart; something had happened to his beloved mother. It had. She was dead by the time he arrived back.

Solemnly the family doctor, old Dr Peters, had ushered him into the dark room. He murmured that death had been instantaneous . . . His mother wouldn't have suffered at all . . . the bomb which had killed her had done its work swiftly . . . painlessly . . .

Numbly he had insisted on seeing the body, now lying on the old oaken table in the centre of the room with its drawn curtain and lilies, and covered by a plush cloth, as if she were royalty. Doctor Peters had tried to convince him not to; it was always better to remember one's loved ones as they had been in life, he had insisted. In the end, Dr Peters, with a worried look on his old wrinkled face, had drawn back the purple covering. Later he had realised that purple showed no blood.

Where his mother's face had been there was a bloody stump sticking up from the white nightgown. The bomb had taken her head off! He had fought back the bitter green bile which had threatened to choke him and gasped thickly, 'The Royal Air Force? . . . The Tommies?'

Peters had not answered immediately. Instead he had replaced the cloth and had escorted Pettinger outside into the fresh air, which still smelled of burned wood and high explosive. 'No,' he said, 'the Americans – the *Amis*. They were aiming at—'

But Pettinger was no longer listening. He had been overcome by a wave of hate. Twenty years before, the Americans had killed his unknown father so treacherously. Now in 1942 they had returned to kill his poor gentle mother who had never knowingly harmed a soul in her life. Now he saw those laughing, open, easygoing people he had known at Yale for what they were – unthinking automatons, who killed from afar with their damned machines, safe from any form of retaliation. Remote murderers, they had shot his father with a sniper's rifle and now his mother with one of those Flying Fortresses of which the *Amis* were so proud, from five kilometres up in the sky, perhaps not even aware of what suffering they were causing so far below. What had the narrator said of Tom and Daisy, the smart people in Fitzgerald's *Great Gatsby*: 'They were careless people, who broke things and didn't pick up the pieces'. Something like that, and that's what the Americans were. That day in Stuttgart he had sworn he would have his revenge on the *Amis* who had fooled him so easily at Yale with their glittering, open-handed, but superficial, heartless world.

Two days later he had volunteered for the *Abwehr*'s section dealing with North America. He had thrown himself into the dirty work of that particular section, heart and soul. He had arranged the sexual seduction by whores of young American POWs so that they'd spy on their comrades in the camps. He had blackmailed US businessmen in neutral Switzerland who had not been too ethical in their dealings with German front men in that country. He had bribed US consular officials in neutral Madrid, Stockholm, Ankara to reveal diplomatic secrets etc. for the 'good 'ole US greenback'. No job had been too dirty or underhand for the '*Herr Doktor*'.

But although he had enjoyed his work immensely, relishing the Americans' downfall with true German *schadenfreude*, Pettinger had longed for a clearcut, decisive intelligence mission.

Two months before, he had been given it. By no less a person than that scar-faced giant Skorzeny. Just as Skorzeny's daring rescue of Mussolini from his mountain fastness in 1943 had changed the course of the war in Italy, now he was going to help to do the same in the West. If things worked out as Skorzeny planned, the Western Allies would have to negotiate better terms with the Führer than Roosevelt's demand for an 'unconditional surrender' on the part of the Germans. The Fatherland might well be saved yet.

Sitting there in the truck, speeding ever westwards to the new mission, the little *Herr Doktor* told himself that whatever happened on the political front in the future, one thing was certain: this was going to be America's Black Christmas! He sighed contentedly. He closed his eyes. Moments later he was breathing gently and fast asleep, as if he hadn't a care in the world. The truck sped on . . .

Six

Lt Washington Lee had been in the Cherbourg replacement depot for nearly a week. But although he knew he ought to be making ever greater efforts to get to his new posting with the US 11th Armored Division in England, the delights of Marie-Claire's bed oftentimes made him forget his duty – and his desire to prove himself at the fighting front. Besides, he could always justify his lack of action by the fact that the camp authorities didn't seem to have the slightest interest in speeding his passage across that narrow stretch of water to Southampton. Indeed, the portmasters were more dutiful in expediting the hundreds of German prisoners who came flooding into the supply port every day. He could understand why. The Germans, all fit and in the prime of their youth, presented a permanent danger to the security of the Allies' major supply port for the fighting front. After all, there were simply not enough GIs there to guard them. Besides, he guessed the powers-that-be weren't particularly impressed by a black officer belonging to a non-combatant outfit such as the Corps of Counter-Intelligence.

So he passed the days and, when he could work it, his nights with the pretty, well-bred French girl and it wasn't only French eighteenth-century port architecture and irregular verbs, as he told himself, that was the great attraction. For Marie-Claire was very sexually sophisticated for a girl so young. If it had a name, she knew it, and if it didn't, she'd work out those delightful sexual antics, not to say perversions, in their rumpled, sweat-stained four-poster as they went along. 'Holy cow, MC,' he would howl in mock anguish, as she ran her long manicured nails down the length of his sweat-glazed, black body yet again suggestively, 'give a guy a break, can't ya? Remember I'm only a weak man.'

But, weak or not, she was relentless in her pursuit of sexual satisfaction and those cunning fingers – and lips – would be soon engaged arousing him yet again for another delightful session 'in the hay', as she called it since she'd picked up the phrase from him. Indeed the word had become their secret sexual code word, with 'Hay?' and a delightful shrug of her pretty shoulders meaning, 'Now?' – and sometimes she wasn't particularly careful where she picked to utter the code word. Twice he had been forced (in the nicest sense of the word) to take action when she had uttered the word. Indeed in one case when they had found it somewhat difficult to arrange a place for a hurried copulation, he had had her doggy fashion behind a derrick on what they had supposed to be an empty dock.

It was not, and they had been surprised, almost at the moment of climax, by an elderly French angler, pushing his bike, with his rod over his shoulder, whose eyes had virtually popped out of his head at the sight: MC with her silken knickers around her ankles, her dress thrown up to reveal her shapely behind, while he pounded her furiously and she gasped, equally furiously, with every stroke. The French girl had not hesitated a single second. She had turned on the astonished Frenchman and barked as if she were a bitch on heat, not wanting to be disturbed (she, of course, was). He had dropped his rod and, with surprising speed for an old man, hopped on board his bike and fled at top speed. She hadn't even stopped moving. All that indicated that she had felt herself disturbed was an urgent wiggle of her delightful butt and the command, 'Hay!' Obediently he had given more of the strawy stuff . . .

Still, Marie-Claire Jondral remained something of a mystery to the young officer, whenever he had time to think about the matter, which admittedly, due to her good company and sexual demands, wasn't very often that week. According to her own story, her parents had dispatched her to an uncle in Cherbourg just before the invasion. They had felt that Paris would be too dangerous once the Allies landed, not only because of the latter but also due to the French communists (she was clearly afraid of the 'Reds', as she always called the communist underground), who might well attempt to take over the government by force 'on Moscow's orders'. But when he asked where her uncle was now and why she was staying, not with him, but in one of the few hotels not damaged or requisitioned by the American authorities, she never seemed to have a satisfactory answer.

Nor was Marie-Claire, alias 'MC', able to explain how she managed to live off the black market on her worthless francs. Naturally he brought US canned goods, cigarettes and the like from the camp, which helped out considerably. All the same, she never seemed to run out of those priceless sheer silk stockings she favoured; nor did she appear to work. But she always had money.

Once he had asked her right out, 'MC, how do you manage? Where do you get your money for all this?' He indicated the luxurious bedroom, which even had running hot-and-cold water, a great luxury then. By way of an answer, she had laughed cheekily and thrown up the back of her flounced skirt to reveal her delightful, sheer silk-clad rump and giggled, 'I have lovers of course . . .' And that was that.

But as besotted as he was with this first white girl he had slept with who was intelligent and beautiful, totally uninhibited about sex and his colour, (and, handsome and intelligent as he was, Lee had slept with several during his days at Harvard in the supposedly liberated North of the United States), his training in Intelligence had begun to reassert itself after the first few days of passionate, all-consuming lovemaking. Why had she picked on him out of all the free young intelligent white lieutenants who flooded Cherbourg waiting to be sent to an early death at the front? It wasn't because he was black in the sexual sense – MC had no erotic fantasiss in that direction. He knew; he'd asked her. How did she live? Why, now that Paris was liberated, didn't she return to her family and the excitements of the capital and flee this grim half-ruined port, dominated by soldiers and the dreary business of war?

Was it because of the port and its role as the Allies' major supply centre that she was here? Yet she never asked military questions. All that had interested her was where he was stationed – the reinforcement barracks – and how much free time he had available for that delightful, exciting business of the 'hay'. Indeed, any casual observer of Marie-Clare would have concluded she was totally uninterested in the war; it seemed to mean nothing to her. He would have maintained she was completely selfish, wrapped up exclusively in her own body and its pleasures.

But, as Lt Lee told himself a couple of times rather ruefully, *he* wasn't a casual observer. He was a counter-intelligence agent who had already gained experience in the field, which had included the arrest of two 'sleeper' German agents at the US airfield at Etain near Verdun and that of an active agent caught working in Verdun's eighteenth-century citadel, who now rested six foot under the ground after being shot as a spy on the same ground where Marshal Petain had had his French Army mutineers shot back in 1917 in the Old War.

As a result he wasn't totally surprised when one dawn, while she snored softly in the rumpled bed, he had slipped naked to the vase on the mantlepiece which he used to piss in during the night, lifted it and found a piece of paper stuck to its bottom. His first inclination had been to crumple it up and hurry back to bed to snuggle up to her warm, inviting naked body. Something had stopped him.

He had urinated noiselessly in the vase and then, walking with it and the paper to the window, he had opened it, shivering a little at the sudden cold air, emptied the jug – it saved a long walk down the creaky corridor to the WC – and held the scrap of paper up to the spectral light cast by the full moon.

Outside, all was silent in the blacked-out port save for the steady tread of some patrolling gendarme and, far away at the docks, the rusty rattle of a jackhammer as the port engineers worked day and night to repair the place which the Germans had successfully sabotaged before they had fled. Eyes narrowed to catch the faint light, he stared at the paper. There wasn't much on it, just a set of initials and a rough, badly executed sketch of an animal or something of that nature which he recognised, as he did the initials, almost immediately.

It was the Egyptian Sphinx and, although it was in black and white pencil and not the gold or yellow of the original, there was no missing the fact that it was the insignia of his own corps, Counter-Intelligence, the CIC.

For what seemed an eternity he stared at it and wondered why she had copied the insignia from the lapel of his 'Ike Jacket' (for it could only be the work of 'MC'). What interest could his mistress have in such matters? She had always seemed totally uninterested in the military. Why this? How long he stood there naked, his black body taking on a greenish hue in the light of the moon, he couldn't recollect afterwards. In the end he gave up, the puzzle unsolved, and returned to the warmth of her nubile body. In the morning when he woke up and she had gone to fetch the fresh croissants upon which she insisted for breakfast, as if there wasn't such a thing as bread rationing – the note under the vase had vanished.

But not his suspicions. For he had realised by then that all was not what it seemed with Marie-Claire. He started to watch her . . .

The *Herr Doktor* was watching, too. The truck they had abandoned on a 'D' road, 10 kilometres outside Cherbourg, setting fire to it and its now dead occupants, the white guard and the black driver. There would be an investigation, once the truck was found. But that wouldn't be for a long time yet. First the French would strip it of anything of value and anything they could barter on the black market before the charred carcass would be reported to the local gendarmerie, who would wait till they passed on the information in case they, too, could profit from this unexpected American treasure. In the meantime Pettinger had smuggled the half a dozen Skorzeny toughs into the great holding cage for German POWs who had already been checked and cross-examined for the next stage of their journey across the sea to Southampton and distribution to POW camps throughout the enemy country.

Now with the Skorzeny men – some of the elite from his
Hunting Commando, stationed in that remote castle outside
Berlin – taken care of, Pettinger concentrated on his second
task: the reactivation of the sleeper network that Skorzeny and
the *Abwehr* had left behind when the German Army had fled
France.

The 'sleepers' were a mixed bunch, the remains of that
confused mess that France had been in immediately after her
alleged 'liberation', that – Pettinger told himself cynically –
most Frenchmen didn't want or weren't one bit interested in.
'The Liberation of the Oppressed Europeans' (to the man brave
resistance fighters) was something, he always opined, that the
fat Jewish plutocorats in Hollywood had foisted on the gullible
young men who had landed on the beaches to die and fight for
them. The 'sleepers' were all sorts, nationalities and political
creeds. There were communist agitators who would employ any
means, even colloboration with the Nazis, to bring down de
Gaulle's provisional government in France. There were fugitives from Petain's Vichy – right-wing fascists who had gone
underground and were prepared to do anything to save their
treacherous necks. There were German-speaking Alsatians who
had thrown in their lot with the Greater Germany and still
wouldn't believe they were fighting for a lost cause. There were
adventurers, petty crooks, whores who had bestowed their
favours too lavishly on the German occupiers, unmarried
mothers who had produced German bastards and had fled
their native villages and provincial towns and who now had to
accept German money to support themselves and their bastards. As Pettinger tried to put a sleeper organisation back
together in occupied Cherbourg right under the noses of the
Amis, he told himself he was dealing with everything from noble
idealists, who still believed in that old Nazi fable of a 'New
Europe' under 'German Leadership'* to treacherous venial
assassins who would knife you in the back for a couple of

* Nazi Germany had founded the first 'Common Market' (at least in paper)
back in 1942.

sous. But he often remarked to himself, in the manner of lonely men who talk to themselves a lot, 'Beggars can't be chosers'.

And that fact worried him; for he knew that men and women who had betrayed a cause once, for whatever reason – change of political allegiance or simply hard cash – could do the same again. It would be necessary to have someone in authority on the other side, another traitor, of course, who could warn him in time in case of that eventuality. Now, as he watched Marie-Clare Schneider saunter along the quayside on this fine autumn morning, together with her black lieutenant of the Intelligence, making a handsome, if strange couple, with the breeze whipping her skirt up and about her delightfully long, silk-clad legs, the little *Herr Doktor*, at whom no one would have given a second glance, told himself he had found the ideal man for that particular piece of double-dealing . . .

Seven

'You know, I think you're trying to corrupt me totally,' Lt Lee said, and he was only half-joking, as he pushed his way with MC through the crowd of excited and mostly drunk officers attempting to enter the back-street waterfront dive. 'Besides they only serve alleged champagne here and you know what that kind of soda pop costs . . . Remember I'm only a lowly first looey on sixty bucks a week.'

She gave that silvery careless laugh of hers, 'Why worry about money, *cherie*. Where do you think those officers get their money from?' She indicated the officers already seated with the giggling, excited 'hostesses' in the smoke-filled underground room, buying bottles of champagne at ten dollars a time, as if they couldn't get rid of their great wads of greasy French notes quickly enough.

'Keep it to a low roar, for God's sake,' he hissed, as a few heads turned their way. 'You don't want me to get into trouble, do you?' He might well have added, 'and lynched, too'. For there wasn't a black face in the whole joint. White officers didn't like black ones watching them let their hair down – even the liberal ones from the North. That was going too far. In this kind of club, he wanted to keep a low profile. Drunken US officers and temporary gentlemen were just as unpredictable with blacks as were drunken, hairy-assed GIs.

By way of a reply, she let her right arm slip behind her back and, under the cover of the throng, pressed his penis encouragingly. As always she was completely outrageous; Marie-Clare simply didn't care about convention or anything else for that matter. She lived for the moment and whatever pleasures it

59

brought. '*So why does she frigging well make sketches of your insignia?*' a harsh little voice rasped at the back of his mind, but at that moment, with all the noise, the drunken laughter, the blast of a record of Glenn Miller heading off for Pennsylvania yet again, it was a question that he didn't have the inclination to answer.

The slim, cute waitress with the cropped hair and the man's dickey suit, placed them at a table behind a pillar at the back of the room, something for which Lee was grateful (though naturally MC protested) and even without their ordering brought them the obligatory bottle of champagne and three glasses, one for herself, it seemed. It appeared to be that kind of place, where women could do exactly as they liked, as long as they performed afterwards; and judging by the worn looks on the rouged, raddled faces of the Frenchwomen all around, Lee surmised that most of them had never ceased 'performing' ever since the Yanks had captured Cherbourg in the summer.

Once again, the French girl pressed his penis underneath the table, twining her legs with his, while the waitress drank a swift glass of champagne without being asked to, saying, 'They say it's very exciting. Oh, la, la . . . women, you know.' Her dark eyes flashed.

Lee didn't know. He didn't care though, for already she had him half aroused and he hoped he didn't have to get up to take a piss in the '*cour*'. He'd knock the damned champagne glssses off the table if he did in his present condition.

Moments later the drums rolled, the lights lowered save round the little stage, suddenly illuminated by a blood-red spot, and the show could begin. But suddenly Lee was not particularly interested in whatever pornographic spectacle she had brought him to see, but in MC herself. For her gaze wasn't fixed on the stage expectantly like virtually everyone else's in that tight, smoke-filled room, but on the exit which led to the yard and the *pissoir*.

He followed the direction of her gaze, somehow feeling that it was important to do so; for since the incident with the sketch he had started to watch MC in the way he might a suspect and not a woman who had done things with him in the 'hay' that he had never experienced with any another female. He blinked in the bad light and for a moment he wasn't sure that his watering eyes weren't misleading him. There was a small man standing there, as if he might well not have come through the front door but had slipped in through the exit in the fashion of some kid in a movie theatre back home trying to avoid paying a quarter to see the Saturday afternoon Andy Hardy movie or *Buck Rogers in the 25th Century.*

He blinked and, when he opened his eyes again, the little man had vanished, as if he hadn't been there in the first place, and she was saying in an alcohol-thickened voice, 'Would you like to put your hand up between the waitress's legs? I could arrange it for you. It'll make you ready for later,' and she rolled her eyes in that comic manner with which she always indicated that unbridled naughtiness was in the offing.

However, before he could even consider the offer, the red spot had moved to reveal two women standing perfectly still and totally naked in the shadows to the rear of the little stage. The audience gasped collectively, as they were caught completely by surprise by the spectacle.

One of the naked women was older. Her face was stamped with a kind of aristocratic hawk-like dissipation. She sat in a straight-backed chair, bolt-upright like some pornographic queen. But it was clear to Lee that she wasn't doing this just for the money; she looked as if she really *enjoyed* the work.

The other was young, barely out of her teens. Her slim body was painted a bronze colour, beautiful and gleaming, the nipples of her tiny breasts tinted a bright pink. Even her sparse pubic hair had been brushed to make it appear fuller. 'Beauty and the beast,' Marie-Clare whispered, and giggled.

Lee frowned, as if he suddenly didn't like what he saw. But the rest of the audience was on tenterhooks, fascinated by what *they* saw, obviously wondering what form this particular '*exhibition*' was going to take.

For what seemed a long time nothing happened. To Lee's right a chaplain in the US Army polished his pince-nez yet again, as if he was going to make the most of the spectacle when it commenced. As for the rest or the viewers, they seemed to be sitting on the edge of their seats, not talking, not even drinking. Why, the whores themselves had fallen silent. Lee bit his bottom lip abruptly; suddenly he felt very out of place here. There was something wrong, but he couldn't quite put his finger on what it was.

The bass drum started to sound softly. Its rhythm suggested the throb of a human heart. The young woman reached out slowly and delicately. She released the gold band that held the older woman's raven-black dyed hair in place. It cascaded down to her naked, skinny shoulders. The other woman seemed not to notice. She continued to sit there bolt upright, staring into space. Using an ivory-backed brush, the blonde began to brush the long black hair. She gave it long, languid strokes, as the sound of the solitary drum grew almost imperceptibly louder. In the room, a tense silence continued to reign.

Lee took a look round carefully. Nothing!

On the little stage, the older woman relaxed. She sank back in the chair. She thrust her full, slightly hanging breasts forward voluptuously. Her legs opened, as if of their own volition. The audience gave a collective gasp at the new sight. Next to him, MC suddenly sank her long nails into his free hand. He winced with pain and suppressed his little cry just in time. He could feel the cold sweat running down the small of his back now. Lee didn't like it.

The young girl had ceased her brushing. In a hoarse voice the older woman broke the heavy silence. 'Paint me,' she said in English in a hoarse, tense voice, as if her throat had suddenly dried up with passion or something.

The girl took up the brush from the little table next to the chair. She dipped it into the open pot of water paint. The woman shivered in anticipation. She drew in her stomach and thrust out her hanging breasts in anticipation. Next to Lee, the bespectacled chaplain gasped in the plaintive tones of the Middle West, 'Oh, my Gawd, what's she gonna do?' No one answered his question.

The girl toyed with the brush for what seemed a long time. The woman trembled even more. Lee could see the sweat pearls begin to trickle down her contorted, dissipated face. She was really enjoying this for God knows whatever perverted reason. Finally the girl touched her with the brush, a malicious smile on her girlish face. The woman gasped audibly. It was as if someone had dropped something burningly hot on her naked flesh.

Next to him Marie-Clare gasped, 'Isn't it exciting?'

Lee looked hard at her face in the blood-red light, as if seeing it for the very first time. He didn't like what he saw. Her face seemed to have aged, grown coarse and as dissipated as that of the older woman up there on the stage; both were indulging themselves, he realised abruptly, in their perverted fantasies. Suddenly he felt nauseated, even sick to his stomach.

Behind the man with the red spot, in the impenetrable darkess outside the light cast by the spot, the watching *Herr Doktor* saw the black man's look and, with the instant total recognition of a vision, realised that Lee had tumbled to the whole plot. Nigger, he might be, but the little Doctor knew that their would-be stooge was an intelligent, quick-thinking man: that was why they had picked him in the first place, once they had learned of what had happened in Verdun.

Now, the *Herr Doktor* reasoned, Lee was unrolling the whole plot in his brain, as the latter looked at the show, decadent and nauseating as it was, then back to Marie-Clare, who was drinking the disgusting spectacle in greedily, her crazy, drugged mind enjoying every perverted moment. He had to do something before the situation exploded. It wouldn't take the nigger long to put the finger on the girl. She'd talk. Keep her off the drugs for twenty-four hours and she'd be singing like a shitting canary. What was he going to do – and do *now*?

On the stage, the older woman's teeth were bared now like those of a wild animal. Her nostrils were flared. Sweat was pouring from her. The music was getting ever louder. The audience, carried away by the crazy frenzy of it all, had broken the tense silence. They were baying like animals. The chaplain

63

was standing on his chair, collar askew, pince-nez steamed up, snarling, face contorted, shouting, 'Grind it, baby . . . Come on . . . *GRIND!*'

Far off in the port yet another of the German delayed charges, laid a month or so before when they had fled Cherbourg, exploded. The little dive trembled. No one noticed. They were all too preoccupied with the frenzied spectacle on the stage, as the younger woman painted the older one's abdomen, getting ever closer to her spread legs, slapping on the red paint with wild abandon – grinning crazily as she did – so that it ran in a blood-red stream into that hairy groin.

By now the victim, for that was what she was, an angry Lee told himself, had virtually lost control of herself. Her hair was dishevelled, as she thrashed her head from side to side in wild abandon. Harsh, choked gasps came from deep down inside her. Her eyes popped out of her head like those of someone demented. Her long skinny fingers, tipped in blood-red varnish, were crooked into claws of frustrated lust. And all the while, that malicious, vicious smile on her young face, the other woman enjoyed herself. This wasn't simply an act to titivate a bunch of sex-starved crude soldiers who were paying for it; this was real torture that gave her pleasure.

Lee swallowed hard. He shook his head like a man trying to wake from some terrible nightmare. What the hell was he doing here? He'd come to Europe to fight for his country against fascism and perhaps, indirectly one day, for his race. After all, black Americans could only prove that they were real, one hundred per cent Americans, if they suffered the same hardships, ran the same risks and perhaps suffered the same ultimate penalty in the cause of freedom as did their white compatriots. Now he had been reduced to this. 'Goddamit,' he cursed under his breath, his handsome, intelligent face full of self-disgust, 'what a helluva mess!'

In the circle of darkness, ears deafened by the frenzied noise on the stage, the little *Herr Doktor* hurriedly wound the big silencer on to the muzzle of his pistol. The nigger had to be killed – and there was no better place to do it than this dive. By the time the *Ami* bulls had gotten round to investigating the matter properly, Trojan Horse would be well underway, and no one would give a damn about what they discovered, if they discovered anything . . .

Suddenly, startlingly, the older woman threw back her head and laughed hysterically; it was almost like the baying of a crazy hound at the full moon. Way off there was another explosion at the port. In the audience flushed, sweating men were on their feet shouting at the two women on the stage. The whores were cackling wildly, too. Marie-Clare's drug-crazed eyes were almost popping from her glazed face. Next to her, Lee pushed back his chair and sprang to his feet. He'd had enough. He grabbed at his throat, as if he were choking. He had to get outside into the cold clean air of the night, away from this fetid, stinking, perverted dive that exhaled decadence and corruption.

Marie-Clare suddenly, it seemed, became aware of him again for the first time in a long while, 'What . . . what?' she stuttered.

For the first time he spoke to her in his fluent French. '*Tu con*! *Ne dit*—'

The curse died on his lips.

A slight crack. The faint whiff of burnt cordite. Marie-Clare's face froze in a look of absolute surprised horror. On the stage, the music faltered away. The older woman fell into the arms of the younger, sobbing. The noise died instantly. Lee stared open-mouthed at the sudden dark-red hole that had appeared in his lover's left breast, as if he could not comprehend what was going on. She moaned faintly and just once. Next moment she fell face forward on to the table, shattering glasses everywhere in the same instant that *Herr Doktor* fired again and Lee found himself being propelled backwards, as if he had just been struck by a gigantic fist.

BOOK TWO:

MARCH OR CROAK

One

The November night was crystal clear, and cold – very cold. It was for that reason that *Oberscharführer* Heidreich had picked it to venture out beneath the wire at Devizes with the recce party. He knew the *Amis*; he had fought against them both in Italy and France. They didn't like to be out at night and they certainly didn't like the night cold; then they sought shelter and the steam heat without which even their hardiest young men couldn't appear to live.

Now, in the icy cold silver sky, studded with the hard unfeeling stars, the little group of Germans in the recce party, followed by the 'burial detail', as Heidreich cynically called the bearers of the bundle, crept carefully through the lines of the 11th US Armored Division. Everywhere there were Sherman tanks and white sout cars shrouded by their tarpaulins, already glittering in the hoar frost, but so far, the SS non-com was pleased to note, not a sign of an *Ami* sentry.

It was all to the good, he told himself. They had a long way to go yet to the US military hospital, which was the objective of tonight's reconnaissance. Already they had checked the 11th's tank park, its armoury and naturally the great sprawling motor transport park, which housed the hundreds of vehicles that these rich *Amis* needed to move their supposed foot soldiers. As Heidreich saw it, American infantry never walked anywhere. One day, he supposed, they'd come equipped with wheels instead of feet. He smiled at the thought. Next moment the smile vanished as he concentrated on the task in front of him.

Naturally a hospital, which dealt with the day-to-day injuries of some 15,000 men in training, functioned differently than the training division. The 11th Armored, Heidreich told himself, was playing at war. The hospital, on the other hand, was doing its normal job. As a consequence, they could expect the night staff at Waller Camp to be just as alert as the Tommies back at Camp 23, Devizes, from which they had just 'escaped' temporarily. Heidreich grinned to himself at that 'escape'. Still, although the hospital staff would be working and alert, in an emergency they wouldn't be in a position to guard their vehicles as would the regular fighting troops of the 11th Armored. It was for that reason that they were carrying out this reconnaissance this icy November night when they would have dearly loved to be tucked up in their warm bunks back at Camp 23 – or at least part of it.

For, when Trojan Horse really commenced, they would need 'wheels' to execute their particular mission just as much as those lazy *Ami* infantrymen, who wouldn't walk to take a shit if they could ride to the crapper instead.

Now it was well past midnight. To the south, where Southampton and the coast lay, searchlights parted the clouds with silver fingers looking for enemy tip-and-run raiders. But below, visibility was too perfect. The Junkers 88s and Focke-Wulfe 190s were steering clear of Britain's coast this night. They'd be sitting ducks for the enemy night fighters. Otherwise, all was silent. The pubs had been closed for nearly two hours now and the rich GIs, their pockets full of newly minted English pounds, knew that even their money couldn't buy them a drink once the supplies had run out for the night. They, too, had long returned to their barracks and camps.

It was a fact that pleased Heidreich as the squat shape of the US hospital loomed up in the ghostly light. It, too, was well blacked out. But the chinks of light escaping from the windows and doors here and there and the muted hum of generators indicated that Waller Hospital was still in business and functioning. They'd have to be careful now. Heidreich paused and whispered to Zieman, his second-in-command from the 17th Panzer Grenadier Division, naturally a 'black' and SS like himself, 'Pass it back, Otto. Tell the – er – burial party to plant the dear departed here.' He chuckled evilly.

Zieman joined in and hissed, '*Wirds gemacht, Oberschar.*'

Heidreich waited till his order reached the 'burial party' to the rear and the signal came back that they had understood, before ordering, his voice tense now, 'Zieman, you know what to do?'

'*Jawohl.*'

'How many vehicles in their park and check if their tanks are full of gas.'

Zieman nodded his understanding. They had been through the plan often enough, but then Heidreich was a stickler for detail – and a bad bastard to cross.

'I'll get on with the nasty business. All right, *los.*'

Zieman didn't hesitate. '*Mir nach,*' he commanded. Next moment he and the men assigned to him were on their way, disappearing into the skeletal winter trees, as Heidreich prepared to carry out his part of tonight's recce.

The hot air hit Heidreich a physical blow in the face as he eased open the door to the hospital's little mortuary. The others of the recce party hadn't liked his choice of entry, but he had appeased them with a piece of his usual macabre humour, 'Stiffs don't bite, comrades – and they certainly don't squawk.' They certainly didn't. As they passed through the hot corridor back into the sudden cold of the long room with its dead bodies, the results of accidents, suicides, training casualties that any army outfit incurs even out of the line, they shivered. And it wasn't only with the cold; all save Heidreich. For his fertile, cunning mind was already working out the plan of protecting the general area of Waller Hospital's vehicle park, while the others seized the vital transport. This place, filled with dead men, now shrouded and silent under their sheets, would be as good a place as any to station the defensive squad. A machine gun set up at the far door nearest the escape route into the vehicle park, firing down the corridor along which they were currently advancing like silent ghosts risen from their graves, and they could hold off a whole company of *Amis*, especially those greenhorns of the 11th Armored.

Another door. He pressed his ear to it while the others waited tensely, hardly daring to breathe. There was activity on the other side, further down the brightly lit corridor. He could hear subdued voices and the soft creak of rubber-wheeled trolleys. Trying to remember the map of the place that he had seen in Tin Leg's office the last time he had been hauled in for interrogation, he wondered if the corridor led to the operating theatre. It could, for that place – he remembered from his own stay with the 'bone-menders' in Heidelberg the last time he had bought one in Russia – would be in constant use, day and night.

He turned and nodded to the others.

They knew what to do. They pulled out their knives and home-made clubs, old woollen socks packed hard with wet soil. In an emergency they could be emptied swiftly and the club could once again become a harmless old sock. He nodded once more. Now the time for speaking was over. All orders would be given by signs and changes of facial expression. While one of them remained behind to guard the door to the 'stiffs', the other four of the recce party passed noiselessly into the brightly lit corridor, automatically hugging the wall and feeling absurdly naked all of a sudden.

On tiptoe they made their way to the left, noting the overhead signs for later, making a mental plan of the place for defensive purposes when the moment of attack came – and that wouldn't be too far off now; they knew that from 'Radio Loens'.

Suddenly there was the sound of a door opening on rusty squeaking hinges. They froze, pressing themselves instinctively against the wall, as if that would somehow help to make them invisible. A female voice said, 'Remember the officers' dance tomorrow night, Mabel. I'm trying to get some civvies for the occasion. Goddam sick of this uniform.'

'In three devils' name,' Heidreich cursed angrily to himself, 'a shitting *Ami* nurse.' For a moment his brain raced wildly. For once he didn't know what to do. A man would have been different, but a woman – what was he supposed to do with a piece of female gash?

Behind him, as the sound of footsteps started to come in their direction, the man next to him whispered urgently, 'Shall we make ourselves out of the dust, *Scharführer?*'

But even as he posed the question, it was already too late. A hefty woman in white with glasses came into view and saw the men crouched against the wall at once. There was no way they could have hidden. They were trapped there against the glaringly white wall under the powerful hospital lamps like flies pinned on a card in some collector's office.

The military nurse – she was a captain, Heidreich could see that from the two silver bars pinned on the shoulders of her white uniform – was totally unafraid to find herself confronted by what was obviously half a dozen German POWs in the middle of the night. She had that overweening confidence and arrogance of all military nursing personnel, who believed that they were always in total charge of the situation, however strange. If anything, she was angry, as she might have been on discovering a patient had disobeyed her orders and gotten out of bed without her permission. She peered at them angrily through her glasses and demanded, 'What's going on here . . . eh?'

Heidreich reacted quickly. He knew these American women; he had encountered a few of them when he had been captured first and taken to an American hospital in Normandy. The GIs maintained they were all lesbians, which he didn't believe. They were sexually all right; they were just typical *Ami* women who liked to dominate their menfolk. If the latter obeyed them, then they *might* be rewarded by a five-minute fuck on a Sunday afternoon. Now he reacted as he thought the ugly bespectacled *Ami* would expect.

In a humble, slightly frightened voice, he said in his best English, 'Repair party, Major.'

'Repair party?' she echoed, puzzled. 'At this time of the night?'

That pleased Heidreich, though he had just decided that the woman had to die; there was no other way. Sooner or later, when questioned, she'd give them away and then all hell would be let loose. 'Yes, Major – ' he emphasised the new rank he had

Leo Kessler

just given her – 'one of the boilers has gone. We've been ordered over here to repair it. Now – ' he shrugged and gave a hesitant, but winning smile – 'we are lost.'

The nurse relaxed. 'But you mustn't wake the patients or disturb anything. The new CG of the 11th is going to inspect us tomorrow.'

Heidreich didn't know what the 'CG' was, but it didn't matter. Her suspicions had been lulled. All he needed now was to get close to her to strike. 'No, we will not do that, Major,' he said. 'But perhaps you can point out where the boiler room is?' He rubbed his big hands together like some yellow-arsed crawler of a pen-pushing clerk, he couldn't help thinking with disgust.

'Well, I'm just going off shift, you know,' she began petulantly, then changed her mind and added, 'Oh all right. I'll come along with you. It's on the way to the nurses' quarters.'

'Thank you . . . thank you,' he said in that crawling manner which he knew would please the ugly American woman with her glasses and flat feet in the white rubber-soled shoes.

'All right,' she snapped severely. 'Don't waste any more of my time. Get your crew up here and follow me . . . and don't make any noise as we pass the wards, is that clear?'

'Yes Major,' Heidreich said humbly.

Bent-shouldered and humble, as was to be expected of enemy prisoners in the presence of a superior person such as she, they advanced down the corridor, while she looked severe and tapped her right foot on the highly polished floor impatiently.

'All right,' she snapped in the same fashion as before. 'This way and make it snappy.'

Heidreich looked at the man behind him. He nodded. The other man looked frightened abruptly, but he nodded back. They set off, with Heidreich's gaze darting from side to side, looking for a suitable place for what he knew he must carry out now, though it wasn't something he had bargained for on this night's reconnaissance mission.

Their footsteps echoed down the empty corridor. There was some activity behind the doors of the wards on each side, but it

74

was muted and the wards themselves were illuminated by subdued lighting, with the nurse in charge seated at a table in the centre, doing her paperwork in the circle of brighter light cast by the table lamp. There was no sign of male orderlies or doctors, which, Heidreich told himself, would have made things more difficult. As usual at night, most of the hospital was left in charge of the female nurses. Still, he knew she'd be no pushover and there would be men somewhere. He'd have to be quick and silent, and he knew, too, that he didn't have much time left. If the big *Ami* female captain was going off duty, there'd be others, too.

'Here.' She stopped so abruptly that he almost bumped into her big corsetted arse. 'To your right. That's the entrance to the boiler room.' She didn't even bother to turn and look at him. He was merely a German prisoner of war; he had lost his power, his ability to frighten. In her eyes, he had lost his manhood too. It was something that made him very angry suddenly. 'Do you understand?' she demanded when he didn't respond. Still she didn't turn around. It was a fatal mistake. But at least it would earn her the Purple Heart.

'Yes,' he said through gritted teeth, and there was something in his tone that made her begin to turn. Too late! His big hands slid around her neck. The cry which had welled up inside her throat died the same instant. Hastily he brought up his knee and jammed it into the centre of her back. He dragged her close to him. He could smell her overly clean odour. The scent and soap she used eradicated all her women's smells; there was none of that earthy odour which attracted men sexually. It made him madder.

Gritting his teeth, he exerted more pressure. His big hands dug into her throat. Strange little stifled, strangled sounds were coming from her throat. She weaved from side to side, trying to break that killing grip, her long fingernails clawing at his hands till the blood came. Still he didn't let go.

Now he was breathing hard as if he were running a great race. The others watched, wide-eyed with shock and fear. But there was nothing they could do; he had to kill her by himself. And

Heidreich knew that. Digging his knee cruelly into her back, hearing the bands of her corset snap as he did so, he gripped harder, the sweat streaming down his crimson face and threatening to blind him.

She made one last attempt to free herself. To no avail. He held on with all his strength. Her eyes bulged from her skull. Now her mouth was wide and gaping, her tongue hanging out like a piece of wet red leather. Her knees started to crumple. Still she hung on. '*Die . . . die, you shitting bitch!*' he gasped, near to tears. 'For God's sake – *die!*'

Footsteps began further down the corridor. In a minute they'd be discovered. The eyes of the others darted back and forth. They'd break and run in a minute, Heidreich knew that. He had to finish her off. *Now!*'

With the sweat streaming down his face in hot gleaming beads, he exerted the last of his strength, sobbing and trembling like a man at the very end of his tether. His big knee bored into the small of her back. He grunted. It was a savage animal sound. He pulled hard. In that same instant, he propelled his knee into her back.

There was an audible snap like a dry twig breaking underfoot in a bone-dry wood in the heat of the summer. Suddenly, very suddenly, she went limp. Heidreich seemed puzzled. It was as if he had not understood what had happened. For what seemed an age, the two of them clung together there like eternal lovers.

'*Scharführer,*' one of the men hissed. 'There's someone coming! Quick!'

Abruptly Heidreich became aware of the impending danger. He let the body slip from his grasp with a sudden look of repulsion. It slumped to the floor, legs spread so that the big nurse seemed to lie in a kind of obscene invitation.

But the Germans had no time for such things. The footsteps were getting ever closer. Everything forgotten now, even the reason for this reconnaissance which had ended in murder, they threw caution to the wind and fled, desperate to get back to Camp 23 before the inevitable roll-call and the investigations commenced . . .

Two

'**D**er *Katzenjammer Kid*' or 'Fat Cat', the GIs of the newly arrived 11th Armored Division called him, according to his particular mood of the day; and it must be admitted that Colonel Karl-Gustavus Katz, fat and pompous, and a senior member of the Division's staff, did change his moods as often as he did his silk, customised, voluminous shorts. One day he could be smooth and relatively easy-going; another he could be miserable and moody, inclined to shout at any subordinate who did the slightest thing wrong. At Divisional Headquarters, Katz – bespectacled, middle-aged and fat, who had never heard a shot fired in anger in a quarter of a century in the US Regular Army – was an officer who was both feared and heartily disliked. He was also one that his clerks and other irreverent younger subordinates made fun of (behind his back naturally) whenever it was safe to do so, which was quite often. For Colonel Karl-Gustavus Katz was so pompous, self-centred and conscious of his own importance that he never even dreamed that anyone might ridicule him.

On the cold, foggy November morning after the murder of Captain McKendrick of the Army Nursing Corps, when Major Clapton was ushered hurriedly into Katz's office at 11th Armored Division, the Britisher, too, was not particularly impressed by the fat staff officer. He had seen plenty of the type in the British Army in the 'last show', as he still called the Great War in that dated slang of his. Since 1942 when the Yanks had first 'invaded' this part of England, he had seen even more of them in the US Army and he had liked *them* even less.

Not particularly because they were American. It was because

they were useless and knew it, yet covered up the fact that they were too old, too fat and totally unprepared for total war by what he could only characterise as 'bullshit'. Most of them had never seen any action even in the 'last show' and had concentrated over the last quarter of a century of peacetime duty in those remote American 'forts' on recovering the rank they had once enjoyed as 25-year-old majors and colonels back in 1918. That had been the mainspring of their existence. They had learned nothing and, although they were constantly being sent to 'schools' in the US Army fashion, all they were really concerned with was 'keeping their noses clean' as the Yanks usually phrased the process.

Now they had spent a couple of years in the UK and had become even grander, having their uniforms tailored in Savile Row and their shoes hand-made in Bond Street. All of them insisted on a personal car, usually tremendously large Packard sedans and Cadillacs, when three or four years before only the Chief of Staff of the US Army was allowed an official car. And over the years they had begun to regard the English as some kind of better class of occupied nation: 'natives', like Red Indians tucked away on a US Government reservation, glad of any hand out their occupiers deigned to give them.

It had rankled with Clapton every time he came into contact with the type, and in his non-combatant post, it was the type he usually had dealings with. Now it rankled even more when Katz, without even attempting to shake hands and introduce himself, snorted, 'Now, Major, what can you tell me about this bad business? Your camp and its prisoners seem to be the most likely place from which the culprits came. Eh?' Katz shot what he took to be a hard, searching look at the one-legged major, his jowls wobbling with the effort.

Deliberately Clapton took his time. He put his cap and stick down on the corner of Katz's desk and then, ignoring the latter's look, took off his gas mask and did the same with that.

Katz waited impatiently as he did so and Clapton *made* him wait, enjoying the angry look on the fat American's face. It pleased him to take a rise out of such self-important people as Katz.

But when he was ready, Katz moved into the attack immediately, as if he, Clapton, was responsible for the events of the previous night. He snorted, 'How do you explain it, Major? One of your damned Kraut POWs found dead in the lines of the 11th and now this poor nurse brutally strangled like that and, from all indications, sexually abused too – the autopsy'll probably show that later. Again one of your escapees, presumably.' He paused for breath, chest heaving with the outburst.

Coldly Clapton looked at the fat American. He took his time. He was not going to let himself be flustered into making a hot, angry retort by the plump prick in his fancy uniform. He said, 'Naturally, you understand, Colonel, you have absolutely no jurisdiction over Camp 23. This is a totally British affair, although it did certainly involve American service personnel. However, we shall try to accommodate our American allies—'

'*Accommodate . . . American allies!*' Katz snorted, outraged. 'What the Sam Hill do you think this is? Our people have been murdered by Krauts in your custody. You can't bury your heads in—'

Clapton raised his big right hand like some slow, ponderous bobby using all his authority to stop the flow of traffic on a busy street. 'Colonel, let me tell you that the GOC Southern Command has already been in touch with your Divisional Commander and an agreement was reached earlier this morning that this is a matter for the British authorities, though naturally we welcome any assistance that you and your officers might be able to give us.'

He waited while Katz shrunk or, so it seemed, deflated like a barrage balloon which had just taken a burst of bullets from some marauding enemy fighter plane. Then in what he, Clapton, thought was a very reasonable tone, he gave Katz his standard lecture, prior to going on to the murder of the previous night. 'You see, when we get round to it, we do an assessment of the political leanings of every Jerry prisoner who comes into our cage . . .'

Katz listened, still apparently numb from having learned that he was going be Clapton's subordinate in the murder case, although he was senior in rank. He had never felt so miserable since Ike had told him the previous month that he was too old to be given a fighting regiment; he had to stay on the staff.

'So, we have three categories of prisoners, Colonel. We have the hard cases, the bad boys from the SS, U-Boat arm and the German Paras. They are the "Blacks". We've found that it is fatal to put them in a camp by themselves. They simply take over the place. So we mix them with the rest. But that's dangerous too, in a way. Although they are a minority, real hard-core Nazis, they wield a lot of power over the rest with threats to them and their loved ones back in Germany – beatings, kangaroo courts and the like.'

Outside, a jeep had arrived and there was some kind of a scene taking place, as if the big non-com in charge of the HQ's staff car park was objecting to the jeep being parked there. Katz looked out, but didn't respond. Perhaps his spirit had been broken temporarily by Clapton putting him in his place. Normally he would have been rushing out red-faced and furious at such a scene.

'Then there is the great majority of the Hun POWs,' Clapton was continuing. 'These we call the "Greys". They're the sheep. They're not Nazis and they're not democrats in our sense of the term. They're just followers doing what those who are in power tell them to do. Finally there is the minority. They're entitled the "Whites", and I think the designation is self-explanatory, Colonel, don't you?'

If it was, Katz didn't respond. Instead he stared gloomily at the scene outside, his fat face puzzled as if he was not really taking it in.

'The "Whites" are our problem children, Colonel, because they are the ones who stand up against the majority – the "Greys", egged on by the bad bastards, the "Blacks".'

Finally Katz seemed to find his voice, though it took him an obvious effort of willpower to do so. 'But what has all this got to do with our murder, Major?'

'This, Colonel. There's something going on here at Devizes and at other camps too, all over Britain, as I'll explain later.

This is the second "White" who has been killed in Camp 23. Why?' Clapton answered his own question. 'Because they knew too much and the "Blacks" wanted to get rid of them for purposes of their own.'

'But how did that nurse get involved with your Blacks, Whites and all the rest of your colour scheme, Major?' There was anger and contempt for this obviously bumbling limey in Colonel Katz's voice once more as his feeling of superiority to the British reasserted itself. Goddamit, he thought, all they're good for is parades and tea breaks.

Clapton frowned. It was a question he had asked himself several times since he had been so rudely awakened by Hawkins at three o'clock that morning. 'I don't know, frankly,' he admitted. 'All I know is that something strange is going on and the Blacks are getting cockier by the day. Last week alone there were fifty breakouts by Blacks throughout the United Kingdom from Bridge End Camp in Wales to the north of Ayrshire.' Clapton paused significantly, then added in a low tone so that Katz had to strain to hear his comment. 'And the bloody frustrating thing about these fifty escapes is this.'

'What?'

'All the escapees came back of their own volition.'

'Came back?' Colonel Katz echoed, totally out of his depth now.

'Yes. They were posted as missing and the usual alert was instigated – you know, police, local troops, Home Guard, Boy Scouts and the like. But it was unnecessary. They all returned and gave themselves up. A couple of cheeky Black buggers at Bridge End actually knocked on the guardroom door and asked formally to be taking back into the camp. The cheek of the Hun bastards!'

'Dames?' Katz suggested, as puzzled as Clapton.

'We thought of that, Colonel. But Blacks aren't allowed out of the camps in the work parties. They have no opportunity to meet willing girls. So that possibility is out. Not on at all.' He let the Colonel consider his words. Besides, his mind was else-where. This was really a courtesy call to appease Southern

Command. He couldn't see how Katz and the other big shots of the 11th Armored Division could help him with his problem. They'd soon be crossing the Channel, heading for the front. Thereafter they'd be too busy trying to avoid having their heads shot off. Still, he'd give the fat fool another few minutes and then he'd be on his way back to the damned problem of these Blacks who disappeared and just when one thought they'd done a bunk for good, they reappear and beg, like in the old prison joke, to be allowed back in again to the security, warmth and reassurance of the 'nick'.

'As we see it, Colonel,' he made an attempt to sum up for Katz so he could write his report to SHAEF HQ and get on with his real job of preparing the 11th for the blood-letting at the front soon to come, 'the Blacks are up to something. What, we don't know exactly. They go out, check something or other and, when they're satisfied, they surrender themselves to us once more. What they're checking out,' Clapton shrugged eloquently, 'God only knows.'

'Be that as it may,' Katz said, 'I'm concerned with that nurse. What are we gonna do about her, Major?'

But before Major Clapton could answer that particularly awkward question there was what seemed an urgent knock on the door of the Colonel's office. 'Come,' Katz called in a grand manner.

The door opened. The master-sergeant in charge of the orderly room stood, mouth open with shock, big slab-like drinker's face aghast. Beyond, a slim young man with a bandaged hand stood to attention, a sheaf of papers under his good arm, a musette bag at his feet.

'Yes?' Katz began, and then he saw the reason for the big top sergeant's shocked look.

'Sir,' the latter stuttered. 'First Lieutenant Lee reporting for duty, sir.'

His words trailed away to nothing; he could say no more. In all his long US Army career he had seen nothing like it: a nigger reporting to a white man's outfit! What was the goddam army coming to?

The same alarming thought had obviously occurred to Colonel Katz. For while Major Clapton watched the unexpected scene with a mixture of amused contempt and bewilderment, noting as he did so just how trim and intelligent (unlike the other two white Americans) the young black officer appeared, Katz choked and said, 'Reporting – *here to the 11?*'

Numbly the master-sergeant nodded, obviously unable to speak; he was that shocked.

Katz let his fat head fall into his pudgy hands like a broken man and said, 'Oh, my God . . . Oh, my God . . . !'

Three

'The Krauts keep blowing kisses at me all the time,' Lee said, as he sipped the mug of tea, well laced with British Army rum. 'Why? Do they think I'm some sort of a fag?'

Clapton grinned at the young black American. They were huddled around the pot-bellied stove in the Intelligence office, together with Sergeant Hawkins, enjoying the illegal Quartermaster rum, while, outside, the winter gale howled and flurries of snow lashed the little window angrily. 'No,' he said. 'Behind your back, you see, Lee, they call you *"Negerkuss"*.'

'Nigger Kiss,' Lee translated. Like his French, his German was fluent, but not as colloquial as it should be, Clapton told himself; while Hawkins, unconcerned by these intellectual problems, which he left to these officers and gentlemen, buried his red nose in the steam from his mug and told himself, 'Cor, ferk a duck, this rum could take the frigging enamel off yer choppers!'

'Yes, but it's the German name for a cake – chocolate on top with a soft filling. They probably think you're black and soft . . . a typical American.' He grinned even more. 'But we know that isn't true. You're a hard, *black* American.'

Lee returned his grin. 'Thank you for the kind word,' he said and told himself that these first two Englishmen he had ever met were different from his concept of the race, based on literature and, more basically, Hollywood movies. In their presence he felt naturally that he was a black man, different on account of the colour of his skin, but all the same that they were assessing him on his ability to do his job. The two middle-aged limeys were too old and wise to be fooled by bullshit like Colonel Katz and his ilk.

He frowned at the thought of Katz. As soon as *he* had gotten over his obvious shock at being confronted by a black officer posted to the all-white 11th Armored, he had started planning to get rid of him. 'Lee,' he had snapped, glancing at the lieutenant's papers, 'despite your education, you have been a nuisance and a problem everywhere you have been posted since you joined the Army. Verdun . . . now Cherbourg in some sort of an affair with a Frenchwoman.' He had shaken his head as if shocked and his jowls had wobbled yet again. 'I shall accept you, however, as our new head of the CI outfit, yet to be formed. But on sufferance. I want you to keep your nose clean – and then some.'

Lee had said nothing; he had willed himself to keep his mouth shut. He knew that Katz was probably already plotting to get rid of him as soon as possible. He was right, for Katz had said after some thought, 'OK, this old limey Clapton from the POW Camp thinks there is something going on among all the Kraut prisoners in this godforsaken country. Be that as it may, *I'm* concerned with what happened to that poor nurse. So, Lee,' he had said with an air of finality, 'I'm going to see that you are attached to Clapton as the 11th Armored's representative for the duration of this investigation. I'll fix it with the Commanding General. I want the killer of that woman nailed, whether he's a Kraut or a frigging Red Indian. Got it, Lee?'

'Got it, sir,' he had replied laconically, not even arguing. He knew Katz was attempting to hide him, keep him out of view as far as his supposed comrades of the 11th were concerned. In the mean-time Katz would attempt to have him posted. There and then he had told himself, 'Fuck you, Colonel Katz . . . you're not going to get rid of Mrs Lee's handsome black son as easily as that.'

For the last forty-eight hours, he had spent most of his waking hours prowling about the camp, accepting the seemingly good-natured taunts of the Kraut prisoners and the gawping of the guards at the sight of a black man, now seemingly on the staff of Camp 23, checking out the place.

A couple of times he had sneaked out of the bunk allotted him in the middle of the night, and lay in the cold observing the huts, swept at periodic intervals by the searchlights positioned on the stork-legged towers.

Nothing happened. Yet, all the same, Lee, sensitive as he was to men's feelings and moods, felt that somewhere in those silent huts, broken only by occasional snores, there were desperate men, as wide awake as he was. They were timing the Limey soldiers on their beats outside the wire, ascertaining when they let their guard slip towards dawn as they tired; how they perked up when they knew the orderly officer and the guard commander were in the offing, that sort of thing.

He had already done the circuit more than once, watching for tell-tale signs of earth disturbance, prisoners who lingered too long in the 'death zone' just inside the wire, brighter marks on the rusting wire where someone might have attempted to saw through it and the like.

In the main he had not discovered anything of importance, not even how the prisoners might have got out on the night of the nurse's murder and how they had managed to get the body of a White through the wire with them. All the same, he had come to agree with Major Clapton and his old sergeant – both wise old buggers, he had to admit, despite Katz's comments on 'those senile Limey farts' – that there was something going on at Camp 23. And not only at Camp 23.

For, as Clapton said again while they sipped the powerful, warming drink, 'The Blacks are gaining power all over the UK. Imagine it – we've got exactly five active divisions left in the whole of the country, two British and three of your American ones, Lee. All have slated to go to the Continent in due course, once they have finished their active training. By Christmas, we won't have an active fighting division left in the country.' He paused and stared at the red-glowing metal of the old stove as if he could see something there, known only to him. 'But what we *will* have, Lee, is a quarter of a million able-bodied Jerries in their prime, guarded by handfuls of third-class British squaddies, unfit for active service.'

Lee nodded his understanding. He could see that Clapton was very worried at the prospect of what might happen once the fighting troops had shipped to the Continent. He said, trying to take the Major's mind off that gloomy prospect, 'Well, sir, we can't do much about the big picture. But if we could find that radio you've talked about, it might give us a clue.'

Clapton didn't respond immediately. Instead he took out his old briar pipe, saying as he always did, 'Filthy habit', made a great fuss of tamping down the tobacco, lighting it and blowing into the bowl before exhaling a stream of acrid blue smoke, pointing the stem at the amused Hawkins and Lee, with: 'You've hit the nail on the head, Lee.'

'Not bad for a Yank, sir,' Hawkins agreed with a flash of his yellow false teeth. 'Only we've been trying to find the bugger for about a month now, Lieutenant.' He would have dearly loved to have pronounced the rank in the Yankee fashion, 'lootenant', but he knew the Major would have been down on him like a ton of bricks; so he refrained.

'Perhaps, Sergeant,' Lee said carefully, for he didn't want to offend his new-found friends, 'you haven't been looking for it in the right manner.'

Clapton wasn't offended. He said, taking another puff at the old pipe, which had survived the trenches and the German POW camp at Holzminden, 'Pray, how do you mean?'

'Now, gentlemen, don't think I'm trying to upstage you. I'm not pulling the smart Yank thing, as I believe you call it.'

The two older men listened, but said nothing. He felt they were not about to give him a hard time, so he continued, feeling ever more confident with his new plan. 'You see, I've contacted one of our propaganda outfits, attached to the 11th. They broadcast propaganda to the Krauts, or they will do. They're all German and Austrian Jews, who fled to America—'

'All right, Lee,' Clapton interrupted him gently. 'Don't give us a lesson in recent history. Get on with it.'

'Wilco. Now, they're expecting the Krauts – naturally – to drown out their broadcasts with their own radio vans. You know, German brass band music, marching songs and the like. So they need a protective device which—'

'Which will detect the Jerry radio van and make it easy for them to call up the guns and blow the Jerries to kingdom come,' Hawkins interrupted. 'A detector van in other words, sir!'

The two of them looked at the wrinkled sergeant in sudden amazement, Clapton in particular. He'd never heard the old sweat talk so much in one go before. 'Have you been at that GS rum before we came in, Sergeant?' he asked.

'No sir,' Hawkins answered cheerfully. 'All out of my own head, sir, not out of a bottle.'

Lee smiled. 'Well, Major, he's hit the nail right on the head. The radio guys have a limited-range detector antenna which they can use in combat to locate the Krauts. Now, they're prepared to let us have their services – they hate those Blacks of yours with a passion, naturally – to detect and translate the POW broadcast.'

Clapton took his old pipe out of his mouth, saying, 'I say, young Lee, that's a really splendid idea. I must be getting senile. Why didn't I think of it before?'

But neither Hawkins nor Lee were prepared to answer that question . . . So, while the cold wind howled outside, the flurries of snow rattling and battering the windows, the three of them hugged the red-hot stove and planned the operation. Outside, *Oberscharführer* Heidreich, the veteran of Russia and seemingly oblivious to the piercing cold and the whirling snow, watched and wondered. They were up to something, he knew, but what?

Abruptly the big former SS man shivered violently. But it wasn't the cold that caused him to do so. It was something else which he couldn't quite define. Perhaps it was fear, he told himself, apprehension. Later he realised it was neither. It was the sudden knowledge that comes to all men in the end, that realisation that nothing is really worthwhile; that all our efforts will end in despair and failure.

Inside the fug of the little Nissen hut, the three men, the two white Englishmen and the black American, were not afflicted by such thoughts. They were happy and it wasn't just the rum. It was the knowledge that they had come up with a workable solution and, if things worked out as planned, they might well uncover the mystery of Camp 23. As a delighted Major Clapton put it, still sucking on that evil-smelling pipe of his, 'I'd just love to see the looks on the ugly mugs of those damned arrogant Blacks when we find out what the buggers are up to!' To which Sergeant Hawkins closed his eyes momentarily in mock reverence and folded his hands, as if in prayer. 'Amen to that sir.'

Lee grinned. The two Limeys were really cards. For the time being he was happy in their company. What the morrow might bring, even if things went wrong, he didn't care. For, at that one moment, he was happy – happy without qualifications and imponderables. It was a damned good feeling.

Four

They had hit Regensburg that night. Their aiming point had been the centre of the Messerschmitt Works producing engines for the Messerschmitt 109. They had been briefed back in North Africa, 'If you guys knock out the Kraut plant, you'll destroy thirty per cent of all German fighter-aircraft production.' It had sounded impressive then – after all, most of the US bomber crews were new boys straight from the 'land of the round doorknob', i.e. the States. They hadn't yet learned the 109 was obsolete. Now the Germans were concentrating on the Messerschmitt jet fighter.

The attack had gone pretty well. They had come in over the Alps, protected by Mustang fighters from Allied bases in Italy most of the way, before attacking from the south in two boxes, with each box consisting of a wing. They had dropped their long-range 'Tokio' tanks to give them additional speed and commenced their mission. The flak, as expected, was bad. But they'd coped, and aerial attack had been weak. 'Like taking candy off a blind man,' they had quipped to each other excitedly over the intercom until their harassed skippers in their heated leather flying suits had told them to 'pipe down . . . we ain't home yet.'

They certainly weren't.

Half an hour later, as they flew along the upper Rhine, an easy marker for inexperienced navigators, the Krauts had attacked in force. They had come in in swarms, juggling from side to side, zooming down from above, firing their new secret cannon from below into the bombers' fat bellies – firing and dodging like eager little gadflies, taunting these big, heavy, slow

Amis. Immediately the 'weak sisters' had dropped out of the formations. Over their radios the pilots shrieked, 'Engine trouble!' or something similar and, with their undercarriages lowered to indicate they were out of the fight, they hedge-hopped for neutral Switzerland, only miles away, and safe internment for the rest of the war.

The rest, made of sterner stuff, though mostly frightened out of their minds – especially when the pilots saw their first enemy jets coming at an unbelievable speed, in and out of the deci-mated boxes before the waist gunners could even range their heavy machine guns on the attackers – flew on. They tightened their boxes in order to bring maximum firepower to bear and radioed urgently to England for fighter cover; for already there were dozens of Allied advanced fighter bases in newly captured Normandy and the Flanders Plain.

They were out of luck. The Germans had picked their day well. All the fields to the west were 'socked in'. Visibility was down almost to zero over Northern France and Belgium. For the time being the 'Seventh Cavalry', in the form of the Allied tactical air forces, was not coming to the rescue. And the Germans, who knew all about the attack, were already aware that that same fog would spread to the *Ami* fields in East Anglia. The Flying Fortresses could expect no help from that quarter; their skippers and crews would have to fight out all the way till death or landfall on the emergency fields dotted about Britain's south coast. For once, since the great terror raids by these '*Ami* air gangsters' had commenced the year before, the advantage was on the side of the Germans.

And they took it.

At eight o'clock that winter's morning, as the Flying For-tresses broke through into French airspace, with the blood-red ball of the sun lying on the horizon, tinting the perspex of their portholes and gun blisters the colour of sudden death, a fresh wave of attackers came racing in from their fields in the Eifel and Rhineland. They knew this would be their last chance; and they pressed home their attack with the fury of desperate young fanatics. For them it was 'march or croak'; for these German pilots brought up in the creed of the German 'New Order' were the closest thing to Kamikaze pilots that there was in continental Europe.

Below, the German flak opened up. Shards of hot metal rapped at the Forts' eggshells of aluminium and perspex like the hard beak of some gigantic bird of prey. The gunners' intention was obvious. They wanted to keep the enemy bombers at the right height for the success of the fighter attack. The American skippers reacted as they had been taught – 'Tighten the boxes,' the wing commanders ordered urgently. 'Get those frigging Forts right up close to one another – come on, guys. Let's get on the fucking stick.'

The pilots needed no urging. Now they had to rely on their firepower. The tighter the 'box', the more effective their massed point five machine guns firing in every direction. It was like the old nineteenth-century wagon train forming a circle to fight off the Indians on their fast wiry ponies. They hoped, just like the pioneers had, that in the end the attackers would be sick of their losses from the defended prairie schooners and ride away.

Now the intercom was filled with excited orders and directions, the snarl of fighter engines coming in from all sides to attack, the cries of pain from wounded gunners, the pleas for help from anguished skippers whose mortally damaged Forts were going into their last dive of death. '*Bogies . . . two o'clock high . . . Bandits . . . BANDITS . . . Starboard engine out . . . feathering port props . . . Holy Mother of God, I can't see a frigging thing . . . GUYS, HELP ME . . . I'M BLIND . . . I CAN'T . . .*' From all sides, those desperate cries came for help and assistance . . . But now, with the 'Boxes' crumbling and threatening to break up at any moment, it was every man for himself, with B-17s streaming down to earth and certain destruction, trailing thick black smoke from shattered engines behind them. It was no longer a battle; it was a massacre.

It was about then that the strange Fort appeared out of the clouds, cruising quite slowly and keeping out of range of the enemy fighters attacking the boxes, retreating back into cloud cover every time it appeared that a German was about to investigate the long four-engined bomber.

For a while the harassed skippers, sweating and red-faced beneath their oxygen masks, were puzzled. What was going on? But they were all relatively inexperienced and unaware of the many tricks that the Germans played on enemy bomber formations, and in the end they assumed that the lone Fort was some kind of 'master bomber' of the kind the RAF had introduced the year before, or perhaps a substitute for their own commander and deputy commander, who usually gave orders in battle, both of whom had been shot down as they had crossed into France over the Rhine.

Their guess was confirmed a little time later when, speaking in clear, a cool, calm voice from the lone Fort started issuing instructions and encouragement to the hard-pressed bomber skippers: *'Four yellow noses twelve o'clock high . . . Two more two o'clock low . . . Gunners, don't waste your ammo . . . lead the bastards in before you give 'em it . . . Talk slow, skipper . . . don't panic . . . we're winning . . .'*

Once, as one of the great four-engined planes was hit smoke started to pour from its starboard engine. A silver rectangle of metal sailed past its shattered, cracked cockpit – the B-17's main exit door. An instant later it was followed by a dark object. It hurtled through the box, narrowly missing several props. It was a pilot making a delayed drop. He was crouched in the foetal position, revolving like a crack high diver attempting a triple somersault at some display. Hardly had he shot through the box safely, than the B-17 blew up in a ball of flaming purple and thick white smoke. When it had cleared, all that was visible were four balls of whirling fire: the fuel tanks streaming downwards.

But the escape of the pilot and the encouraging, soothing voice of the speaker in the lone Fort, saying, 'That's the way to do it, guys . . . don't panic and you'll come out of this smelling of frigging roses', encouraged the defenders. It made them feel they hadn't been abandoned totally. So, once they had tightened what was left of the two boxes, they prepared to meet the next German attackers. Carefully the lone Fortress flew away and positioned itself at the edge of the clouds, obviously ready to disappear into the fleecy cover if the German fighters came too close.

They didn't. They concentrated on the groups. In they came again, machine guns and cannon chattering. In a lethal white morse the tracer bullets and 20mm explosive shells slammed into the Forts. Great chunks of gleaming metal were ripped off them. Here and there cherry-red flames burst from the fuselages. A gunner, ripped from his turret by a burst, but still alive, fell out of the plane, arms and legs flailing wildly, mouth gaping in silent screams as he plummeted to his death far below in the increasing low-level fog.

And then it was over. They were closing with the English Channel. Here and there the crew of the lone Fortress could catch glimpses of the white cliffs beyond in gaps in the fog and cloud. It was time for the Germans to turn back, heading for the flak cover of the Breton ports still in German hands, before turning and running along the dogleg back to the occupied Alsace, where again there'd be German flak cover.

Slowly, almost painfully, the two boxes merged, while the radio operator in the lone Fort encouraged them with, 'Keep formation and keep up your guard. One of their frigging jets might try to sneak a flanker yet.' But the unknown operator's warning was unnecessary. The Germans had had enough. For a few losses they had inflicted severe casualties on the *Amis*. The latter wouldn't attempt another raid on the Messerschmitt factory in Regensburg so soon again. Here and there a jet roared in, fired off a long burst at the limping, smoking Fortresses and then turned south-west, disappearing from sight at a tremendous speed. Occasionally one of the pilots in the ragged boxes looked back at the lone Fortress. It seemed to be in difficulty now. Smoke was pouring from one of the two port engines and the big plane was slowing down, losing height all the time. Still it plodded on and the exhausted pilots were too concerned about their own safety. So they turned their heads and left the Fortress to it. Its pilots were probably old-time hotshots; they'd fly with the seat of their pants. They'd make it.

Gradually the box disappeared from sight and the morning sky was empty of both friend and foe. Abruptly the great lumbering Fortress picked up speed. As if by magic, the lone plume of ugly black smoke, tinged with oil, which it had been trailing behind it for the last fifteen minutes or so went out. It gained height, the blister guns hanging down, as if the gunners had gone back forward, all thoughts of danger thrown to the wind. To a casual observer it might have seemed the Flying Fortress was a training flight, far from the scene of battle, with the pilot concentrating solely on his flying with no worries of being attacked to bother him.

Inside, the crew of Skorzeny's special 'Squadron 200', which for years now had carried out clandestine missions behind enemy lines for the scar-faced SS officer, definitely *had* worries. But not about flying. That was second nature to them. Their concern was to put the little agent, already clad in his jump suit, in the right position, height etc. so that he'd float with his parachute well over the Tommy coast, with its guards and lookouts, into the interior. It wasn't an easy thing to do. But the dispatchers had dropped scores of Skorzeny's agents into the highly dangerous territory of the Russian Soviet Workers' and Farmers' Paradise. They thought the Tommies with their buck teeth and extended tea breaks would be easy in comparison.

Finally, as they were about halfway across the water that separated England from Europe and the pilot was beginning to get worried – for the fog was thinning and it was obvious that he would have been picked up by the Tommy radar by now – the sergeant dispatcher was satisfied. 'We've got the height and the right distance, skipper,' he reported. 'He should do it.'

'He's a small shit,' the skipper answered, already searching the fog wall for the first sight of a prowling Tommy fighter, 'and he's never done it before.'

The big burly dispatcher grinned and lowered his voice a little as if the little man laden with his parachute and now crouched like some sort of blue-clad hunchback near the open hatch might hear above the roar of the Fortress's four engines, 'Well, let's hope he'll make a handsome corpse, skipper.'

'On your way, you heartless bastard,' was the skipper's only comment as he jerked his gloved thumb to the rear.

'Nothing too good for the boys in the service, sir.' And then he was gone, waddling back to where Pettinger waited anxiously.

The little '*Herr Doktor*' had never jumped out of a plane in his life before. It didn't worry him. Hugging the small radio to his chest with one hand and prepared with the other one for the opening of the chute, he waited.

The winking red light changed to an urgent green. '*Los!*' the burly dispatcher cried, the wind tearing at his words.

'*Heil Hitler!*' Pettinger shouted, carried away by the overwhelming excitement of it all.

'Yer, if you see him,' the dispatcher cried back cynically. Then he planted his big boot firmly in the little academic's skinny arse and Pettinger flew into the unknown. His last mission had commenced . . .

Five

D ressed in the uniform of a lance corporal in *Sanitats-dienst*, complete with Red Cross armband and army spectacles, which he didn't need, the little *Herr Doktor* had reported at the remote Bavarian camp at Grafenwöhr where Skorzeny was training. If he had been capable of surprise still, he would have found the place very strange indeed. But he had long come to regard the unusual as usual and so it didn't surprise Pettinger very much.

All the same, Grafenwöhr Camp and its occupants, set in this Bavarian heartland, did seem strange. The sentries, dressed as they were in the uniform of the *Waffen SS*, were surly, even aggressive, looking as if they had itchy trigger fingers, and to the man they didn't speak a word of German save for a few curse-words. In the end it took an officer and a sergeant of the Secret Field Police to convince them that the humble little corporal in the Medical Corps should be allowed in through the barbed-wire gates, which were then closed with an air of finality behind him. He smiled faintly as he remembered the old cliché from Dante's *Inferno*, but he decided he wasn't going to abandon all hope, yet.

Skorzeny made him wait. It was all part of the great deception, of course. Why should a senior colonel in the SS, a national hero and favourite of the Führer, rush to see this humble little corporal? After all, there could even be spies here in this great sprawling secret camp. In November 1944, no one could be trusted in the Thousand Year Reich, not even the most important general.

In the meantime, the little *Herr Doktor* stood in the shelter of a hut, as the first soft woolly flakes of the winter snow drifted down aimlessly, heralding the heavy fall soon to come, watching the activity all around him. Anyone surveying him would have taken him for the average thick-witted squaddie, snatching a few draws at the 'lung torpedo' hidden in the cup of his hand, bored and lazy, waiting for the midday bowl of 'fart soup' and mug of 'nigger sweat'.* But Pettinger's keen eyes were everywhere, as he began to grasp the boldness and enormity of Skorzeny's great clandestine operation.

There was captured American and British equipment everywhere, being refurbished by greasy-overalled mechanics, and all bore the bright new white star of the Allied forces, together with unit numbers. There were a handful of Panthers, too. They were having their barrels shortened and turrets altered so that from a distance they looked like American Shermans. They, too, bore the white star of the enemy.

But it wasn't the vehicles which really caught Pettinger's covert attention; it was the soldiers. For, one and all, they were wearing bits and pieces of American uniform, strolling about with that typical American way of walking from the hips which looked decidedly unmilitary in the eyes of a man who had been trained in strict Prussian Army fashion; and all of them were chewing gum, even when marching – very slackly – in little squads. It was something, Pettinger told himself with an amused grin, which would have turned the average German NCO drill instructor hairless. Even as a sergeant-major crooked a finger at him from the brigade office, indicating he should come forward, he was stopped in his tracks by a squad of pseudo-*Amis* chanting by rote, '*Crap in ya hat, buddy . . . Crap in ya hat.*' As he moved off again, he surmised the pseudo-*Amis* were being instructed in the niceties of American slang. Why, he hadn't the faintest idea.

The sergeant-major looked the little lance corporal up and down suspiciously with his pig-like eyes. He was old-school, obviously, his burly chest heavy with 'tin' – German Cross in

* Pea soup and black ersatz coffee. *Transl.*

98

Gold, Silver Close Combat Badge, Silver Wound Medal, Iron Cross, the works. But instead of the usual explosion at the sight of such an unlikely, sloppy soldier, he said wearily, like a man long resigned to failure, 'Go through there, knock at the adjutant's door, wait for the pen-pusher – ' he meant the adjutant's clerk – 'he'll tell you what to do next.' With that he sat down at his desk, swung up his heavy 'dicebeakers'* and opened a pornographic magazine depicting two crop-haired naked women doing something Pettinger thought was impossible to each other on an old-fashioned chaise longue.

Five minutes later the scar-faced giant was advancing towards him, mighty paw extended, full of that fake Viennese charm with his 'What a pleasure to meet you again, *Herr Doktor*! Here we talk about your amazing exploits all the time.' Pettinger was flattered, but he knew it was all that typical Austrian bullshit all the same. 'Now, what about a cognac – French – or a cup of real bean coffee, my dear fellow?'

Then they were smoking cigars and drinking *café-cognac*, ignoring the *Ami* chants of the trainees and the snow which was coming down heavily now, while now and again the SS Colonel eased his gigantic bulk out of his chair to illustrate a point he was making on the full-scale map of the Western Front pinned on the wall behind him by means of two bayonets. Drawing pins would have done, Pettinger told himself, but Skorzeny loved dramatic gestures, so it had to be bayonets. Perhaps he should have dipped the blades in blood? He dismissed the idle thought and concentrated on what the other man had to say about the new offensive.

'In essence, therefore, we shall attack with three armies through the sixty- to ninety-kilometre front on the *Ami*-held Ardennes. With the superiority of four to one we enjoy, and the surprise, we should be on the River Meuse within twenty-four hours. My *Ami* brigade – ' he smirked at the thought – 'will lead the SS armour and capture key bridges across that river for our Sixth Panzer Army to pass on to their objectives in Brussels and

* Jackboots.

Antwerp, thus splitting the Tommy and the *Ami* armies. For this, speed and surprise are essential.'

As Skorzeny puffed his cigar, the little *Herr Doktor* nodded his agreement. Outside, another squad was plodding through the falling snow like white ghosts, doggedly chanting, '*Blow it outa ya barracks bag, you crummy jerk.*' Idly Pettinger wondered when the supposed *Amis* would have occasion to use that particular coarse American phrase.

'That will be the end of the mission for my special panzer troops,' Skorzeny continued. He lowered his voice, as if he half-expected an agent of the infamous English Secret Service to be listening outside the door, Pettinger couldn't help thinking. 'The most important part of the Hunting Commando's work will now commence. Sabotage, sedition, murder and, in your case, *mein lieber Herr Doktor*, the English Trojan Horse operation.'

Pettinger lowered his glass and waited, a nerve ticking electrically at his right temple. Outside, a captured US jeep ploughed its way through the new snow, at the wheel a Skorzeny commando dressed in US uniform, complete with American head-liner perched at a cocky angle. To the little *Herr Doktor's* eyes, *he* looked like a real Yankee.

Skorzeny must have been able to read the little man's mind for he said, 'Yes, he is the real thing – almost. A German-American to be exact. One of my key elite team which will carry the war far behind enemy lines. All will be provided with thousands of dollars, francs, pounds etc. for bribes. All are fluent speakers of the American dialect and if necessary – ' Skorzeny stared directly at the other man – 'they will be infiltrated or parachuted into that English island to help you with your special mission, which I don't need to remind you is of key importance to the success of the Führer's great surprise offensive.'

'Yes, agreed,' he said hastily, responding to Skorzeny's words. 'The six I smuggled into the UK are now in place. But for a while it was nip-and-tuck. There was an unpleasant incident at Cherbourg which might well have jeopardised the whole undertaking.'

'I know . . . I know. But, with your usual skill and expertise, you managed the matter very well. So they are in place with their plans for the construction of illicit radios. But I fear we shall need more of these brave chaps, who will undoubtedly be shot by the Tommies as spies if they are apprehended.' He casually flicked the ash from his expensive cigar into the ashtray, as if he had just disposed of the six SS men whom Pettinger had escorted to the POW cage at Cherbourg personally.

'If that is so, *Oberstammführer*, then the land route through Cherbourg is too time-consuming and dangerous. It will have to be by parachute as you have just said.'

They chatted a while longer, as it got progressively darker and the falling snow deadened the roar of the American tanks and the shouts and chants of the troops under training. Not that either of them noticed the snow; they were too engrossed in their planning. Finally Skorzeny broke off, as if in obedience to an inner command, and snapped as if he were addressing a complete stranger, his voice no longer that of a friendly Viennese charmer but of a strict superior, 'You will keep this secret on pain of death, *Herr Doktor Pettinger*. We march at dawn on Saturday the sixteenth of December. By then, you will be in place in England, ready and waiting to launch Operation Trojan Horse.'

Now, as he lay there on that lonely heath, his chute collapsed all around him, badly winded by the impact of his fall, the little German recalled once again the total shock of that announcement of Skorzeny's. He had been as surprised as he was now to find himself lying on the ground, with the Fortress droning away in the distance. At the beginning of the whole operation he had felt it would be his duty to simply dispatch others into danger and possible death by firing squad. Now he realised, for the first time with the full chilling impact of that knowledge, that he, too, might well suffer the same dreadful fate if he were caught. The Tommies, as was universally known, were a cruel people. It came from the manner in which they had treated the natives of their Empire for centuries. They would shoot him out of hand, without a second thought.

That grim realisation seemed to paralyse him. He just lay there, swamped in his chute, seemingly unable to summon up enough strength to remove it, dig a hole and hide it as he had been trained to do.

There was no sound now, save the soft rustle of the firs in the wind. Even the faint drone of the decoy bomber from Skorzeny's special squadron had vanished. For all he knew at that moment he might well have been the last man alive in the whole wide world.

The hoarse, hysterical barking of a day a long way off broke into his consciousness. He knew it couldn't be a hunting dog or anything like that. Still, it suggested human beings in the offing and possible danger. By a sheer effort of naked willpower he raised himself to his feet and started folding the awkward chute. It was as if he could have lain there for ever, avoiding starting whatever might come in the near future.

Finally he had the chute buried. For a moment he stood there, looking to left and right, as if puzzled about which way to go. Then he remembered Skorzeny's words, '*Herr Doktor, we march at dawn on Saturday the sixteenth of December.*' Suddenly he was fully alert again. He knew time was running out. Clutching his little radio to his skinny chest, he set off. Moments later he had disappeared behind some skeletal trees. Operation Trojan Horse was getting ever closer.

Six

T he amateur camp barber was clipping the hair of a new POW. There were still a few lice left in his long matted hair. But it didn't matter. The shears took care of them. Opposite, in the crowded wooden hut, heavy with the burned smell of clothes drying too close to the pot-bellied iron stove, a tall gangling *Obergefreiter* played a sad lullaby. He held the home-made violin under his chin, his prominent Adam's apple rushing up his skinny throat every time he struck a high note. On the bunk nearest the stove a group of bored prisoners played skat for matchsticks. They were so bored that they didn't slap their cards down with a shout in the German fashion. It was a typical long winter Saturday afternoon in Camp 23. Now all the POWs had to look forward to, it appeared, was an early tea of pilchards, jam and bread and weak English coffee, perhaps with an extra spoonful of sugar, if they were lucky.

Oberfeldwebel Wirtz and *Scharführer* Heidreich watched the cardplayers without interest. They yawned every now and again. Occasionally they cast what seemed disinterested glances out of the window. Perhaps they were looking for the *Essen-holer*, who would bring the dixies with their food from the camp cookhouse. It all appeared to be just another Saturday, a grey day in a grey war that seemed as if it had gone on for ever.

But a more acute observer would have noted that every action of those present in the hut – the violinist, the barber, the skat players – was calculated, played out to a scheme, too bored to be real. For, indeed, all of their eyes were wary, alert, darting from side to side as if they expected to be taken unawares at any moment, and were prepared to react to a pre-prepared plan.

Again time passed leadenly. Over at the Tommies' wet canteen, someone was trying out the NAAFI piano for the customary Saturday night piss-up and sing-song, singing along with the tune he was playing, '*They say there's a troopship* . . . *filled with time-expired men bound for the land they adore* . . . *Bless 'em all, the long, the short and the tall* . . . *you'll get no promotion this side of the ocean* . . .' The POWs had heard the Tommies bawling often enough before. Soon, when they were drunk on that warm beer of theirs, they'd be substituting 'Fuck 'em all' for the 'blessed' bit. No matter. The Tommies didn't have any firm masculine marching songs like the German Army did. '*Auf der Heide bluht eine Roselein* . . . *und es heisst Erika* . . .' No, sir!

Now it was almost dark. Tea was on its way and soon the sentries would be doing their last rounds before banging up the prisoners for the night. On Saturday night, if they could get away with it, the Tommies weren't too careful. They wanted to get away to their girlfriends, pubs, dance halls. Saturday night was holy for the average English soldier, Heidreich told himself, and it was good that it was. The prisoners had a lot to do this night.

Almost as soon as the *Essenholer* were through, the first of the tunnelers appeared, his shift ended. Tunneling made too much noise in the stillness of the night. He was totally naked, stained with sweat and sand, and he crawled up from the hole on all fours, a bag tied around his neck with a string. He looked like an animal, a very tired one.

He nodded to Heidreich but disappeared towards the ablutions without a word to the others, dragging another bag behind him attached by string to his skinny waist. Heidreich smiled. He looked as if he were trailing a particularly large set of balls. The others continued their activities. It was part of the plan. Anyone watching the room from outside through binoculars would not even note a change in the facial expression of the violinist, barber and the Skat players.

The Great Escape

Suddenly the scraggy violinist ceased playing. Heidreich's heart skipped a beat. The trap closed immediately. The skat players started to play the usual noisy card-slapping game. The barber continued to cut his unfortunate client's hair at a tremendous rate, slicing off huge chunks blindly. The man in the chair let it happen. Nothing should cause suspicion now.

Heidreich waited. He knew what the violinist had spotted through the window, though he hadn't yet seen the man himself. He'd seen a 'ferret', one of the younger, keener guards who smuggled themselves into the compound, prowled around in silent, rubber-soled shoes, occasionally prodding beneath the raised huts with their canes, or attaching mirrors to them to peer underneath.

He licked suddenly parched lips. A cold bead of sweat was trickling down the small of his back unpleasantly. But he daren't change his position in case he was being observed from outside. Instead he sat there woodenly, a rigid smile set on his haggard face.

He caught a glimpse of the ferret. He looked tired and frozen. Still his eyes were keen and alert. He was doing his duty right to the end of his shift, which would be soon. He passed without looking inside; it was part of his attempt to trick the POWs into a false sense of security.

Still Heidreich didn't move. He knew his ferrets. They could easily turn and double back noiselessly in the hope of catching the prisoners doing something they shouldn't. He continued to wait. Up at the far end of the hut, someone shouted, in one of those apparently mad rages that all prisoners succumbed to now and again, '*Heaven, arse and cloudburst, I cant stand this*! *Somebody's nicked my "Emil and the Detective" again*!'

It was the signal. The ferret had passed on to the next hut. They were out of danger. Once more the trap behind the stove opened. Another naked tunneler emerged. He was tired, Heidreich could see that. Still, he carefully dusted the sand from his body on to the newspaper. Wirtz crossed and waited while the next man did the same and the next. It was an old practise, one that was always carried out silently and without any speech. The 'old hares' of Camp 23, the veterans, had long established the routine, just in case the Tommy ferrets had buried mikes beneath the huts to listen to the prisoners' conversations. They would not have put it past old 'Tin Leg'. He was a cunning old bastard, who was up to every low-down trick.

Wirtz waited till the last naked tunneler appeared, Hartmann, a giant of a fellow, who actually gave the NCO a dirty-faced grin, although he must have been exhausted by two hours' hard work six metres down in the fetid, poor air of the escape tunnel. He clambered out, pushed his penis to one side to dislodge some earth in the left side of his crotch and then, while the others swept the sand from the paper into the waiting bags, held up the fingers of his right hand three times and then three individual fingers, which looked to Wirtz like hairy pork sausages.

Then the tunnelers vanished carrying their bags, which would be distributed throughout the compound on the following morning by the means of bags inside the POWs' trousers, activated by strings attached to them and worked through the holes in their pockets.

Wirtz walked over to a waiting Heidreich. He repeated the big tunneler's movement with his own fingers. Heidreich nodded his approval and said in a whisper, 'Relax everybody,' and then, bringing his mouth closer to his fellow non-com's ear, said softly, 'Three three metres.'

'Yes, thirty-three,' Wirtz agreed, eyes shining. 'That should mean—'

'Yes, just under the wire,' Heidreich interrupted hastily. 'It won't be long now.' He rose and walked over to the plain wooden table, made from the boxes that the Swiss Red Cross parcels came in, and picked up a mug, adorned with the skeleton key of his old outfit, the 1st SS Panzer, 'The Adolf Hitler Bodyguard', and drank slowly and thoughtfully from the lukewarm coffee it contained.

For once he wasn't hungry, although food was the prisoners' only real pleasure, a break from the awful soul-destroying monotony of the Devizes camp. His mind was too preoccupied. At this rate of progress with 'Otto', as they had code-named the tunnel, they'd be ready to leave it where it joined the rough track from Camp 23 to the US Army Hospital and its vital car park within forty-eight hours. All they needed was the signal from high command and two days' work would see them through, every escaper prepared and armed. Once they'd seized the US vehicles and they had 'wheels', the *Amis'* arms store would be next and they could march.

For a minute his face glowed again at the thought. There was a kind of almost religious fervour to it. Once as a young recruit he had marched west under 'Old Pappa' Dietrich, the first commander of the 'Bodyguard', full of patriotism and highly charged tension that had made him feel he was impervious to enemy bullets and, even if he were hit, it would not have mattered; he was dying for the holy cause of National Socialist Germany and the Führer.

Since then, naturally, he had lost a lot of that youthful enthusiasm. There had been too many battles, too many losses, too many retreats. The whole 'Bodyguard' had been turned over more than once due to horrendous casualties. Still, as he sat there with the darkness growing rapidly outside as the November weekend commenced, he felt a trace of that old fervour. He knew that this was the last chance. All the same, the prospect of putting one over on the fat, cocky *Amis* and their skinny, worn-out cousins-in-arms, the Tommies, gave him a lift. He smiled suddenly. At nothing that anyone could see. But, in his mind's eye, he could see himself once more as that proud confident boy, garlanded with flowers by the cheering Berlin crowd, goose-stepping with the rest of the giant blond heroes in front of a smiling Führer himself. Victory was theirs. They were the masters of Western Europe. Germany's century had commenced . . .

Four hundred yards away, Tin Leg put down his powerful binoculars. He had seen nothing really save the abrupt look of happiness on the Chief Black's face just now. But it wasn't enough. He dropped back on his rough-and-ready seat in the hide which Sergeant Hawkins had built for them in one of the dense bramble thickets which fringed the outer wire here and there. 'The big bastard looks full of piss and vinegar,' he announced to the other two who crouched there muffled in their greatcoats, camp comforters underneath their caps, trying to keep their heads warm in the bone-chilling November cold.

Hawkins nodded. 'Been like it for days now, Major,' he agreed. 'The Jerry bugger's up to no good, mark my words.'

They didn't need to. They felt the same as the wrinkled old sweat.

At the phone, Lee said, 'Thank you, over and out,' then turned to the others and said quietly, though there was no mistaking the note of triumph in his voice, 'The seismograph operator picked 'em up again. He's located the tunnel, heading in a south-south-westerly direction. They're near the wire or even beyond.'

Tin Leg nodded his approval. 'I don't think we need a crystal ball to find out which way they're heading. The track to the Waller Hospital. Why?' He shrugged. 'Search me.'

Washington Lee frowned, but Sergeant Hawkins took the half-smoked Woodbine from behind his left ear and lit it deliberately. 'Easy option, sir.'

'Easy option?' the other two echoed, puzzled.

'Yes sir. Look at it like this.' He coughed as the first coarse smoke hit his lungs, cursing: 'Bloody things. I swear they make 'em outa nag droppings these days. Not like yer Camels and Chesterfields.' He looked hopefully at the black officer.

'Get on with it, Sergeant Hawkins, for God's sake,' Tin Leg cut him short. 'It's going to be a long night.'

Washington Lee smiled and behind the Major's back mouthed the words, 'I'll get you some.'

'Vehicles . . . transport . . . there's plenty of unguarded transport at that Yankee dock. Easy to nab 'em and be off like a shot.'

'But to where, Hawkins?' Tin Leg protested, airing that same old damned question, the answer to which had been plaguing him for days now. 'What are the buggers going to do once they're out in force? They've been out before, as we know, but they've only stuck it out a night or so before coming back with their tails between their legs. They didn't even go on the rampage and force us to call out the bobbies, the Home Guard and alert the whole bloody county. So what are they going to do, eh?'

But there was no answer to that particular overwhelming question and in the end when, over the road, the tarts from the big towns started to get out of the buses and taxis which had brought them here en masse for the weekend Yank pay day, ready to sell their pathetic wares to the Americans, they decided to call it a day for the time being.

The two officers would eat at the mess, get their heads down for a while and then, when the blackout and the US military curfew had put an end to the local jollification this Saturday, they would wait for the US radio detection van to make its secret appearance. Then perhaps they might get a few answers at last. *Perhaps*?

As Sergeant Hawkins said to himself, as they crept carefully behind the cover of the hedge to the little van waiting for them, with the legend '*Smith, Grocer, Freshly Ground Coffee and Fine Wines*' painted in fading gold letters on its once shiny-black sides, 'What a fuckin' war! I'd be better off in the front line getting my balls shot off.'

And in the light of what was to come, perhaps the old sweat wasn't too far wrong there . . .

Seven

C aptain Hurwitz – he liked that, 'the Whore's Joke' – trudged along the shingle, feeling warm from the effort and somehow 'loose', unable to think of another word. Perhaps it was because the war was so far away in this haunted, remote place and he had no real responsibilities. He knew that some people would be terrified out of their wits to be in his position at this moment: dressed in enemy uniform with the nearest enemy camp only a mile or so away on the heights above Slapton and in the midst of the enemy country, where he could be shot out of hand as a spy at the whim of the first knuckle-headed nigger officer who discovered his true identity. Yet all that didn't worry him one bit. He almost felt as if he were on vacation for the first time in five years of total war. Up on the heights, where once Conan Doyle's Hound of the Baskervilles had howled and hunted down its prey, it was foggy and wintry. Soon, he surmised, it would snow on those Devon moors and tors. Here on the beach, pitted everywhere and, he supposed, dangerous with undetected live ammo, it was so hot and summery that he was tempted to take off his 'Ike Jacket'. But in the end he decided against it. If he came up against one of those mush-mouthed bumbling niggers with his shovel, it was better that the poor creature from the Graves Registration Command should see the twin silver bars of a captain on his shoulder. Then they'd go through that Hollywood nigger routine of rolling their poor black eyes, saluting the best they could and giving him all that 'Yessuh, Mister Captain sah.' *Scheisse*. He laughed to himself and stopped. Perhaps there was some kind of significance in the fact, though for the life of him he couldn't quite put his finger on it, that other whites killed the *Ami* whites, but it

110

was the Yankee niggers who buried them and presumably went back to their billets to sleep the sleep of the just. Some sort of poetic justice?

He paused, the wavelets crawling around the soles of his boots like white worms, and looked down at the swollen dead body, lying on what was left of its face. It wasn't the first he had seen since he had come here and, even if it had been, it wouldn't have shocked him; in the past five years he had seen more than enough stiffs. 'Well, Hurwitz, you whore's son,' he asked in the fashion of lonely men, 'what are we going to do about this one, eh?' He put his foot under the waterlogged corpse and turned it over unfeelingly. 'Call in these black fighters for freedom and the future of US big business?'

The body was that of a young man, perhaps twenty or so. The face had been nibbled by fish, but it wasn't too bad and the uniform, torn here and there, covered whatever the tide and rocks offshore had done to the torso. By now he had come to recognise the ivy-shaped green patch of the US 4th Infantry Division, and this stiff had it on the arm of his olive drab sleeve. So he must have been one of the 600 GIs from that Division killed on 'Operation Tiger' two months before the *Ami* invasion of Utah Beach.

Hurwitz sniffed and it wasn't at the smell the body gave off; it was at something else, perhaps at the stink of history and the fortunes of men. The stiff would have stood a better chance of surviving if he had gone in at Utah on 6 June, facing real enemy fire. Instead he had been killed on an exercise without ever having fired a shot in anger. He shook his head.

For what seemed a long time he stared down at the stiff. The tide was washing it back and forth. Soon the sea would reclaim it. Should he leave it at that? Or should he tab it as was expected from an officer of the Graves Registration? Just in case someone was observing him from the heights to his rear, he decided to go through with it. He walked over, dodging the shell craters from the last bombardment of Slapton Sands before D-Day and pulled a grave marker out of the sand – there were scores of them dotting the beach everywhere – and then stuck it in the shingle next to the body. He bent his head in mock solemnity, again for the sake of any watcher, and, turning, started up the incline which led past the mere towards the ruined village beyond.

He didn't take any special precautions. Why should he? This was a haunted place. The civvies had long been evacuated and the blacks stuck to their camp – safety in numbers, he guessed – when they weren't working on the bodies still being found nearly six months after the Operation Tiger debacle. Indeed, no one in his right mind would come down here, especially when it was getting darker. That was why Skorzeny's planners had selected the place for him as a hideout for the first stage of Trojan Horse. The English and the Americans had abandoned this killing ground and the niggers wouldn't bother a white officer, so he could come and go without hindrance.

Besides, Hurwitz told himself, the same *Kapitänleutnant* Krause who had led the murderous attack on the troop transports during Operation Tiger was just over the water at German-held Lorient, ready to race out at the head of his flotilla of high-speed E-boats at a moment's notice. Skorzeny had known what he was talking about when at Grafenwöhr he had placed his heavy hand on his shoulder and had intoned solemnly, 'You have my word on it, *Herr Doktor* . . . Nothing is going to happen to you at this – er – Slapton Sands . . .'

They had been 'banged up' now for over two hours. Over at the NAAFI wet canteen, the Tommies' ale was already flowing freely to judge from the racket. Somebody was pounding the piano's keys as if he intended to break them sooner or later and they were already bellowing, '*Now this is number one and I've got her on the run, lay me down and do it again . . . Roll me over in the clover . . .*'

Heidreich sighed as he squatted on his bunk, sewing one of the trouser-leg bags for the transportation of the tunnel's soil. The English were a damned noisy people, always shouting and commanding in that harsh guttural manner of theirs. The Germans were a quiet race in comparison. Still, it was a good sign. This was going be a typical Saturday night like all the other Saturday nights that had gone before it ever since he had arrived at Camp 23 as a new and angry prisoner of war.

All the same it was unbearably hot in the small, crowded room, despite the cold outside. The wooden blackout shutters were up and barred from the outside so not a breath of air circulated. Now it was stale and thick with cigarette smoke.

He tried to take his mind off the heat and concentrate on what was to come. Already they had the stooge on guard outside in the corridor which connected the various rooms of their hut. He was supposed to be reading a book in the poor yellow light of the single naked bulb. But it was only a pretext. His job was strictly to keep a lookout for an unexpected raid by the shitting Tommy ferrets.

Heidreich found it hard to concentrate. Through the thin partition wall to the left he could hear some damned fool playing the same old sentimental record over and over again. '*Nach jedem Dezember gibt's wieder ein Mai . . . Es geht alles vorüber . . . es geht alles vorbei.*' Angrily Heidreich told himself if the bastard didn't stop playing the shitting record soon, he'd never live to see another 'May' after the coming 'December'. He sighed and tried not to hear the angry discussion going on between the two 'warm brothers' on the other side of the partition to the right. God, wouldn't he be glad to get out of this damned place, cost what it may.

In the end, he gave up trying to concentrate. He walked over to his own personal 'refrigerator', pushing others to one side if they were too slow in getting out of his way. He'd have a cool drink. After all it *was* Saturday night; he deserved a little treat, didn't he?

The 'refrigerator' was an open-sided wooden cupboard, standing on two bricks in a shallow tray of water. A loose cover cut from an old grey Army blanket was fitted over the cupboard, its ends falling into the water in the tray. Another tray of water was on top of the cupboard and what they called 'feeders' – narrow strips cut from the same blanket – led from the upper tray on to the loose cover. By keeping both tins full of water, the absorbent loose cover was always moist and the constant evaporation of this moisture lowered the temperature inside the cupboard. This 'refrigerator' was so effective that cans of food placed inside it soon became coated with beads of moisture.

Heidreich had made his 'private fridge' not long after he had entered the camp, before he had been categorised as 'black' and removed from privileges. Then, due to a piece of good work for the camp office and the German 'Camp Elder', Old Tin Leg had rewarded him with a bottle of ale: an unbelievable treasure. Indeed, he had slept with it beneath his pillow in case of theft until he had decided to build the fridge for it so that the ale could be suitably chilled before he drank it. One Saturday night he had drunk the ale, slowly and with due ceremony, while the rest of the hut had looked on, eyes full of longing, greed and admiration.

Thereafter the fridge – 'Heidreich's Fridge' – had become a centre of attraction, always shown to newcomers and high-ranking visitors to the camp. Naturally the ferrets gave it an inspection every time they turned the hut over, but even for them it was a matter of half-hearted routine. They thought that Heidreich would never chance his precious fridge, the only one of its kind in the whole camp, to hide some unimportant piece of contraband.

Now, as he pulled out the ice-cold bottle of milk stolen from the kitchen bulls in the Tommies' cookhouse and his hands savoured the freshness of the glass, Heidreich glanced hastily at the top container, wet and soggy where the blanket strips overlapped. He put the bottle down for instant and reached up. He felt inside the water, stretching up on his toes to do so. There it was – the rubber container made out of stolen hot water bottles in which it lay safe, snug and dry. He smiled and dropped the blanket strips once more. 'Radio Loens' was ready for use . . .

'Now get this, Lee,' Katz snapped over the phone, and the latter could tell his boss was drunk. They were having the usual Saturday night shindig at the 11th Armored's senior officers' club, and the rye and the Scotch would be flowing freely. Katz, it appeared, had already had his share. 'You're getting no further with those Limey jerks. All the CG wants to know is what happened to that GI with the built-in foxhole.' He laughed at the crude GI expression.

'You mean the murdered nurse, sir?'

'I didn't mean my Aunt Mabel from Buffalo,' Katz said obscurely. 'So you'd better get on the stick, Lee. The CG has given you till the end of the week and then he's hauling your ass off the case. Your job is to get the CIC outfit set up before we go over there, not frigging around in a Kraut POW camp.'

'But we're getting closer, sir,' Lee protested. He could hear the noise of the detector van's engine now. Tin Leg and Sergeant Hawkins, muffled up to the eyeballs in the November cold, were already outside the Camp Mess waiting for the Jewish GIs to arrive. 'Perhaps even tonight we might make a breakthrough—'

'Wait a minute, honey,' Katz said to some unknown third party and it was obvious it was a person with that celebrated 'built-in foxhole'. 'I'm ready when you are, but I've got to deal with this guy first.' Katz's voice rose and he said as if he were suddenly in great haste, ''Kay, you've got the message. Till next week. Waste no more time. Over and out.' Even before a harassed Lee had time to protest further, the phone went dead.

For a few moments Lee stood there, dead phone in hand, wondering what he should do next. Again he felt that awful sense of isolation as a black man in a white society where there was no one of his own kind to whom he could turn and discuss his problems. He shrugged. Abruptly he put the phone down, new determination in his handsome black face. It had always been that way ever since he had decided to get an education – the best – and make his way in a white man's world. If he was fifty years ahead of his time, as Malloy had suggested back in Verdun, well that was just too bad. This was the here and now and he was in it. There was no other way.

He put on his cap and coat and shivered a little as he went out into the night cold. A full moon was shining. Everything was hard and silvery. There was an unrelenting quality about the night, which even the drunken bawling from the British NAAFI across the way could not lighten.

'*Tight as a drum, never been done . . . queen of all the fairies*

*. . . Isn't it a pity she's only got one titty to feed the baby on . . .
Poor little bugger's only got one udder . . .'*

Lee shook his head in mock wonder and walked over to where the other two were waiting, Major Clapton indulging in his 'filthy habit' once again, puffing at his old briar, while Sergeant Hawkins was saying, 'One sniff of the barmaid's apron and they're one over the eight. Soldiers – I've shat 'em!'

Clapton took the pipe out of his mouth and remarked, 'Nice night for it, Lee.'

'Let's hope so.' He didn't tell the old Englishman about Katz's ultimatum; he knew if he did, Clapton would go in to bat for him; they had gotten on very well these last few days of the investigation. And if Clapton intervened, Katz would only dig his heels in and make matters worse. So he refrained and said, 'I hope so, Major. If we can pick up the signal, at the worst we'll discover where on the Continent it's coming from and that might give us a clue to what the Krauts are playing at.'

'Who knows what the Jerries are up to?' Hawkins moaned. 'I don't bloody well think *they* know.' He broke off and said swiftly, 'Here come the radio boffins.'

Moments later the van came into view, two blacked-out slits of light with, in the silver glare of the moonlight, its radio transmitters discreetly covered with a tarpaulin to conceal the van's real use. 'Yeah, it's them. Come on, gentlemen. Let's say hello.'

But their reception wasn't exactly warm. As the narrow door to the back of the high-sided van opened to emit a shaft of yellow light, the tall skinny sergeant standing there saw the black officer waiting in welcome and blurted out to the man seated at the receiver behind, '*Hermann, das ist doch ein Schwarzer.*' There was a definite note of shock and distaste in his voice. The next moment, he recovered from his surprise and said in accented English, 'Hi, Lieutenant. Right on time, eh?'

'Right on time,' Lee agreed hastily.

Behind him Clapton, who had understood the reference to Lee's colour too, told himself sadly, 'What a world. The persecuted are prejudiced against the persecuted! Shit, will it never end . . . ?'

Nine

'Hurwitz, you never had it so good,' the little man said to himself in English. 'Why,' he added, remembering his days as a graduate student in the States, 'you'll be wanting eggs in ya beer next, buddy!' He laughed shortly at his own humour.

In essence, there was some truth in the lonely spymaster's words. The village was his to use and abuse as he wished. It might well appear to be in ruins, but there were plenty of pickings left for a smart operator to use to his advantage. He hadn't selected the cellar of the wrecked village inn for his hideout, although there was still plenty of drink buried in the shell-wreckage; that would have been too obvious. He had chosen 'Rose Cottage' at the end of the abandoned village instead. It was one of those ancient, sunken seventeenth-century places one finds in that part of the world, with two exits, both concealed by the garden and the subsidence.

Someone, perhaps the departed Yanks, had rigged up a power supply to the 'olde worlde' place's outer wall, but he had declined to use it, being content with the candles he had found during his scavenging all over the village. Now, as he prepared to transmit from Rose Cottage's cellar, surrounded by the looted possessions which made his life tolerably comfortable (plus the tommy gun, in addition to the Walther pistol hidden in his pocket) he did not use the easily available power supply. That might well have been a dead giveaway.

He knew from his training and experience in the field that enemy detectors were apt to use the old trick of turning off the power supply from area to area. Once a particular area had had its electricity cut and an illegal transmission ceased, they knew

117

exactly where to search. No, that would have made it too damned easy for the Tommies to find him.

Instead he had attached the transmittor to a six-volt battery taken from the local blacksmith-cum-garage. When the Americans had forced the locals to evacuate the Slapton area so that it could become a D-Day training ground in the fall of 1943, the civvies had been able to take most things with them. But, as always in such cases, they forgot the things they would eventually need to keep those they had taken away working. So they had moved their tractors, lorries and the few cars that still had a petrol allowance, but had overlooked the batteries. The garage had been full of them and there had been a charger too.

Now Hurwitz was profiting from that oversight. He had enough batteries to keep transmitting way into the New Year, though he already knew that after that December Saturday, he wouldn't be needing any more oily car batteries. As he squatted there in his cellar, surrounded by his looted treasure trove, he told himself, 'No, my little whore's son, by then I should imagine it will be home to Mother and yet another piece of cheap tin from a grateful Homeland.'

The thought cheered him no end and, taking a final drink from a bottle of Bass Light Ale, found in the cellar ruins of the pub, he turned to the job in hand. He would commence transmitting at the witching hour – midnight. By then, he imagined, the enemy would be fast asleep, pissed or totally occupied with what every red-blooded, right-thinking male should be doing on a Saturday night – dancing a hearty mattress polka with a nubile and willing piece of female gash. Happy, for some reason known only to himself, Hurwitz began to whistle the *Horst Wessellied*, wondering idly whether it was appropriate for a supposed Jew. All that stuff about *Judenblut**wasn't exactly kosher, was it?

All was silent now. Somewhere an owl hooted. The orderly sergeant was long gone after closing the NAAFI and gently

* Jewish blood. *Transl.*

urging the last drunks on their way back to their Nissen huts
with a friendly, 'Move it, you pregnant penguins . . . the last
man out's feet won't touch the frigging ground on the way to
the frigging guardroom!' They'd moved it. Here and there was
the soft footfall of some lonely sentry, wrapped up in a cocoon
of his own thoughts, patrolling the outer side of the wire.

But, in the detector van, they were all wide awake, as they
crouched there in the green-glowing gloom of the interior, all
eyes fixed on the long row of instruments in front of the
operator, a pair of earphones clamped to his ears, which he
kept touching nervously, as if he wanted to be absolutely sure
that they were functioning correctly.

Stiff and feeling his 'phantom leg' beginning to ache again as
it always did at times of stress, Major Clapton would have given
anything for a smoke. But the Jewish sergeant in charge had
been strict in insisting no one should smoke. 'Every faculty has
to be acute,' he had lectured in his heavy accent. 'We must be
alert to everything all the time in our job. Therefore, I am
saying, please no smoking.'

'Pain in the arse,' had been Hawkins' opinion. 'Bloody
foreigners . . . worse than the Yanks.'

And to that, Clapton had told himself with an amused smile,
there was absolutely no answer.

Time passed leadenly and Clapton, fighting off the desire for
a pipe, could see that Lee was growing increasingly nervous. He
could guess why. His chiefs were putting pressure on him. There
was no particular love lost between the 11th Armored Division
and the military authorities in Devizes. The former felt themselves to be fighting soldiers, whereas 'the locals' or 'natives', as
they called the soldiers in Devizes, were second-line troops who
would never see action. What did they say? 'One man in the
line, six men to bring up the coca-cola.' He guessed, in the
opinion of Lt Lee's superiors, the former was wasting his time,
running with those old Limeys whose job was to look after a
bunch of tame Germans who would be shipped off to the States
sooner or later as it was.

At that moment Lee would have agreed with his new-found

friend, Clapton, especially after Katz's warning. All the same, he was determined to see this thing through to the end. It was a matter of principle, not just a job of work.

Midnight came and went. It was getting even colder. Inside the van it was icy. But they daren't attempt to warm the place up with the engine. That might well have alerted any watcher in the POWs' huts. Now the operators changed every thirty minutes so that they could stand up and get their circulation working once more. For Clapton it was like the old days in the last show when they had been waiting in the forward trenches for the order to go over the top on some damned patrol that GHQ had ordered. The same mixture of tension and wonder at the peace and beauty of the night, which had hidden the terrible lunar landscape below; and no-man's land waiting, with its dangers, terrors, sudden alarms soon to come. God, he told himself, it seems like another age – which he supposed it really was. He had started his life fighting the Huns and it looked as if he was going to end it doing the same thing.

'*Achtung!*' In his excitement, the man with the earphones spoke German, which he corrected the next moment with 'Attention . . . there is something coming through.'

They forgot the cold and their weariness instantly. Immediately they were fully alert, nerves tingling electrically, as the operator, crouched over his instruments, gave instructions to the haughty sergeant who didn't like blacks and who had poked his head through a sort of glass bubble in the van's roof and was working at his direction finder, as the aerial turned and jerked back and forth. The two of them were obviously trying to pinpoint the direction of the signals. Lee and Clapton had been right after all. Not only could the Huns receive secret signals; they could *send* them, too!

Without being ordered to do so, Hawkins slipped the mike attached to its webbing strap around his neck, blew hard into it and prepared to relay any orders that Major Clapton might give him. They would go to the waiting 'snatch squad' in the guardroom. They were armed with Stens and pick-handles. As soon as the hut from which the broadcast came was located,

they would rush it and finally capture the unknown operaters of
'Radio Loens' red-handed.

Lee smiled for the first time that evening. Everything was
going to plan. He'd show that prejudiced, self-opinionated
bastard, Katz . . .

'The goons are in their boxes . . . all's well with the world,' the
duty stooge stuck his head round the door and reported to
Sergeant Wirtz, who was guarding the door, sock filled with wet
sand ready in his hand. He was the senior guard. Anyone
breaking in would have to pass him first. Behind him in the
shadows, not far from the radio was Girowitz, the crazy one.
He held the home-made pistol. In an emergency he'd use it. He
wasn't the best of shots. But he hadn't been picked for his
accuracy. He'd been selected to use the pistol because he was
crazy. If he was ever caught using it and charged, the Tommies
wouldn't be able to top him. He'd already been certified by their
doctors, who were waiting to find some asylum or mental home
where they could deposit a mad POW before he was repatriated
on the SS *Gripsholm*, the Swedish Red Cross ship used for such
purposes. Now he stood there trembling as if he had a fever,
muttering over and over again, 'Buried alive, gentlemen, buried
alive for three long days . . .'

Crouched over the radio, the earphones off his head and
placed in the entre of a tin bowl to amplify the weak sound, the
Oberscharführer listened entranced and at the same time
puzzled. The instructions were in clear, but they wouldn't be
readily understood save by anyone in the know. But it wasn't
the instructions now crackling over the airways which pleased
and yet bewildered Heidreich. It was the place they were
coming from.

Prior to this night, he had always thought (correctly, he had
discovered later) that the secret transmitter had been based in
Lorient, then in Dunkirk, the two ports still held by the
Wehrmacht after the debacle of Normandy. For a while he
had assumed his instructions had been sent from one of the
German-occupied Channel Islands. His method of discovery

had been simple. By twisting the earphones around until the signal was at its loudest, he had ascertained that it was coming from the south-east and, as Devizes wasn't far from the coast, it meant that the transmitter was located somewhere beyond the water. That could only be on the Continent, probably in German-held coastal France.

This signal was coming from a totally different, an almost unbelievable, direction, namely from the south-south-west, which meant the transmitter was situated somewhere in the enemy country itself. The spymaster who was now at this very moment giving him his instructions for the future was actually located in England, not more than a hundred kilometres from Devizes itself!

It was something that almost made him forget to take accurate mental notes of the good, exciting, definitely hopeful news that was coming his way this dark November Saturday night. The unknown German agent who was going to give the signal that would set everything in motion at last was already in place. That could mean only one thing, Heidreich knew. *THE GREAT ESCAPE WAS READY TO GO . . .*

BOOK THREE:

THE GAME'S AFOOT

One

O ne minute after midnight on Saturday 16 December 1944, the night shift at the British Government Decoding Centre at Bletchley Park was put on an immediate 'red alert'. It shocked the hundreds working there, both civilian and military.

For weeks now, virtually no messages of any importance had come in for decoding from Nazi Germany and the Western Front. The Enigmas, the captured German coding machines which enabled the British boffins to receive Hitler's orders as early as his generals (sometimes sooner) had remained obstinately silent. The *Wehrmacht*, it appeared, had drifted off into a winter sleep on the 400-mile long front that ran from Southern Holland to neutral Switzerland. Perhaps, the boffins told each other over their games of croquet and tea and crumpets, the Germans were just waiting for the correct opportunity to surrender.

Tired and jaded by the months of intense activity when they had worked all out, prior to and after D-Day, they had begun to relax, to ease the mental and even physical strain of those long days and nights of decoding and interpretation.

Suddenly, however, the Enigma machines were clattering away furiously once more. Clerks and typists ran back and forth with messages to be decoded. 'The Green Goddess', as the first, room-filling, gigantic computer was nicknamed, glowed and glowered and prepared to spit forth a decode. The balloon had gone up, it was clear. Now the boffins and their military assistants wondered and waited. Why?

The first 'flimsy' bearing the initial decode was rushed into

125

the Nissen huts in the old Victorian mansion's park, the heart of the whole war-winning secret operation. Hurriedly the top boffins grouped around the translator as he put the German text into English by the light of a single, small-watt bulb.

It was from Field Marshal Gerd von Rundstedt, aged and alcoholic, but the most able of all Hitler's field commanders. It read:

> The hour of Destiny has struck. Mighty offensive armies
> face the Allies. Everything is at stake. More than mortal
> deeds are required, as a holy duty to the Fatherland.

What did the bombast mean? they asked. Where were these 'mighty offensive armies'? What precisely was 'at stake'? A score of questions ran through the heads of the boffins and their military bosses as the dispatch riders were readied for their 60-mile dash to London to inform Churchill of the latest surprise development: a score of questions without answers . . .

A hundred and fifty miles away at the rugged, wooded front of the Ardennes, the answer was all too obvious. At exactly five-thirty that morning, while the US Top Brass slept off their hangovers of the previous Friday way back at their grand headquarters in Paris, Luxembourg and Nancy, the complete front of a whole US Army corps, some 60,000 men strong, erupted startlingly into flames, fury and sudden death.

The total artillery of three whole German armies, ranging from 16-inch guns to 3-inch mortars, descended upon the surprised Americans. As the morning stillness was ripped apart by 1,000 guns firing the kind of barrage that the GIs had never seen from the German side since they had landed in Normandy the previous June, white-clad German infantry burst from the snow-bound, wooded heights. Hundreds, thousands of them. Drunk, drugged or both, they came staggering towards the American positions, cheering like madmen as they did so. Behind them came the tanks – battalions, regiments, whole divisions of them. They rolled forward, churning up a white wake, their long, overhanging cannon turning slowly from side to side like the snouts of primeval monsters seeking out their prey. The great counter-offensive in the West, which Hitler had been planning ever since September, had commenced at last and it had, it appeared, caught the American High Command completely off guard.

For one, long, unending hour the tremendous barrage boomed and boomed. Then with startling suddennness it ended, leaving behind a loud echoing silence which seemed to go on for ever. Now the GIs could see the damage the bombardment had done to their positions. They could see, too, the German infantry in their 'spook suits' and their white-painted Tigers and Panthers advancing upon them. They were young and for the most part green. They hadn't been warned to expect this sort of thing. They panicked. They broke. At first in companies, then in battalions, in the end even in whole regiments. Within forty hours one division would be broken, another surrounded, ready to surrender. Everywhere the GIs began 'bugging out'.

Now the back roads leading from the front were packed with fleeing soldiers and vehicles, jammed nose to tail. Order broke down. No one seemed to be in control. Colonels fled side by side with corporals. It was *sauve qui peut*; everyone for himself and the Devil take the hindmost.

It was not surprising, therefore, that panic-stricken fleeing soldiers paid no heed to the strangers in their midst: soldiers who bore different unit patches than they did and whose vehicles didn't look altogether American, especially their armoured ones. Why should they be surprised? Besides, who would attempt to stop well-armed men, four to a jeep (that in itself was suspicious – American GIs always drove only three to a jeep), who seemed to know exactly where they were going? Which they did. For they were heading for the key bridges over the River Meuse, spying and sabotaging as they went, cutting landlines, pulling down overhead telephone connections, changing army road signs, misdirecting convoys attempting to head for the front. For these were Skorzeny's people, the same pseudo-GIs who had trained so long and so well at that remote Bavarian camp at Grafenwöhr. Now, carrying out the Führer's orders to the letter, their scar-faced leader was ready to set the rear area aflame, and not only in Belgium and Luxembourg, but also at the vital ports of Le Havre, Cherbourg, Marseilles and in the end those of Great Britain itself. Soon, Skorzeny knew, the Americans would rally. New leaders would take charge. The panicked GIs would be brought to order. Supplies would be brought up and the Americans, shaken and badly disorganised at the moment, would be formed into a solid front once more. But all those attempts would come to naught if that island off the coast of Europe which the GIs cracked was 'America's floating aircraft carrier', was racked by revolt, armed insurrection and eventual chaos. Then the 'floating aircraft carrier' would undoubtedly sink and victory would be in the hands of Germany. The history of the Second World War in the West would be irrevocably changed . . .

On that same morning, at exactly the same time that the tremendous bombardment swept the front of the US VIII Corps in the Ardennes so alarmingly, Major 'Tin Leg' Clapton finally died. For nearly twenty days he had fought the wound which had torn his stomach apart as the mad German had fired directly at him, muttering that crazy gibberish of his about being buried alive 'for three days'.

He hadn't died peacefully, as the obituaries usually have it; he had fought death, writhing back and forth with his tin leg hanging over the edge of the white-painted cot ready for him to get up and get on with it, business as usual. But that wasn't to be. All that night, Lee and Hawkins, who had already drunk a whole bottle of class VI bourbon, courtesy of the former, had watched over him, trying to cool him down, helping the doctor, whose only real contribution was to shake his head almost angrily, as if the whole long-drawn-out business was a waste of his time.

Of course, he had been right. What penicillin had been

available (again there was an acute shortage of the wonder drug at the front) had been given to the dying Major too late. The wound infection from the badly splintered, home-made bullet fired by the crazy POW had been too great. Thus it was that Major Clapton, DSO, MC and bar, had passed away, fighting still and angry, it seemed, at his fate, in that same hour when the Germans had launched their great surprise attack on the other side of the Channel.

Numbly the two disparate friends, the wizened old British sergeant and the young, handsome black officer, were ushered into the December darkness by the Matron and left standing there shivering, left to their own devices and wondering what they should do next.

Somewhere a bugle started to call reveille and from a long way off there came the rattle of mess tins and dixies. The noise roused Lee, for he said tonelessly, 'Did he have any next-of-kin – wife, kids?'

'No sir,' Hawkins answered, playing with his swagger stick, 'he lost his missus in the blitz in 1940 and I think his only son went missing in the Desert a year later. That's why he liked this job – at the camp. He was back in the Kate Karney – Army, to you, sir,' he added quickly, explaining the rhyming slang. 'He'd been a regular as a young officer before the bastards blew off his leg. He loved the Army and the life . . . No, sir' his voice was suddenly reflective, 'he had nobody except us.'

Again they stood there in silence, listening to the early morning noises of an Army unit coming to life, but only vaguely aware of them. A 'jankers man'* rushed by them at full speed carrying two heavy buckets, chased by a heavy-set regimental policeman who saluted as he pursued his victim to whatever his destination was. 'Never changes,' Hawkins mused, as if speaking to himself. 'But it's discipline and order. Yer miss it.'

---

* Soldiers, who were being punished in off-duty hours for minor military crimes.

Lee nodded silently. Discipline and order? he wondered. Neither the British nor the American authorities had reacted to the shoot-out at Camp 23, which had now resulted in Major Clapton's death and the clearing up of the nurse's murder (Heidreich had confessed on his deathbed). But so far nothing had been done about their discovery that Heidreich and his fellow tunnellers at Camp 23 had been receiving their orders from inside Britain, somewhere in the Devon area to be exact. Indeed, the German-American propaganda experts had reported their discovery independently to 11th Armored Divisional HQ – perhaps they didn't trust the '*Schwarzer*' to do so properly, Lee had told himself bitterly – but nothing had come of it. The Commanding General had apparently not been interested. 'Beyond our line of duty,' he had said to Colonel Katz. 'We're combat soldiers. Leave that to the cloak-and-dagger boys.' It was a message that Colonel Katz had been only too pleased to pass on to Lee.

In the two weeks since that fatal shoot-out in November nothing had happened to give Lee an opportunity to take up the matter once more. In the first twenty-four hours since the German Jews had picked up the signal from Devon, unrest had been reported from German POW camps throughout the United Kingdom. Comrie in Scotland, Penkridge on the main road between Stafford and Wolverhampton, Bridge End in Wales, even Eden Camp in Yorkshire – everywhere where the 'Blacks' were in control, there had been disturbances: an outbreak of Nazi saluting, beatings of the 'Whites', sit-down strikes, insolence to the guards and the like. Then overnight it had all ceased, as if in obedience to some unknown order, and the camps went back to being their usual selves. Even the 'Blacks' tamed down and went back to preparing for the usual sentimental German Christmas, making decorations for the Christmas trees, wrapping gifts for their people in the Reich, practising their Christmas Carols – 'yon bloody "Silent Night"' as Hawkins had commented bitterly. At times, Lee could hardly believe that the incident – as it was now called by those in authority – at Camp 23 had ever even happened.

Time and time again he asked himself angrily, 'What the Sam Hill is going on?' But he knew that he could only find the answer to that damned question – if there was one – by a full-time investigation into the Devon area from which the original message had come. But, as long as Colonel Katz was his boss, he knew there was no chance of that. 'You're here, Lieutenant,' Katz had snapped, 'to form a CIC unit, not go frigging about with your Limey friends. This is the United States Army and we're a fighting division – remember. If you don't like it – ' he had shrugged his fat shoulders, jowls wobbling as usual whenever he exerted himself – 'you know the alternative.' Lee did. It would be a transfer to the 'Louisiana Shit-Shovellers'.

Now, as the two men walked slowly to the cookhouse in the hope that they might beg 'a char and a wad from them greedy gits, the cooks', as Hawkins put it, they were barely aware of the little camouflaged van heading their way, flashing its blacked-out lights at them urgently. It was only when it skidded to a stop – dangerously – on the black ice in front of them that the two awoke from their reverie and cried as one, 'What's up?'

'What's up?' the hearty, beer-thickened voice of the company sergeant-major bellowed back over the noise of the little van's racing engine, 'The bloody balloon's up. A bunch o' Eyetie parachute officers have broken out of their frigging camp in Scotland. All you cushy camp wallahs have been recalled. You're on frigging alert. Now jump to it!'

They jumped.

131

Two

The 'Little Doctor' was slightly puzzled. It was obvious the German-trained parachutists of the Italian Folgori Parachute Division, fascist to a man, had jumped the gun at Comrie. Why, he didn't know.

Operation Trojan Horse was not scheduled to go into action until the leading elements of Skorzeny's 150th Brigade had reached the River Meuse and had seized the key bridges so that Dietrich's Sixth Panzer Army could continue its great drive for Antwerp and the Belgian coast. The combination of that capture of the bridges and what was to take place in England, so the German High Command supposed, would throw the Western Allies into a headless panic. Now, as he waited for the next stage of the great operation to take place, he wondered whether the escape of the damned Macaronis might affect the whole plan.

In the end, squatting in his hiding place, he decided that the Comrie breakout in Scotland was too far from the scene of the main action to rouse the suspicions of some nosey English intelligence officer. So he concentrated on his own position now and what he should do once Operation Trojan Horse commenced.

England in 1944 had opened his eyes somewhat. The 'Little Doctor' wasn't easily taken in by propaganda and the like. All the same, he had been subjected to the 'Poison Dwarf's'* propaganda machine for five years of war and *had* come to

---

* Doctor Goebbels, the German Minister of Propaganda, so named on account of his vitriolic tongue and small stature.

132

believe some of it. But the enemy country hadn't been the bombed wasteland he had come to expect. Mass destruction with the new 'terror weapons', as Goebbels had predicted over the radio, hadn't taken place.

After half a decade of Admiral Doenitz's U-boat blockade, the natives looked well fed, and one thing especially had caught his attention: the quality of the uniforms the British wore. They were made of top-grade wool and not the synthetic rubbish of the German Army. No, he decided, as he half-listened to the sea wind howling outside on that lonely cratered beach at Slapton, England was not on its last legs. Nor, he suspected now, would the great new surprise offensive in Europe bring England to its knees. She was still an island and possessed the greatest Empire the world had ever seen – nearly a third of the globe.

He frowned at his own thoughts. He still wanted revenge on the damned, loud-mouthed *Amis* for what they had done to his parents – and he would have it, too. All the same, he wanted to survive as well. But how? There had to be a way to have his revenge and at the same time save himself for a quiet academic life in the peacetime world. By now, he told himself, he had had enough adventures to last him for the rest of his existence. Now all he wanted was a quiet life.

Perhaps some obscure German provincial university, teaching an obscure subject so that he wasn't bothered by too many students. Switzerland – the German-speaking part would be best – would be an even more attractive choice. Nothing ever happened in that delightfully boring country, where the good, fat citizens' main concern was making money, lots of it.

The 'Little Doctor's' face brightened at the prospect. He'd teach German philology perhaps, specialising in that really obscure subject, the sound changes in German language between the eighth and twelfth centuries. He'd rent one single room, a large one, of course, for his books and papers; and he'd need a proper Swiss balcony for his potted plants. What would a good, peace-loving Swiss burgher do without his balcony and plants?

He'd never cook, save his morning coffee, prepared over a spirit burner. He'd eat at the university's student *Mensa* or in the local *Ratskeller*; and if he needed a woman he'd go to the nearest big town. All Swiss cities with over a 100,000 population were allowed to have red light districts. All in all he'd spend his days in boring, dusty routine, growing fat and old without a care in the world. Now he was postively beaming at the prospect.

He had made up his mind. He forgot the delights of peacetime provincial Switzerland. As always he had a contingency plan forming at the back of his mind. Operation Trojan Horse, he told himself, could go ahead as planned once he received the signal from Skorzeny. *But it would end without him!* For now the 'Little Doctor' realised he had to make his own escape before the balloon went up. What happened then wouldn't concern him in the least. He peered out from his hiding place in the deserted, wrecked village, across the cratered beach with its rusting barbed wire and bits of wreckage from the American fiasco of the previous April. It would have to start here, he decided. But, by the time it did, he would be long gone on the first stage of his escape. Then let the *Amis* and their running dogs, the decadent Tommies, try to catch him.

The same afternoon that the 'Little Doctor' made his decision, Hawkins and Lee kidnapped Sergeant Wirtz from the 'cooler'. It couldn't have been easier. Hawkins had done the introductions to the Guard Commander and Lee, wearing his stolen gold stars of a major in the US Army, had come over big, yelling out orders and demands, all the while smoking a fat cigar in the fashion of self-important high-ranking US officers. The corporal in charge of the guard hadn't known whether he was coming or going. Wirtz, surly and truculent, had been turfed out of the 'cooler' and escorted to the waiting stolen Packard sedan, hands chained behind his broad back, before he had really understood what was going on; and by then it had been too late.

Now, lodged in the empty basement of the US Army Hospital, where they had once broken in prior to the 'disaster', as the POWs called it, he faced the two of them, a worried look now on his tough, scarred face. For he realised that he was confronted by enemies who wouldn't hesitate to use third-degree tactics if they didn't get their way. All the same, Wirtz was a hard man who knew that the Anglo-Americans, in general, were basically soft. So the German pressed his lips together tightly, as if to indicate they'd have to wait till hell froze over before they'd get him to talk.

Sergeant Hawkins noted the look. He grinned. But there was nothing pleasant about that grin. He lifted up his battle blouse to reveal the thick leather belt beneath. Arranged around the leather belt there were the silver and brass badges of what Wirtz knew to be various British regiments. He had seen others of his captors, brown, hard-faced little men with service stripes on their sleeves indicating long-time service, wear similar ones.

'An old sweat's belt, mate. Got to get yer knees well and truly brown before yer can wear one of these, chum.'

If Wirtz understood, he made no sign. All the same, he gave Hawkins his undivided attention as he pointed to one of the badges and commented. 'That's a rare 'un. Took it off a cheeky Mick bugger when the Irish regiments mutinied in India in 1922. I was only a kid – a drummer boy – but I gave the treacherous sod a real pasting, even if I sez it mesen.'

Lee frowned and wondered where all this was going, but as Hawkins pulled the belt free and started to roll it around his fist, Wirtz made a frightened guess at what the old sweat was about to do and he didn't like it one bit.

'Got this one off a big streak o' piss in the Tank Corps in Mespot in 1930,' Hawkins was saying now, lovingly wrapping the belt around his fist. 'La-di-da bugger like them tank corps fellers were in them days. But I soon cut him down to size. Yessir,' he addressed a somewhat bemused Lee. 'Every one of them badges has got a fond memory for yours truly. I could write a book about—'

By now it had dawned on the young American officer what

Hawkins was about to do and he interrupted the monologue with, 'You're not going to hit him with that, Sergeant Hawkins, are you?'

Hawkins didn't lose his malicious grin. He said, clenching his fist, 'Well, let's put it like this, sir . . . I'm not gonna frigging well french-kiss him into telling us what we want to know.'

'But that's against international military law.'

'Lots of things are agin the law, sir, *if* yer gets caught.' Hawkins looked threateningly at the big German NCO.

'No hit please!' Wirtz quavered suddenly in broken English. 'Please no hit.' His bottom lip quivered as if he might cry. 'I talk . . . please, sir.' He looked appeallingly at Lee.

'Okay.' Lee took over hastily now that Wirtz seemed ready to talk. 'What's the deal? You had a radio?'

'*Jawohl, Herr Leutnant.*' Wirtz suddenly spoke German instead of the broken English of which he had been proud. 'It was tuned to the Reich. To report back.'

'Then you started getting orders,' Lee persisted, not giving Wirtz a chance to recover his nerve. Next to him, Hawkins, not understanding the interchange, kept slapping the belt into the open palm of his other hand threateningly. Out of the corner of his eye the German watched him carefully. 'From England?'

'Only once. Before from Germany, sir. We were told to get ready to break out.'

Lee restrained himself just in time. 'You mean only in Devizes?'

'Everywhere in England, sir . . . every camp where we true Germans—' he lowered his voice swiftly as if he realised he had overstepped the mark with the remark about the 'true Germans'. 'Here in Devizes we were to break out several times to discover where the *Amis* had their trucks, ammunition, arms and the like, which we did.'

Hurriedly Lee turned to the British non-com and explained what the German had just said.

Hawkins nodded. 'Keep the pot boiling, sir.' He gave the

German a malevolent look and slapped the belt against his open palm once more. 'Don't give the Jerry bugger a chance to go broody on us.'

Briefly Lee grinned at the little Britisher's choice of vocabulary. Then he turned back to Wirtz. 'But the last message you received – or Heidreich did – came from England, hey?'

Wirtz nodded his head numbly.

'And what did that signal say?' Lee rasped, feeling his nerves begin to race electrically, as he realised that he was coming very close to the truth now.

Wirtz didn't answer.

Hawkins looked down at him, fist wrapped in the belt, with the brutal brass buckle to the front, ready to smash in the German's broad face at any moment.

That did it. 'I don't know exactly, sir.'

'But you know something, Wirtz?'

'Yes . . .' Wirtz hesitated and Lee guessed he did so, not because he didn't want to reveal the message, whatever it was, but because he wasn't quite clear what it was about.

'*Na?*' Lee demanded, "*Raus mit der Sprache. Los, Mensch . . . Wird's bald?*'

'It's difficult, sir, that's all . . . But it is a code-word.'

'What code-word?'

'I don't know exactly, sir . . . Honestly.' There was a note of despair in Wirtz's voice as he flashed a look at Hawkins, as if he half-expected the wizened sergeant to strike him at any moment. 'Heidreich wouldn't tell me. All he'd say was that the code was connected with the Führer . . .' His voice trailed away to nothing, as if he didn't believe his own words. 'I know.' He shrugged apologetically.

Hastily Lee translated his words for Hawkins' benefit. The latter nodded and for a few minutes the two men fell silent, their faces puzzled and moody, while an anxious Wirtz stared from one to the other, as if he were trying to read their thoughts.

Finally Hawkins said, 'But sir, if anybody here in the UK tried to broadcast a code using Hitler's moniker, he'd have half the detector stations in the country down on him like a ton o' frigging bricks.'

Silently a very puzzled Lee nodded his agreement, and with that particular conclusion the handsome black officer had to be content for the time being.

Three

Automatically *Obersturmbannführer* Otto Skorzeny clicked his heels together as that well-known voice came over the line. 'Skorzeny?'

'*Jawohl, mein Führer*,' he barked back over the noise coming from outside. The *Amis* were shelling Dietrich's Sixth SS Panzer HQ once more. They were firing their huge 155mm cannon and, every time a shell landed, the very earth trembled like a live thing. But most of their shells were landing in the thick forests around the little village of Meyerode. The firs were snapping like dry matchsticks. All the same they were suffering casualties and the walking wounded were trailing by in the usual sad procession, the customary look of outrage in their shocked eyes, as if they were asking themselves, 'Why has this happened *to me?*'

Skorzeny didn't notice. He'd seen enough wounded soldiers – and plenty of dead ones, too – since 1940. Besides, he was about to talk to the greatest soldier of all times, Adolf Hitler.

'Things are going splendidly,' Hitler said enthusiastically, new confidence in his voice. 'But we're still being held up before the Meuse . . . Is that gunfire I hear, Skorzeny?' he asked abruptly. 'You know I ordered you not to cross the frontier into Belgium. You are too valuable for me to lose now when everything is at stake.'

'Long-distance enemy artillery, *mein Führer*,' Skorzeny lied glibly. He was like an old warhorse; he couldn't avoid the smell of gunpowder. He had to be near the scene of action, whether the Führer liked it or not.

'Good,' Hitler said and dismissed the matter. 'Now, what is

the situation with Trojan Horse? It is vital that the operation starts within the next twenty-four hours, Skorzeny. A major incident in England will shake the enemy's morale tremendously. Whatever defences they have in front of the River Meuse will inevitably crumple. So?'

Fortunately Skorzeny had his answers ready, even if some of them were lies. But then these days, the big scar-faced Viennese soldier knew, the Führer often preferred lies to the truth. The naked truth was simply too hard for his fellow Austrian to bear. 'Already there has been a premature breakout in the northern part of England called Scotland. But there is no need to be alarmed, the Tommies are no wiser to the full extent of the Trojan Horse operation.'

'*Ausgezeichnet, mein lieber Skorzeny*,' Hitler retorted happily. 'And now?'

'As I speak, *mein Führer*,' Skorzeny lied, 'the first stage is in progress. Our agent is being contacted by our people in the *Kriegsmarine*, who are to take in special weapons for the breakout.'

'*Kolossal*!' Hitler enthused. 'A quarter of a million of our best manhood erupting in armed revolt to the enemy's rear. My God, the Tommies and those Jew-Americans will have the surprise of their lives. Good. Keep me informed, Skorzeny. *Hals und Beinbruch!*'* The phone went dead.

Skorzeny allowed the orderly to take the scrambled phone from his hand, the man taking the apparatus through which the Führer had just spoken as if it were a very precious object indeed. He stared through the window. The wounded were streaming by in ever increasing numbers. He watched as a badly wounded panzer grenadier, staggering to the dressing station, holding his bloody hands to the gaping hole in his stomach, slipped. His guts uncoiled from his torn abdomen like a grey steaming ugly snake and dropped to the ground. Hastily, a medic grabbed his arm and then helped him to stuff back the obscene pulsating tubes.

* Literally 'Break your neck and bones', i.e. 'happy landings'.

Skorzeny turned, sickened, just as Dietrich, the commander of the Sixth SS Panzer Army, came striding through the door, a black look on his broad Bavarian peasant face. 'You spoke with Hitler?' he said without ceremony.

'Yes, *Obergruppenführer*.'

'Did you tell him to call this shitting foolish offensive off before it's too late?'

Skorzeny knew Dietrich of old; he knew he was no respecter of persons. All the same, he was shocked by the directness of the Army Commander's comment. If high-ranking SS officers were talking like this, the most loyal of the loyal, what were the regular army generals and commanders thinking? 'No,' he stuttered, shocked and caught off guard for once.

'Then you should have. Someone ought to tell the old fool which way the train goes.' He sighed wearily, clicked his fingers and downed the cognac the orderly had produced, as if by magic, in one gulp. He dismissed Hitler and said, 'Well, your fellows are causing tremendous disruption behind the *Ami* lines. All the same, Skorzeny, we are still no closer to getting those bridges across the Meuse and I don't have to tell you that, every day we are held up, the enemy will be pushing ever more troops into the line in front of the river. The going will get tougher and tougher.' Again he clicked his fingers and again the orderly dutifully produced another cognac which Dietrich downed in the same swift, greedy manner.

Skorzeny cleared his throat and stared at the general, slumped and gloomily looking into space, while outside the enemy guns thundered and ever more SS wounded streamed back to the already overflowing dressing station. 'There is hope, *Obergruppenführer*,' he said, trying to inject a note of confidence into his voice. 'We start Operation Trojan Horse – ' he glanced swiftly at his watch – 'in one hour's time. If it is successful, you can rest assured, sir, that the pressure'll be off. The Sixth will be celebrating victory in Antwerp with good Belgian gin before this week is out.' He smiled winningly at Dietrich.

The burly Bavarian looked at him, as if he had suddenly gone raving mad. 'Heaven, arse and cloudburst, man—' he commenced, then he thought better of it and signalled for another cognac. He sat there morosely, while Skorzeny remained standing, at a sudden loss as to what to do. Outside, the panzergrenadier whose stomach had been shot away slipped again and lay dying in the mud like an animal . . .

Almost silently, some 200 miles away from the Ardennes, the first lean grey shapes slid out of the sea mist. Like ghosts the three E-boats under the command of Lt Commander Krause approached the beach at Slapton. Everywhere the ratings who were to unload the special stores – pistol grenades, Panzerfausts* and the like – were poised in readiness. Their orders were to unload and be back on board in double-quick time. The Royal Navy was very active in these waters ever since the Operation Tiger debacle and they knew it. Still they knew, too, they had a guide already ashore, who would warn them of any impending danger from sea or land.

On the bridge of the lead craft, Krause peered anxiously through the grey murk. The signal from the 'Little Doctor' had predicted the fog, which made cover for an op of this kind; but, landlubber that the key agent was, he hadn't realised it made equally good cover for the enemy too. Krause had to be on his toes.

'Pretty shitty,' his Number One observed. 'I'd have thought he'd give us some kind of signal to help us in.'

Krause grunted. He thought the same, too. But he hadn't the time to comment on the matter. Instead he searched his front for a signal torch or the like. The agent could risk it. The beach was supposedly deserted save for a few kaffirs. Once he'd landed the 'goodies', he was supposed to fire a few rounds into Kingsbridge as a diversion and then belt like hell for the security of German-held Dunkirk on the other side of the Channel. In meantine, the agent could do a bunk with the special stores. But where was the damned piss-pansy?

'Don't fancy his job, *Kalo*,' the young second-in-command spoke again. 'If they catch him, they'll put the little wet fart up

* A primitive form of anti-tank rocket launcher.

against the nearest wall, tell him to close his glassy orbs and prepare to make a handsome corpse, eh?'

Up at the bows, *Obermaat* Hansen, the craft's senior petty officer, swung his leaded line once more and then sang out, 'Ten metres draught, skipper.'

'Keep it to a low roar, *Obermaat*,' Krause commented and looked even more worried. If they had to do a swift bunk, the shallow water would make it more difficult. Besides, this wasn't the time for them to run aground.

Behind him the two other E-boats came ever closer – close enough, but hard to see in the swirling wet mist. He cursed the weather once more and the elusive agent somewhere on that deserted shore too. What in three devils' name was he playing at? He turned to the young pinch-faced rating just behind him on the tiny bridge, 'Give him another whirl, Flags,' he ordered.

'Sir,' the sailor answered promptly, glad to have the chance to move in the freezing December fog.

While the skipper focused his big binoculars, the signaller started to click his Aldis lamp off and on rapidly, knowing that he had to send his message at top speed if he didn't want to give them away to any watching enemy.

Krause swung from left to right carefully. But the circles of calibrated glass of the binoculars remained obstinately empty. Nothing moved in that deserted still vista of roofless cottages, holed church and cratered fields. It was as if he were viewing some empty alien landscape, long abandoned by whatever creatures had once inhabited it. '*Um Himmelswillen*,' he cursed once again with frustration. 'Where is the damned fellow? Does he think we like farting around like this in full view at a depth of six fathoms.' He sighed and let the big binoculars drop to his chest.

Next to him, his Number One looked away, as if he couldn't bear to see the skipper agitated in this manner. Up front *Obermaat* Hansen said, 'Three fathoms, sir.'

Krause reacted promptly. He daren't go any closer. 'Stop both,' he snapped down the tube to the engine room and clicked the telegraph. The engines died and the lean, high-powered craft came to a stop. Behind it, the other two did the same.

Suddenly there was a heavy silence, broken only by the soft mournful howl of the wind and the subdued lap-lap of the wavelets against the crafts' bows. Abruptly Number One felt helpless and very vulnerable. It was always the same for him when the boat wasn't moving on an active patrol. 'What now, skipper?' he forced himself to ask.

Before Krause could answer, the first salvo of enemy shells came howling in like some great speeding express through a silent midnight station. The noise was tremendous, awe-inspiring, terrifying. 'God in heaven—' the Number One commenced, as the shells plummeted down 50 or so metres away. The E-boat rocked violently. Next moment, as the smoke erupted, shrapnel scythed lethally across the German craft's deck, as she heeled to port.

The main mast came tumbling down in a shower of angry blue sparks. The superstructure was suddenly riddled with gaping, gleaming metal holes. Men and metal were ripped apart effortlessly. Everywhere, as the first British torpedo boat came racing out of the fog, a bone in her teeth, there were dead and dying men, writhing and squirming in their death agonies, choking in shallow steaming pools of their own dark red blood.

The deck stowage caught light immediately. Even as the gunner behind the bridge took up the challenge, turning his twin machine guns on the racing Tommy, the flames were reaching upwards, crackling and blazing fiercely. Like a gigantic blowtorch they seared the deck. Ratings were turned instantly into crouched, charred pygmies, shrunk by that tremendous heat.

Behind the lead craft another E-boat was hit. It started to burn like tinderwood. The grey wartime paint bubbled and sizzled. Huge paint blisters shot up on the hull like the symptoms of some loathsome skin disease. In a flash all was horror and sudden violent death. Even as he fell to the deck, his right arm severed, blood jetting from the horrific wounded stump in a bright scarlet arc, Krause breathed, 'Betrayed . . . betrayed, Number One.' He closed his eyes as if very weary. Next moment he was unconscious.

The E-boats didn't have a chance. The British gunboats had taken them completely by surprise. Now they proceeded to slaughter them, as they floundered there in the shallows, their screws racing and churning up white wakes impotently. Perhaps the British were taking their revenge for what had happened here at Slapton Beach eight months earlier. No one knew later, for this was a secret battle that was never revealed to the public.

Five hundred metres away, the 'Little Doctor' rose from his hiding place and dusted the wet sand from his knees. He had seen enough. The signal in the least secure code he could remember had done the trick. The English had picked it up and deciphered it as quickly as he had anticipated. They had been waiting for the unfortunate Krause and his delivery. Now the whole of Southern England would be alerted and in uproar; it was an ideal opportunity for him to commence his journey northwards and avoid the flak. Then he'd send his message, the camps would rise and, whatever the outcome, he would have fulfilled his duties to the Homeland. Thereafter, he'd be on his own, looking after Number One.

He took one last look at that scene of desolation on the shoreline below – the dead, the dying, the sinking E-boats, one of them half submerged but still bravely firing its twin 20mm cannon; while the Tommies pumped shell after shell into the trapped flotilla, showing no mercy, carried away by the atavistic cruelty of war and bloodshed.

The 'Little Doctor' felt no qualms at what he had done. They were Germans dying down there, admittedly, but he felt no special relationship to them. For him they were simply young men in uniform who were fighting – and now dying – on the same side as he himself. Undoubtedly they would have experienced the same feelings if it had been the other way round.

He shouldered the American Army haversack, which contained the special *Abwehr* light radio, and stamped his highly polished US shoes. It was time to go.

He turned. Without another look backwards, he set off up the slope to the road beyond. Behind him the slaughter continued. But the 'Little Doctor' had already forgotten what had happened and what was happening to Lt Commander Krause's flotilla. It was the best way, he knew.

Four

C olonel Katz was full of himself. Now he was no longer the pudgy, desk-bound bureaucrat. No, now he was the lean, keen warrior, ready for combat at a moment's notice: a killing machine in the Patton mould. On his desk rested his lacquered helmet with its silver eagle, and oftentimes his bemused clerks would find him striding about the office in his helmet liner, striking his thigh with a riding crop, again à la General 'Blood an' Guts' Patton.

Naturally the custom-tailored uniform had been replaced by battle fatigues, with a pistol belt digging into his fat midriff. He had even tied the ends of the .45 pistol holster to his thigh with leather thongs, as if he were some old-time Western gunslinger. Thus it was that when he was not practising his 'war face, number one' in front of the mirror as his hero Patton was reputed to do, he was looking mean and 'ornery' in the style of a Western bad man. But, as he could not see well without his horn-rimmed glasses, he dispensed with any gun-drawing exercise, just in case he miscalculated and shot himself in the foot!

Indeed, everything was going splendidly, Colonel Katz told himself, as he sat bolt upright at his desk, eyes set far away on some distant battlefield where he had just won America's highest honour for valour – the Congressional Medal of Honor. He was in a winning mood altogether. Two hours before he had really given the black bastard Lee, with his goddam Harvard accent, a real shaft up his black ass. The cocky coon had come again, full of this goddam Limey business with the escaped prisoners and the supposed mass breakout. According to the upstart prick, the British authorities had already located roughly where the enemy transmitter was. It would be used to signal a general POW rising. In his opinion, the mush-mouth was talking a lot of bull. 'Christ on a crutch, Lee!' he had snorted angrily, glaring at the handsome black, 'don't start that goddam shit again. Don't you know our guys are fighting for their very lives in Belgium. We've got no time for this PW crap. Hellfire, man, we could be over there tomorrow up to our neck in Nazi Krauts!' He had slapped his crop down across his desk to emphasise his point.

Lee had apparently not been impressed. 'But don't you see, sir,' he had objected, voice full of controlled passion, 'this PW thing, as you call it, is all part and parcel of the same operation, sir.'

'Watch your mouth,' he had snorted sternly, not liking that 'as you call it' one bit; after all, he was Lee's commanding officer. Besides, what could you do, Lee, if it were *your* responsibility, which it aint?'

'Sir, as I've said, we've got a fix on this guy. Now we've just heard from the British Navy that there's been some sort of scrap off Slapton Sands, the very same place where we think this Kraut spy is located. Isolated training ground, not used since before D-Day and definitely off limits due to the un-exploded shells everywhere—'

'And goddam off limits for you, too, soldier!' Katz inter-rupted harshly. He pulled his haughty Patton face and added, 'Got the message, eh?'

But Lee hadn't. Desparately he tried again with, 'But sir, this might be of the greatest help to our men over there. We could prevent a murderous stab in the back which might—'

Katz flushed a dark red. 'Don't you understand English, black boy,' he roared, losing his temper completely. 'No more PWs. No more Limeys.' He raised his pudgy hand in warning. 'Clear? Make a false move now, Lee, and I'll have your black ass behind bars in the stockade before you can goddam cry Rastus. Now – *out!*'

That late afternoon in December 1944, when such things happened to men with a different skin colour, Washington Lee

147

deserted the Army of the United States. Later one might have argued that the United States deserted Washington Lee . . .

Krause was dying. Fast. All around in the light of the search-lights from the nearest searchlight battery, which had been rushed to the site of the uneven naval engagement, the naval boarding parties were scavenging the half-sunken E-boats while medics trudged through the wet sand, bearing away the wounded on blood-soaked stretchers. Along the beach the blacks of the Graves Registration units stared in open-mouthed amazement at the scene, not moving, not helping because no one had told them to do so; and blacks in the US Army did nothing without orders from a superior. They weren't supposed to.

Lee, accompanied by Hawkins, was the only exception. After asking the harassed surgeon-commander's permission to do so, he trudged to where Krause was dying, wrapped in a blood-stained blanket, and looked down at him. Krause looked back. All hope had vanished from his faded gaze. But there was still anger there in his dying eyes. For now he looked up at Lee, apparently not at all surprised that this black American spoke fluent German, and answered his question with a bitter, 'We were betrayed. The little bastard . . . led . . . us into a trap.' He grabbed Lee's hand suddenly and surprised the latter. 'A trap, I say, you understand?'

Hawkins knew the signs. The Jerry was dying fast. The sudden rage, the temporary burst of strength, as if raging against the fates, were all sure signs of fast-approaching death.

'But who is the little bastard?' Lee asked gently, lowering the German officer as blood started to trickle once more from the left side of his dark-red lips. It was flecked with tiny bubbles, as if he had been hit in the lungs too.

There was no answer.

Lee repeated his question.

Krause tried. He gasped, his right hand clawed the air and his eyes were intense and fixed on Lee's unsmiling, worried face, as if he were intent on making the American understand; as if it were vitally important for him to do so. But nothing came save a barely audible whisper.

Hastily Lee bent his head almost to the dying man's face in an attempt to hear. Then slowly, very slowly, he raised himself. The weary surgeon-commander, his hands red with blood as he puffed at his limp cigarette, came across. He nodded, as if to confirm something and then, bending down, closed Krause's eyes and nodded to an orderly. Carelessly the latter threw a blanket over the new corpse. The surgeon-lieutenant stomped away without a word. Perhaps he had seen too much for this particular day.

Wordlessly Hawkins offered Lee a Woodbine.

'Coffin-nails', Lee knew the little English non-com called them. The name seemed appropriate for this day and the surroundings. Although he didn't like the cheap taste of the working-class cigarette, he took one and accepted a light from Hawkins' stolen Zippo lighter.

'Well,' he said as he puffed out a stream of acrid blue smoke, 'that didn't get us very far.' He sounded bitter.

'But he said something, sir, I thought, before he snuffed it.'

'Yes, but nothing I could make sense of, Hawkins.'

'What was it?' Hawkins persisted, as on the beach the medics started to turn off the searchlights, at last removing that terrible scene of carnage and human suffering from sight.

'Chocolate Soldier . . . *Schokoladensoldat.*' Lee hesitated before adding the German word, as if that might help, his face perplexed.

'Chocolate soldier . . . hm.' Hawkins considered and Lee let him, for, uneducated as he was, the little Britisher was no fool. He had been around.

'Yes, and I found this in his pocket. Why he should be carrying this, God knows. Men don't usually go into battle, I guess, with a chocolate bar in their pockets, do they, Hawkins?'

Hawkins, who had been into battle many times in his long career with the British Army, peered through the increasing gloom at the bar of chocolate, wrapped in blue paper, but with no marks or writing on it to identify who had manufactured it, his lips moving, as he repeated the words, 'Chocolate soldier . . . chocolate soldier.'

Just offshore one of the E-boats was now beginning to sink completely. The shattered craft was giving off a strange keening, moaning sound, as if it were almost human. It was accompanied by the obscene noise of compressed air rising to the surface and exploding there like an enormous fart. Neither man seemed to hear. Instead they concentrated on this strange business of the chocolate until Lee asked hesitantly, 'Chocolate must have been important . . . Perhaps it was some kind of recognition signal – a sign, you know, Hawkins, like a dollar bill torn in half, which two agents fit . . .' His voice trailed away for he could see that Hawkins wasn't listening.

Abruptly the little NCO said, 'You know, that blue-wrapped bar of chocolate. You know where it comes from?'

Lee shook his head.

'From a British compo ration box. That's the ration box the lads get in the front line. Each bloke gets a bar of bitter chocolate and seven boiled sweets a day as part of the grub ration.'

Lee nodded, though in fact he didn't quite understand what Hawkins was getting at.

'Well, the people who make that chocolate bar is Rowntrees – you know them Quakers who have their factory up north in York. They don't want to fight themsens, but don't mind making a profit on them who does,' he added bitterly.

'Get on with it,' Lee urged.

'Well, sir. I don't know if I can put it all together, like, a compo ration chocolate bar and this poor dead Jerry stiff going on about a chocolate soldier and the fact that our bloke has gone and done a bunk . . .' He took a deep breath, 'But do you think it's giving us a clue?'

'What kind of a clue?' Lee asked swiftly.

'To where he's gone?'

'How do you mean?'

Sergeant Hawkins was unusually flustered. Perhaps he

150

thought he was making a fool of himself, for he said hurriedly, as offshore the E-boat gave one last obscene belch and then disappeared beneath the surface, leaving behind a strange sullen silence, 'York.'

'*York?*'

'Yessir. Does it add up – them things we've just mentioned – that if he's gone far – and we know his nibs will have to have skedaddled out of this part of Devon now – he's gone to the home of the chocolate soldiers?'

'You mean York?'

'Ay,' was Sergeant Hawkins' answer, for already in the far distance he could hear the shrill sound of the sirens like those he remembered from the pre-war Hollywood gangster movies with George Raft and James Cagney. They could only be Yank. And he knew instinctively why they were sounding their warning to clear the coastal road so urgently. They were after him and Mr Lee. It was time to go . . .

Five

'*The cabin boy's name was Ripper . . . He was an ugly nipper . . . He stuffed his arse with broken glass . . .*' Outside on the glistening wet blacked-out platform, the guard shrilled his whistle. The long train bound north shuddered. In the packed corridor, the tightly pressed crowd of civilians and service people grabbed for holds. But not the drunken sailors. They braced themselves and balanced easily, as if they were still on the deck of their ship, while the drunken three-striper continued to warble his dirty song, oblivious to the angry looks of the ATS and WRENS, shocked as they were. '*Filled his arse with broken glass,*' he repeated, leading up to the punchline, '*and circumsised the skipper . . .*!' The end of the dirty ditty was greeted by a round of applause, wild cheers and cries, 'Gie' us another one, Stripey! What about "Tight as a drum, never bin done, queen of all the fairies"?'

In his reserved compartment, Colonel Frank Fisher, Jr, US Corps of Signals, smiled thinly and leaned back more comfortably in the smelly, dusty plush of the first-class seat. Outside, the last of King's Cross Station was beginning to flash by at an ever-increasing speed. For the while he was safe. The train seemed packed with Britishers only and he hadn't seen an American since he had been checked at the ticket barrier by polite British MPs under the supervision of an equally polite RTO.* Somehow he felt the Limeys wouldn't bother an American, especially one of his rank.

* Railway Transport Officer.

He leaned back even more, weary now, but for the time being he fought off the temptation to close his eyes. It wouldn't be wise. With his eyelids almost closed, he watched the activity outside in the blue-lit corridor, the unreal light turning the troops' good, honest, simple faces into the wan ones of people suffering from advanced consumption. Soon, he knew from experience, they would drop off, even in the standing position; they had a twelve-hour journey in front of them till Edinburgh. They'd need all the shuteye they could get. But still they were full of high spirits, fueled by the many pints of ale, weak as it was, that they had consumed at King's Cross, their conversation animated, even hectic, as if they didn't want to think of what was soon to come.

With his mind half on the activities outside in the corridor, the American officer considered his own immediate future. With the square of coloured metal on his left chest, indicating that he had been wounded and received the 'Purple Heart' for his suffering, and the highly polished paratroop combat boots on his small feet, he assumed he would be taken for a 'Yank' who was recovering from a wound and was on vacation. For wounded Americans who had been discharged from US military hospitals in the UK, were always wandering all over the country, wherever the fancy took them, seeing the sights, looking for 'lost' pre-D-Day girlfriends, seeking relatives. The place was full of them. He hoped that the ploy would work if anyone stopped him, for he had no official papers indicating that he had been posted to some US outfit in the north. Indeed, there were few of them left. Those Americans of the pre-D-Day millions who were left were predominately in the south near the Channel ports. Well, that was what he hoped anyway. Besides, once he had reached his destination, the 'sleeper' would take care of his cover and the colonel in the US Army Signal Corps would disappear for good. Till then he had to keep a weather eye opened for danger.

He yawned and dismissed the matter. Instead, he took more interest in what was going on in the smoke-heavy, dark corridor outside. They were the usual service people that one might encounter during one's travels in any country, he told himself. In essence they were small, unimportant cogs in a machine which they could not influence in any way. It directed them hither and thither and they had no recourse but to obey until one day their particular journey came to an end for good.

He frowned. He could not let that happen to him. He had to be master of his own fate. It was difficult and it was a course that bore its own risks. But at least you were giving yourself a chance, making your own decisions, trying to buck the powers-that-be and the fate they had allotted to you.

'Stripey', as the others called the drunken old salt, was being urged on by the younger sailors to sing again. Perhaps they wanted to shock the ATS nearby with his dirty ditties. Someone had handed him a bottle of beer and he was waving it to and fro, as if conducting a band, warbling, '*Up came a spider, sat down beside her, whipped out his old bazooka and this is what he said . . .*' The old salt paused dramatically before he launched himself into the chorus.

An ATS sergeant protested, red-faced.

That did it. The whole bunch of happily drunken sailors joined the soloist as he bellowed, '*Get hold o' this, bash . . . bash. Get hold o' that . . . bash . . . bash. I've got a luvverly bunch o'coconuts . . . I've got a luvverly bunch o' balls . . .*'

A little cynically, the American Colonel told himself, 'Cannonfodder . . . Mere cannonfodder . . . no-hopers.'

Outside, the singers were launching themselves into the second verse: '*Big balls, small balls, balls as big as yer head . . . give 'em a twist around yer wrist and swing 'em right over yer head,*' when the ATS sergeant who had protested turned and beckoned to someone further down the corridor and out of the Colonel's sight.

He craned his neck, suddenly alert and curious, for the singing was beginning to falter rapidly. '*Where was the engine driver when the boiler bust, they found his bollocks and the same to you . . .*' Even the drunken three-striper was beginning to shut up and now the Colonel could see why.

Two redcaps had come into sight, pushing their way through

the throng with practised ease, as if they knew there was going to be no trouble even if many of the travellers were drunk and hardened veterans of five years of war.

Fisher swallowed hard. He didn't like what he saw. The one Limey redcap had an old, hard face, which looked as if it had been carved from solid granite. On his chest he bore the ribbon of the Africa Star and there were two gold wound stripes on his sleeve beneath his sergeant stripes. He was the old soldier, who had probably been wounded with a fighting outfit and then transferred to the military police.

The other redcap was big and powerful, but youthful and somehow innocent. His face bore no experience of actual combat; nor did he wear any medal ribbons. As the two men talked severely to the crestfallen, chastened sailors and then examined their passes, the Colonel told himself that the younger MP might be the easier mark. All the same, he preferred not having to deal with either of the Limey cops. Both of them definitely looked tough babies, who wouldn't be fooled easily. Tensely he waited till they had dealt with the sailors, warding off the bitter comments of the ATS on the former's behaviour. Were the cops going to look in and – seeing that he was a Yank officer-and a high-ranking one at that – leave him in peace? He hoped so. If not, he'd have to act. What would they do in the next few seconds? Abruptly he was wide awake, his nerves tingling electrically. It was the moment of truth. What was he going to do?

Outside, the two MPs had bullied and chivvied the drunken sailors into quietening down and behaving themselves. Now occasionally muttering to themselves under their breath, their happy faces had taken on the sullen, hangdog look of those who know that they are powerless to do anything about their circumstances; they just had to accept orders from their superiors and that was that.

The older of the two MPs looked at the lone American in the compartment. His keen, shaven face showed no emotion. The Colonel's heart leapt. Was he going to get away with it?

He wasn't. The older one nodded to the younger MP. He

nodded back his understanding and, tapping his pistol belt to see if it was in the correct official position, he rapped his knuckles at the door of the first-class compartment and in that same instant slid it back. 'Travel documents, sir,' he said politely. 'Check.'

The Colonel pretended to be a little flustered. Hastily he showed the page of the *Daily Mirror* which displayed 'Jane' losing her skimpy lace panties yet once again. The young MP smiled carefully. Even these officers and gents liked to read 'Jane', just like the ordinary squaddie. All of them, officers and other ranks, were just waiting for the day when she took her knickers off and showed what she had up front. 'Sorry to bother you, sir,' he continued, as the flushed little Yank fiddled in his pocket as if he were searching for his travel warrant and his official ID card. 'Routine, sir. Can't be too careful these days.'

'Yes . . . of course, Corporal,' the Colonel agreed. 'You're only doing your duty—' he broke off suddenly and snapped, 'D'you smell smoke?'

'Smell it, sir?' the corporal cried in sudden alarm. 'It's bloody well coming from right behind yer.'

The Colonel rose hurriedly. Behind him the plush was already smoking while the *Daily Mirror* was beginning to burn. He acted. Later the two MPs thought he *over*-reacted. But that was later. He yelled at the startled corporal, 'For God's sake, man, don't just stand there . . . get an extinguisher . . . The goddam train could catch fire with all this plush. *Move!*'

Caught completely off guard and not accustomed to being shouted at by a colonel, even an American one, the corporal forgot his usual cautious approach to things. Hastily he flung open the door and cried, 'Out of the way there, you matelots . . . there's a fire in here!'

It was definitely the wrong thing to say. An ATS screamed. A burly sailor gave his mate a shove. The latter woke up from his doze and the burly one cried, 'Fuck this for a game o'soldiers . . . the whole bloody train's on fire, Chalky!' '*The train's on fire!*' the cry of alarm went down the crowded corridor. The throng didn't panic. Someone yelled, 'Stand fast . . . Don't panic . . . Remember you're British!' But they didn't have to rely on the traditional British calm and stiff upper lip. They couldn't have panicked even if they had wished to; they were too tightly packed for that. But in that moment of unreasoning alarm, someone did pull the communication chord – 'penalty five pounds'.

With an ear-rending screech of metal brakes trying to get a grip on the tracks while travelling at a speed of sixty miles an hour, they came to a slow, shaking halt that sent even that tightly packed throng tumbling forward and then backwards, with the servicewomen shrieking and a woman crying, 'Someone's just put his hand up me skirt, the dirty bugger!' Which was the only thrill that the sailor in question was going to get in this life before his ship was torpedoed in the English Channel on New Year's Eve, 1944.

By the time the lights had flashed on again and the guard was pushing his way down the corridor, crying angrily, 'Who pulled that communication chord?' and the MPs had returned to their duties and to view the 'blazing compartment', the 'Colonel' had vanished; as had the cartoon strip, to reveal the *Mirror* agony aunt's column, in which the future Barbara Castle advised some unfortunate soldier to 'write to your MP immediately . . . When we take over power, there'll be none of this class distinction in our Fair Land.'

'Well,' said the Eighth Army veteran, eyeing the smouldering seat, 'you really fell for it, Corporal, didn't yer . . . hook, line and sinker . . . You really buggered it up.'

The young corporal looked alarmed. 'What do you mean, Sarge?' he asked anxiously.

'Oldest trick in the world. He used a diversion – the old bit of burning newspaper lit behind his back while you thought he was reaching for his documents.' He shook his head. 'You've got a lot of learning to do yet, laddie, if you're ever gonna get that third tape.' He meant his sergeant's stripes.

'You mean, he weren't what he was supposed to be, Sarge?'

'Of course, I do. Your *colonel* – ' he emphasised the rank –

'could have been a deserter from the frigging Black Watch for all I know. You know what cheeky buggers them kilties are. But one thing is for certain. That Yank colonel was on the trot.*

The corporal's mouth fell open in sheer naked surprise. Slowly the night express started to roll north once more.

* On the run from the authorities.

Six

Nella Mandelbaum, otherwise known to herself as 'Frei-frau von Stolzembourg', placed the swastika badge attached to the silver chain carefully between her deep, hanging breasts, patted the spot warmly and did up the last buttons. She stared at herself in the mirror, tucked away a curl of her dyed blonde hair, which she had fashioned in the popular German Pompador style, and was pleased with what she saw. No one could mistake her in her severe black suit and high-necked blouse for anything else but what she was: a member of the German *Altadel*, the Old Aristocracy. '*Preussische Disziplin und Ordnung!*' she barked at her image in the mirror. 'Prussian discipline and order – that's the way the world should be run.' She grunted and her dark eyes flashed fire. 'Not like these damned decadent English.'

The word 'decadent' must have triggered off her next action. For, turning from the mirror, she took the bottle from its hiding place under the perfectly made bed, which nearly filled the tiny room. She opened it carefully, no longer smelling the toxic biting fumes that came from it. '*Prosit!*' she said to herself and allowed herself a tiny sip, just enough to carry her through the morning.

Again that delightful, almost sexual, sensation surged through her plump ugly body and she was tempted to take a drop more, but she controlled herself with 'Enough, madam. We Prussians are too poor to be self-indulgent.' With a hand that had become firm as a rock once more, the shakes vanished for a while, she replaced the stopper tightly and stowed the bottle in its hiding place again.

Outside, at the end of the narrow, cobbled, sixteenth-century street, the great bell of the Minister chimed the hour. It was time to be going. Naturally the train would be late arriving at the station, but what could one expect from these idle English. She, however, as a Prussian aristocrat in exile from her homeland had to be an example to them of how a poor, but well-disciplined people were never late. She touched her felt hat once more and went out.

It was snowing and Stonegate was virtually deserted. The tourists who had once thronged it when she had first been exiled here in 1938 had long vanished. Now the only sign of life was the elderly milkman and his even more elderly nag and trap, dishing out gills of precious milk from his churn. Further down, however, she just caught a glimpse through the swirling flakes of a special constable in his steel helmet looking in her direction as he crossed the Mansion House Square. Probably he was spying on her once more. No matter. Prussians took that kind of oppression in their stride. She passed into the street and headed for the River Ouse and the LNER station beyond.

The old city looked grey and shabby – even the layer of virgin snow powdering the roofs of the medieval buildings couldn't hide that fact. The civilians in their shabby, dirty macs and cloth caps, with the Rowntree factory workers trying to hide their iron curlers beneath their headscarves, didn't look any better. The sight pleased her. Even though she had lived among them for nearly half a decade or more and they had been kind to her (they had not even sent her to prison on the Isle of Man back in 1940), she still regarded them as the enemy. Now, as she saw the headline scrawled across the front of the *Express* in Lendal, as she approached Lendal Bridge, '*Rundstedt Offensive Still Making Progress in Belgium*', she knew the English were losing the war at last. Soon *her* day would come. After all the humiliations and trials, she would be able to reveal her true self: a loyal follower of the Führer, Adolf Hitler, and a pure-blooded member of Germany's aristocracy. The thought pleased her

160

and, although the effects of the ether were already beginning to wear off now, she still carried herself proudly and erect.

She crossed the bridge. There were two Home Guard men still guarding the nineteenth-century structure over the River Ouse, next to the burned-out chocolate warehouse. But they took no notice of her, however proudly she walked. They were too concerned sheltering from the driving snow, huddled as they were in their gas capes. Though one did remark after she had passed, 'Did yer see the arse on that one, Charlie. Make two of yer old woman.' To which Charlie replied, 'Ay, but did yer see her face, Phil. Like the back of a bus. God, was she ugly!' But as a *Freifrau* of the old aristocracy, she had no ears for the idle chatter of the lower classes.

She climbed the slight rise past the Lutyens memorial to the dead railwaymen of the First World War. It still bore the fading wreathes of the previous November. She had no eyes for them. That sacrifice was no concern of hers. If she were still to sacrifice anything, now that she really had been finally activated after all these years, it would be for the Holy Cause of the Third Reich. Despite the bitter cold and the driving snow, she felt flushed with a sudden warmth. *That* really would be worth giving one's life for.

Poor, dear, long-vanished Hardt von Hartenstein, her one true love, had taught her that lesson and it was one that she would never forget. How could she? It had been a lesson associated with the night that she had first become a real woman, had realised at last what love and passion had really meant.

Back in 1941 when he had arrived in York as a prisoner of war, one of the first Germans of the *Afrika Korps* to be captured there and dispatched to Britain before moving on to Canada, where she had lost touch with him – at first – she had been a simple creature, her life centred on her humble cleaning job in the great Quaker mental hospital near the city centre. After all, it was the best that a 'refugee', as those foolish do-gooders always called her with their hypocritical, fake-pious looks, could expect. They couldn't talk the language properly, they were subject to Police checks as enemy aliens' and a nightly curfew and she had accepted her lot. That is, until she had been co-opted to help as an interpreter with the German POWs who were imprisoned at the one-time racecourse to the west of the city.

She had been attracted to von Hartenstein at once. At first it had been admiration at his cunning and daring in fooling these hypocritical Quakers into believing that he was suffering from some war-induced mental illness that required him to be removed to the Quakers' eighteenth-century asylum, where he would have much more freedom, better rations and a better chance of escape than under the guarded grandstand of the makeshift racecourse POW camp.

Blonde, virile, typically Nordic, he was the ideal officer of the type beloved of the Führer and the New Order in a decadent, old Europe. At first she had felt ashamed of herself in his presence: dark, foreign-looking, dumpy and in no way Nordic. Hardt, as she learned to call him – 'hard as Krupps steel, tough as leather, as swift as a greyhound' – didn't seem to notice. Always he praised her appearance, talking to her on these vital racial characteristics as if she was one of the blonde elite. Time and time again he praised her aryan purity and how, in other circumstances, he would have asked for her hand in marriage so that they could have presented the Führer with a half-dozen future Hitler Youth.

In due course, she had come to believe him, especially after he had made love to her in one of the abandoned eighteenth-century wards, heavy with dust and the passing of time, the only sound that of the creaking woodwork and the scampering of the rats' clawed feet.

It had been Hardt who had introduced her to the ether. 'It relaxes women,' he had whispered in that high room, heavy with the miseries and suffering of two centuries of mad people. 'They need it . . . Believe me, when you get used to it,' he had added fervently, staring down at her dark Jewish face with barely concealed disgust, 'you'll never want to be without it in the – er – act of love.'

The first time she had been sick and had had an headache afterwards. He had consoled her with, 'Next time it will be a hundred per cent better, *Schatz*. Believe me.' And it had. She was confused about the details but, when she had come out of the ether-induced haze, she had felt wonderful, totally relaxed, a warm, glowing, contented feeling unlike any other she had experienced in her life hitherto. It had been tremendous and, long before cruel fate had parted them, when he had been shipped off to Canada by the decadent English, she had become hardly able to wait till he had finished pouring that precious liquid on the cotton wool to press it gently to her mouth and nose.

In May 1942, six months after he had been taken away from her to the other side of the Atlantic, she had been busy in York stealing bottles of ether during the confusion of the great 'Baedeker Raid' of that month, when she had been approached.

With the flames leaping higher and higher in Bootham, outside the eighteenth-century Quaker hospital where there were dead men in the steaming bomb crater next to the entrance in the park, someone had spoken out of the glowing darkness in her native German, '*Fraulein Mandelbaum, Sind Sie das?*'

She had not been shocked; she was too far gone with the stolen ether from the hospital's dispensary for that. Indeed, for a few moments she was convinced that she was suffering from the customary hallucinations that accompanied the ether. But when the hidden voice said softly, again in German, '*Hauptmann von Hartenstein lasst grussen*,'* she knew she wasn't.

The greeting caught her totally off guard. In her excitement she almost dropped one of the precious bottles of looted ether. '*Hardt?*' she breathed. 'Did you say von Hartenstein?'

The voice chuckled, a chuckle which ended abruptly, as yet another stick of Luftwaffe bombs straddled the nearby railway line, heading north to the Russian supply ports of the north-east coast.

---

* 'Captain von Hartenstein sends his regards.'

She shook her head. Everything came into clearer focus. Now she could see the shadowy outline, a stark black against the ruddy glow of the fires opposite. Everywhere, the grand Quaker houses which lined Bootham were on fire. 'Who are you?' she asked. 'How do you know—'

'Please,' the little man crouched there hissed. 'No questions. I'm in danger of my life. I'm just to tell you that Hardt sends his regards . . . and when the time comes, he depends upon you to rally to our holy National Socialist cause. That is—'

Again another stick came hurtling down and she caught the outline of a twin-engined Junkers sweeping in low in the icy-white flickering light of the burning incendiaries. She blinked. The glare had blinded her temporarily. 'What?' she had begun, but then the question had died on her lips. The shadowy figure had vanished as abruptly as it had appeared . . .

For a while, she had been transported with joy. She had sniffed the ether till she had hardly known what she was doing, unable to keep her fingers from her body, which had run wild with unbridled sexual passion. Every day in her drugged stupor she expected Hardt to appear miraculously. More than once she had dreamed that he had made love to her, his slim muscular loins thrusting in and out of her writhing body, so that she had awoken trembling violently, drained of energy and soaked with hot sweat.

Then had come the anti-climax. The months had passed without any further sign that Hardt still lived. For a terrifying period she had felt that the ether had finally softened her brain completely and she had gone mad, imagining the whole thing. That had been until the letter had arrived from Switzerland. It had been forwarded from Germany by the International Swiss Red Cross in Geneva. It purported to come from her mother, but she knew that it couldn't have; her mother and the rest of her family had long vanished into the camps of the German-conquered East. The final PS had convinced her that she was right. It read like a hastily scribbled afterthought: 'By the way, H, who is sick, sends his undying love.'

Time and time again she had kissed that letter with her thick wet lips until finally the ink had begun to run and she had been forced to stop if she didn't want to lose the message, that precious sign of life and 'undying love', altogether. She realised that she needed to pull herself together. Hardt would expect her to exercise National Socialist discipline, wouldn't he? She started to cut down on the ether, limiting herself to her Saturday night 'orgy', as she called it to herself, when she drugged herself into half-consciousness in that little room in the shadow of the great Gothic cathedral and indulged in her solemn, even ritual, act of masturbation.

But, unknown to Nella Mandelbaum, the damage had already been done. Her brain had indeed been irrevocably damaged by the months of ether. Nella Mandelbaum was forgotten, at least in her own crazed imagination. Now she had become a Prussian aristocrat of the old school. While she still spoke their own language to the 'decadent English', as she now called the people who had saved her life and nurtured her when she had been a penniless refugee, in her own mind her inner monologues were always in her native language, now transformed from the easy-going dialect of Frankfurt, her home town, to the harsh, hacked-off, brisk cadences of Prussia. After all, she was a Prussian, just like her beloved Hardt, wasn't she?

She started to read the literature of the 'New Order'. It was clear to her that sooner or later she would receive the call to serve the Führer and her lover. It would be better to understand them and their aims, which, she already knew, would finally cleanse a 'New Europe' of the decadent Jewish plutocrats and those racial, unworthy lick-spittles who served them.

Now each day started with a solemn 'Heil Hitler' to herself in the little mirror. Whenever she knew *he* was going to speak, she thrilled as she listened to his coarse Austrian voice over her tiny radio. More often than not, she sang the *Horst Wessellied* to herself as she wound her crazy, staggering way through the narrow cobbled streets of the ancient city, savouring the references to the 'long knives' and the spilling of 'Jewish blood'. But always she waited for the signal – that call to action –

which, she knew implicitly, would bring her together once more with her beloved Hardt. Now, finally, after all these weary months of praying, hoping and waiting, it had come.

'The call,' she muttered to herself, ignoring the driving snow, eyes glowing feverishly. Up ahead, the square Victorian pile of York railway station loomed up, its walls still blackened from the fire and smoke of the Baedeker Raid of two years before. But the mad woman didn't see a station. Instead she saw the massive stadium of those pre-war days when *he* had strode majestically through the cheering ranks of his brown-shirted followers to present some lucky individual with a medal accompanied by a warm clap on the cheek or a soldierly brave clasping of hands. Soon she, too – she knew it implicitly – she would be meeting him, accompanied by her beloved Hardt to receive some great honour from his very own hands.

Carried away by that heady vision, she raised her hand as she staggered through the snow, a fat, dark, dumpy woman in a masculine suit that she had once bought from Merriman, the Jewish pawnbroker in Petergate, and cried to the wind, '*Heil Hitler!*'

Behind her the special constable who had followed Nella Mandelbaum discreetly ever since he had spotted her in Stonegate shook his old greying head and said pityingly, 'Poor Jewish devil . . . What a life she must have led to end like this . . .'

In front, Freifrau von Stolzembourg knew nothing of this. Her vision was filled exclusively with the war-damaged station which had been transformed by magic in her crazy mind to that great stadium in far-off Nuremberg. It was her date with destiny. Her moment of greatness had come . . .

Seven

'I don't know exactly how to say this, sir,' Hawkins said slowly, hesitantly. The two of them peered through the windscreen of the stolen Packard as the wipers swished back and forth trying to clear the snow which was now falling in a steady sheet. The Oxfordshire countryside was flat as they drove through the night towards the Great North Road, and empty. Lee, at the wheel, was glad. The big sedan would have been a pain in the ass through hilly countryside. A couple of times he had prevented the automobile from skidding into the ditch on the side of the road. 'Say what?' he said, not taking his eyes off the white blur ahead for one moment. The blacked out headlights were not helping much either.

'Well, it's like you being a Yank, sir,' Hawkins muttered, as if he was finding it difficult to articulate his words. 'You see, I'm an old sweat who's served all over the globe with the Kate Karney – in the Empire, like.' He swallowed, apparently with difficulty. 'I mean, for yours truly, they was all wogs, darkies, nig-nogs.' He shot a quick glance at the black officer, but Lee still seemed to be concentrating on the road totally. 'Now and agen we've had a darkie in charge, especially with wogs in India, some rajah or the like that the government wanted to butter up and made a general in the British Army – honorary naturally.'

'Naturally,' Lee commented a little ironically.

But irony was wasted on Hawkins at this moment. 'But he didn't count. They would let him have a parade, a band and a few salutes from our lads but in the end he was still a wog. You see?'

'I do.'

'Yessir. This is the first time that a darkie – I mean a black man – has ever given me an order and I've taken it serious, like.' Hawkins shook his head like a sorely puzzled man, 'I don't know what to make of it all, sir, that's the honest truth.'

Lee jiggled the wheel to avoid some deep snow and remembered his boss in France telling him that he was fifty years ahead of his time. One day the blacks would have a say in the affairs of their country, but not now – thank you very much. 'Perhaps it's because I'm an American and not on account of my being black, Hawkins?' he said gently. He liked the tough little Limey sergeant, but there was no reason why the latter should understand the complexities of segregated America.

'Yessir, perhaps that's it, sir,' the Britisher said, grateful to be let off the hook. 'But I had to say it, sir, you understand.'

Lee nodded and caught a brief glimpse of the convoy sign, posted by some military policeman. He couldn't read the military shorthand, but he did know it indicated that they were approaching the Great North Road and its convoys heading south towards the Channel Ports and the fighting front.

'You're a Yank, you know, sir,' Hawkins stated the obvious, 'and you're the new bosses. I know how the lads make cracks about the Yanks, you know, one man in the line and five men to bring up the coca-cola.'

Lee laughed.

'All the same, you're running the show now and I think you'll keep on running the show when this bloody war ends, if it ever does. Winnie might think he's in charge, but really it's you Yanks. That's why you're giving the orders and I'm tak—' He broke off, sudden alarm in his voice when he spoke again. 'Up front! Police patrol!'

Instantly their discussion was forgotten as they craned their necks to see who was standing in the middle of the little country road, waving a red lantern and obviously indicating they should stop.

Instinctively Lee changed down. The big Packard shimmied a little on the slick wet snow, but he held it, while Hawkins stared intently at the burly figure with the lantern, huddled to the eyeballs in a heavy khaki overcoat. He could just make out the other dark figures on either side of the road, leaning against motor-cycles, with what looked like carbines – American Springfield carbines – slung over their shoulders; or in one case held challengingly at the ready. Suddenly he cried, 'It aint our lads, sir . . . it's yours – *Yanks* . . . an' they're gonna stop us, sir.'

'Christ on a crutch!' Lee exclaimed, automatically changing down to second now and reducing his speed to a safe ten miles per hour, 'you're right. But what—' He didn't finish the question. The big man in the centre of the road was whirling his gloved hand round, indicating that Lee should unwind the window and now, in the faint light cast by the headlight slits, Lee could see that he was faced by a tough, typical redneck, stump of an unlit cigar held in his thick, slack, contemptuous lips, his expression one of complete control, as if nothing on this earth was going to faze him; *he* was the boss.

Lee had known that look ever since he had first gone south to visit his grandparents in the early 1930s. It said, 'I'm gonna get me a nigger . . . an officer nigger, and, brother, I'm gonna put his nuts right through the mangle, you'd better believe it.'

'Why us?' Hawkins put his alarming thoughts into words. 'I mean . . . Yank MPs out here in the middle of the night and in the middle of frigging nowhere?'

'It's us,' Lee answered grimly, his handsome face hard and set. 'That arsehole Colonel Katz has posted me AWOL. He's probably reported me as having stolen Army vehicles as well. That guy wants me in Leavenworth – for life.'

Hawkins swallowed hard. 'Cor, ferk a duck,' he managed to say and added a moment later, as the car slowed down even more and to their front the big MP grinned in spite of the driving snow, as if despite the time and the weather he was set to enjoy what happened next, 'What's the drill now?'

Lee didn't answer immediately. He didn't quite know himself. All he *did* know was that he was going to get out of this. No big redneck was about to give him a hard time in this Godforsaken spot where he could do what he liked to a black who was on the run. 'Hold tight!' he cried with a sudden burst of excitement.

'Sir—' Hawkins began.

Too late. Abruptly Lee put his foot down on the Packard's accelerator – *hard.*

The car shot forward, skidding and shimmying on the snow. Grimly Lee held on, driving straight at the big MP. He yelled something. The red lantern fell to the snow. Next instant he jumped for his life and they were racing through the road block, with the other cops unslinging their carbines and pumping the first slugs on automatic at the departing Packard, while Hawkins gasped and cried, 'That's fuckin' torn it, now sir . . . The bleeding rozzers are after us!'

They were. In the rear-view mirror Lee could see the first of the startled MPs to recover, straddling his big machine and attempting to kick-start it in the freezing dawn air. Lee didn't hesitate. He put his foot down on the accelerator, taking crazy risks on the slick, white surface, heading for the Great North Road, hoping that he could submerge himself in the convoys that roared up and down the trunk road day and night, twenty-four hours a day . . .

'Get me the Limey Provost Marshal,' Katz yelled to the operator, beside himself with rage. While he waited, looking like some fat middle-class, small-town businessman in his dressing gown and minus his glasses, he snapped to his aide, 'Durand, I want this uppity nigger, Lee, crucified, do you understand that? Now he's just attempted to run down and murder an American sergeant and refused a military order to stop. I think that justifies our people taking his black hide. I don't want no candy-assed protocol and all that crap. If our people get him before the Limeys, they're to shoot first and ask questions later.'

Major Durand of the 11th Armored Division's legal office looked horrified. 'But, sir, you can't do that, even in a state of emergency. Lee has to have a proper trial according to the Code of Military Justice, Article 82a, if I'm not mistaken.'

A red-faced Katz looked at the bespectacled ex-civilian lawyer contemptuously. 'Aw, forget the legalities, Durand. This is frigging war. Hundreds of our guys are gonna die soon, without the benefit of Article frigging eighty-two of whatever it frigging is; who gives a shit about one lone nigger?'

'All the same, sir—' Durand tried once more. He didn't get very far.

'There's no two ways about it, Durand,' Katz cut him short. 'Nail the nigger or, Major—'

'Sir?'

'We're awfully short of infantry officers at the front. I could see if I could get you an immediate posting out. You read me?'

Durand 'read' the Colonel. His liberal principles flew out of the window. 'I'll get right on to it, Colonel.'

'You just do that,' Katz said with a knowing smirk on his fat face.

Katz went out and prepared himself mentally for the great search which would soon commence. He hadn't told Durand that the Division was to drive to its assemble area in the Southampton region this very night. Soon there'd be mass confusion. After all, there were over 15,000 GIs and hundreds of tanks and soft-skinned vehicles ready to be moved. Who would care in the light of all that and the fact that the Division was vitally needed at the front (Patton was screaming out for reinforcements for his hard-pressed Third Army) what happened to one lone, black officer, who really didn't belong to a fighting outfit? 'Washington, boy,' he said to himself, as if he were addressing an already arrested Lee, 'you've blotted your copybook by being an uppity nigger . . . Now, Washington, you're gonna have to pay the price for it. Amen.'

Pleased with himself, he put on his helmet liner and then took off his bathrobe so that he could clamber into his combat gear, Lee already forgotten, while he considered whether he should ask the divisional photographer to take a picture of him in full battle gear for the record. The folks back home would be thrilled, and it wouldn't do him any harm with his local masonic lodge. He decided he would go ahead with the idea that very morning before the shit really hit the fan. Pleased with himself, he started to dress. Outside, it continued to snow, as if it would never stop again.

The woman was crazy, absolutely *meschugge*, the 'Little Doctor', alias Colonel Frank Fisher, told himself as he sat on the bed in the tight little low-ceilinged room with its medieval beams. She was parading before him in all her disgusting fat, wearing nothing but a pair of black-patched flannel bloomers and with, of all things, a swastika brooch between her dangling tits. And it was obvious, he told himself with a little shudder of apprehension, what she wanted from him.

He had known she was eccentric. The neutral Spanish diplomat from London who had activated her for the German *Abwehr* had mentioned that. But he had not mentioned that she was stark raving mad. Heaven, arse and cloudburst, she had even spoken German to him when she had made contact at the station. In a shitting very loud voice, too.

Now she paraded back and forth, her fat wobbling disgustingly, barking out her instructions as if she were some damned drill instructor – and again in German. Fortunately the medieval house was empty. There was a fruiterer's shop called *Annan*'s, but as there was no fruit left in England, it seemed, it had long been empty. No one could hear her loud-mouthed ranting. Still, as he squatted, inwardly miserable, he kept smiling encouragingly as if he were hanging on her every word.

'Naturally I will accept your orders, *Herr Leutnant*' (she had decided on account of his appearance that he could not possess a higher rank than that). 'You are after all the one who knows the assignment, but you must remember that while you are a guest at my headquarters here, you come under my command. Naturally you are my subordinate. Is that perfectly clear?' She rapped out the question with so much force that her breasts trembled like great custards.

'Yes, yes,' he said hurriedly. 'But *Freifrau* – ' he thought he'd better use her absurd title – 'I won't be here very long. Two days at the most be—'

172

'The date of the attack?' she interrupted like some high-ranking general staff officer impatient with the bumblings of a junior planner.

'Christmas Eve.'

'Excellent choice – day of celebration for us Germans, what? We will celebrate, too. No matter I shall leave the planning to you.' She ceased shouting and looked at him hard like an officer trying to sum up the quality of his command, which was about to go over the top. 'But I must brief you on the sexual matter.'

His mouth dropped. 'Sexual matter?' he managed to gasp.

'*Jawohl. Ja.*'

'But we have other plans and priorities—' he attempted to object weakly.

'*Unsinn*,' she snapped. 'The sex is vital, you must realise that.'

He swallowed hard and was even frightened at the look which had crept into the crazy Jewish woman's eyes. She was as mad as a March hare. He couldn't work with a demented woman like this. Abruptly he realised that she would have to be got rid of. 'How vital?'

'As a process of purification before battle like our aryan forefathers, those blonde, blue-eyed, brave giants once did. A bath and sex is the only way, you must understand that, although you are a mere humble junior officer?'

'Yes, yes,' he said hastily, trying to humour the grotesque half-naked woman with her patched black bloomers and swastika. 'I see, *Freifrau*.'

He did. Nella Mandelbaum, who now in her madness called herself Freifrau von Stolzembourg (crazy in itself) would not survive for that sexual ritual of Christmas Eve 1944. He couldn't leave such a demented witness behind. If he were going to live – she must die!

Eight

'The guy's nuts!' Lee yelled above the roar of the Packard's motor.

Hawkins shot a glance to his right. They had shaken off the Yank MPs ten minutes ago now; the going was too treacherous for them to keep up any speed on their motorbikes. Now the Great North Road was just beyond the next roundabout and he had thought, as the first harsh, crisp light of a winter dawn broke to the east, they were relatively safe. Now he knew from the alarm in Lee's voice that they weren't. And the black officer was right. Bounding along a snowy field track, skidding and sliding recklessly, was the big cop who had first stopped them, racing to beat them to the crorssroads. His intention was obvious. He was going to block the narrow entrance, probably with his bike, and, if necessary, prevent them getting any further with his weapon. He looked the type who wouldn't hesitate to use his .45 at the first sign of trouble. His fellow cops had already proved that at the first roadblock. 'Put yer foot down, sir!' Hawkins urged, shouting above the roar of the sedan's engine as Lee concentrated on beating the miliary policeman to the crossroads.

Dangerous as it was on the slick surface of the snow, which had now ceased falling, Lee did just that. Hawkins held his breath, his hands turned to claws, as he willed the driver to beat the cop. Once they were on the Great North Road, which would undoubtedly have been cleared of snow – after all, it was the vital military road link between north and south – the Packard with its huge V-8 engine would

174

easily outdistance the 'governed'* motorbike their pursuer was riding so dangerously.

But even as he willed Lee to succeed, a tense Hawkins could see that the cop was beating them. He was riding his bike with absolute disregard for his own safety. Time and time again he seemed about to lose control of the bike in the snow-heavy country lane, but at the very last moment he caught the machine before it skidded and flung him off.

Now Hawkins could see him quite clearly in the harsh light which outlined everything a stark black and white. To the little sergeant he seemed like the Devil incarnate in his leather helmet and huge goggles, his teeth bared despite the biting cold, as if he couldn't wait to bite them into his prey's flesh. Frantically Hawkins prayed he would skid and come off before they reached the crossroads. But that wasn't to be. And already the cop had freed one gloved hand and was fumbling with the flap of his pistol holster. It was now only a matter of moments and the clash would take place.

Lee must have read his dire thoughts, for he said through gritted teeth, 'Hold on to your tit-for-tat, Hawkins.'

Hawkins didn't appreciate the American's use of cockney rhyming slang, presumably for his benefit. He was too concerned with the approaching cop. 'The bastard's gonna do it, sir!' he yelled.

'No he isn't. We're not going to be stopped by anyone now!'

Hawkins flashed a look at the Yank's intent face, his handsome features streaked with sweat so they appeared to be filmed in grease. 'But what—'

The words died on his lips as the motorcycle cop bounced down the verge from the track in a wild flurry of snow, for a moment appeared about to lose control of his bike, caught it just in time and swerved round in a triumphant curve, and, as he pulled out his pistol, started to brake to a stop.

---

* Some military vehicles were fitted with a 'governor' which prevented them going at high speeds. Usually the maximum was 50 m.p.h.

But, if the big MP thought he had finally beaten the fugitives, he was wrong. Now Lee acted instinctively. All his young life he had based his actions on reason, knowing that as a black man he already had several strikes against him. Now he was motivated by hatred and passion. Here he was trying to do his best for his native country and the official representatives of that country were determined, it seemed, to stop him doing so. It wasn't fair, but then life wasn't fair; and now he'd act like them – unfairly and illogically, intent solely on revenge.

It was clear that the MP expected him to turn left in the direction of the great trunk road and then skid to a halt when it became clear that he, the cop, wasn't going to abandon his bike and jump for safety. Lee thought differently. He bit his bottom lip with pent-up rage. His dark eyes flashed with anger. His jaw clenched and then, changing down to third, he drove straight at the cop, while Hawkins, yelling wildly for him to stop, hung on for his very life.

Crazily the big saloon swung round the bend. The cop fired instinctively. It was a lucky shot. The windscreen of the Packard shattered into a glittering spider's web.

'*SIR!*' Hawkins yelled, blinded momentarily with glass splinters. But Washington Lee wasn't listening to sweet reason any more. He shook his head. His vision cleared. Through the bullet hole in the windscreen he could see the cop fumbling wildly with his big Colt. A stoppage perhaps? The man raised the pistol once more. He stood there in the middle of the snowy road, arm extended with the weapon, the other holding on to his bike as if he were back on some peacetime pistol range in the States, with all the time in the world. There was a look of total confidence on the redneck's face. The nigger wasn't going to harm him, it said.

Lee floored the gas pedal. The Packard raced even faster. The cop grew larger and larger. Hawkins shouted something. Lee didn't hear. His whole being was concentrated on that hateful figure. The cop caught on. *The nigger was not going to stop*! He yelled something. His pistol wavered. He let go of the bike. He was going to jump out of the way. The Packard was nearly on him. His mouth opened in what might have been a scream. Too

176

late! Next moment nearly a ton of metal slammed into him. His body flew upwards. A second later it was lying crumpled like a rag doll in the furrowed snow, the bright red blood staining its white into a star of sudden death.

They thundered on. Next to Lee, who was now panting as if he had just run a a great race, Hawkins slumped back in his seat, knowing now that there was no going back. The cop was dead. They were lost . . .

The 'Little Doctor' was glad to get out of the crazy woman's place. It was cold and snowy and he didn't really have warm clothing, but he could stand the cold as long as he could get away from her mad posturing. Idly he wandered the narrow, snow-bound streets of the ancient city. It would be Christmas Eve on the morrow, but he had still not been able to find a suitable place from which to transmit. Her flat was out; the less she knew of his activities the better. The crazy Yid could be picked up at any time with her mad Nazi and openly pro-German attitude. Besides, the one-time tourist haunt, Stonegate, had proved unsuccessful for a transmission. He had tried a fifty-second 'spurt' in morse, but there had been no response from the great *Abwehr* listening centre just outside Hamburg. Later he reasoned why. Most of the medieval houses in the street had long since sunk so that one or two were nearly two metres lower than when they had been originally built some 500 years before. Not only that – York, he had discovered, was situated in the Vale of York. Surrounded by hills to north and east, a message from the city to Wentdorf receiving station across the North Sea and due north-east, would find it difficult to surmount the heights. He had to find a place that would do that for him and yet at the same time be easily accessible after dark on Christmas Eve, which would be about three thirty or four in the afternoon at this time of the year, he estimated.

Slowly he wandered around apparently casually, but with his keen, intelligent eyes searching the little lanes and alleys, which were everywhere in that warren of medieval streets, for some likely spot. There were few people about. The sun had appeared, bright and cold, set in a sparkling-blue, crisp winter sky. But it hadn't encouraged many shoppers, although it was close to the great festival. But the shops were pretty bare and wherever there was something for sale there were long queues of patient women in headscarves, who looked so weary that they didn't even want to gossip.

He supposed it was the same everywhere in Europe. The war had simply gone on too long. People were sick of it, bored with it. Outside the Mansion House a hoarse-voiced old news vendor in a battered cloth cap and raincoat, tied at the waist with rope, was calling, 'Latest from the Western Front . . . Yanks go over to the attack. Get yer *Yorkshire Evening Press*.' But no one seemed particularly interested in the 'Latest from the Western Front' and it looked as if the old man would take a long time to shift his *Yorkshire Evening Press*, whatever that paper was.

He spotted an elderly bobby, pushing an old bike through the dirty, slushy snow, red-faced with the effort. The man was concentrating solely on the task in hand. All the same, he thought it wiser to turn and get out of the cop's way. He turned slowly, eyes raised, as if he were surveying the view like some pre-war tourist. Then he spotted it and could have kicked himself for not having done so earlier. The twin spires of the great Gothic cathedral, which dominated the medieval city below. '*Natürlich,*' he said to himself, using German, which he had always tried to avoid in case he used his native language in his dreams and gave himself away. '*Die beste Lage.*'

It was the best position. Hadn't he read somewhere that it had the highest spires of any cathedral in Northern Europe? Whether that was true or not, any transmission from up there would clear the hills. And wouldn't a church of that kind be open on Christmas Eve, even quite late?

He grew happy at the thought. It had been a long haul and, though he would have his revenge on the *Amis* at the end of it all, he knew that his triumph would be short-lived; they would win finally. After all, they were the new superpower. Now it was time to complete his part in the deal he had made with his native country and then make his own arrangements for survival in

178

the post-war world of a defeated Germany, which would be universally hated. Send the signal for the uprising and, while the Allies were busy trying to sort out the resultant chaos, he would ensure he left Hull – a mere 50-odd kilometres away – for a new life in some neutral country, starting with Sweden.

She was waiting for him when he returned to that tight little apartment. Despite the freezing cold she was half-naked – she had just returned from her job with the Quakers, she explained, and wanted urgently 'to wash off the filth of those wretched cretins and imbeciles from her pure aryan flesh'. He nodded and made no comment as he eyed the rolls of her dark oriental flesh with distaste. 'Aryan flesh, my arse,' he said to himself, as she towelled vigorously beneath her hairy armpits before she pulled down her baggy bloomers to reveal the great tuft of black hair there and began scrubbing away between her fat legs, as if her very life depended upon it.

Finished, she gasped, a little out of breath with the effort. 'Now, orders for Christmas Eve.'

'Yes?' he said without enthusiasm. He would dearly have loved to look away from that gross, half-naked body as she finished her towelling and started to get dressed slowly, as if she wished him to feast his gaze on it. But he knew he dare not. The woman, brain softened by years of sniffing ether, was totally unpredictable. She might well run on to the street outside at any moment and commence shouting their secret to the world. He couldn't risk that. He'd have to stand her and her demented wishes for a little longer – unfortunately.

'On the morrow,' she announced deliberately, as if she had given the matter much thought, the reality of the day – the commencement of Operation Trojan Horse – completely forgotten, 'we will celebrate our holy feast of Christmas Eve. There will be no gifts. We do not need them.' She looked hard at him with crazy eyes. 'We have our superb aryan bodies to exchange – and that is sufficient.'*

* In Germany Christmas presents are exchanged on the afternoon of Christmas Eve in front of a Christmas tree.

'Yes,' he said tonelessly.

'I have obtained two bottles of my – er – medicine from those pious hypocritical Quakers and have stolen a bottle of wine for you.'

She looked at him sharply and he responded with a quick, 'How good you are to me.' Under his breath, he muttered, 'Hell fire, you crazy bitch, get on with it.'

'We shall celebrate,' she continued,' and when we feel ready for the act of sexual congress, this is what you shall do.'

Down the street the great bell boomed once more, as if to remind him of *his* task on the morrow. 'Yes, please tell me,' he said with fake enthusiasm and eagerness.

'One,' she ticked off the figure with a finger like a hairy pork sausage, 'you will remove my clothing until I am clad in my knickers only.'

He nodded.

'Two, I shall then take the last dose of my medicine and turn on to my stomach on that bed over there.'

Again he nodded his agreement.

'Three, I shall be by now completely in your hands and must exact a promise from you to do as exactly as I am now outlining to you.'

'Of course,' he responded swiftly, telling himself he must be as mad as she was, going along with this absurd farce. By the time she had worked her way through the ether, she'd be in some dreamworld from which it would take a very long ladder indeed to bring her down. She wouldn't know where she was and what the hell she was doing.

'Four, I then wish you to impale me – from the rear.' She had the decency to lower her gaze as she said the last words, though he was shocked by the word 'impale'. But he was in for an even greater one, as she continued with, 'It is not just for sexual pleasure that I suggest this method. It is a form of contraception. We shall wait until we have returned safely to the Reich before performing in a more natural manner so that we can offer our beloved Führer the tribute of pure loins.' She raised her dark mad eyes once more and, smiling winningly at the totally shocked agent, whose mind reeled at the thought of taking this mad Jewess back with him to the Reich, where the only tribute she'd be able to make to the Führer would be via the camp ovens.

For a few moments the 'little Doctor' was too shocked to respond. By nature and profession he was a cynical, virtually unshockable man. He had learned it was easier on the nerves to accept the world as it was. But now, for the first time since he had buried what was left of his poor dear mother, he was shocked beyond all measure, realising just how crazy this war-torn world had become. She was mad, but then they were all mad from Hitler downwards. They were all fighting Fate itself, as if the puny weak pygmies that they were could change things. They couldn't. So they retreated into madness. Suddenly the 'little Doctor', who on the morrow was going to start a minor revolution, felt the urgent need to be sick.

Nine

'*Don't fuck me around, Sarge,*' a weary and hot-tempered Hawkins snorted savagely. 'You've got to get yer knees brown before you can lark around with old "Hawk Eye" Hawkins.'

The pale-faced young signals NCO with the crossed flags on his sleeve protested, 'I can't tell you, Sarge. Honest Injun. It's secret.' He licked his lips. 'I'll lose my tapes if the signals officer . . .' he indicated the next office in the busy central block of Northern Command's HQ.

'Don't worry yer pretty head, chum,' Hawkins reassured him, controlling his urgency though he knew every second counted. It wouldn't be long now till the Yanks were signalling every unit, British and American, in the UK to be on the lookout for the two missing deserters. And one of the first places they'd signal up north was Command HQ. He and Lee needed to be out of this place tootsweet – bloody tootsweet indeed. 'I won't split on yer.'

Still the young sergeant hesitated and Hawkins said, 'Look, chum, I'll make it easy for you.'

'How?'

'Like this. Then they can ask you to swear on a stack of Bibles and you can truthfully say you *told* me nothing.' Not giving the younger NCO the chance to consider, he continued with, 'Nod if I'm right. Shake yer nut if I'm wrong. OK? You picked up an illicit station around this way, didn't yer?'

The signals sergeant hesitated. 'Get on with it, mate,' Hawkins urged, knowing that time was running out for him and Lee, sitting outside in the battered Packard, which was virtually out of petrol now. The young sergeant looked around anxiously and then gave a quick nod. 'That's the stuff to give the troops, Sarge!' Hawkins said winningly. 'Now, was the message something to do with Adolf – Hitler, you know?'

The second question put the NCO in a quandary. He frowned and gestured that he couldn't explain without using words. Hawkins reacted immediately, his brain racing frantically. 'Write, then. I promise on my mother's grave that I'll destroy the message immediately. Anyway,' he added when he saw just how reluctant the signals sergeant was, 'in for a penny, in for a pound. You've spilled yer guts already now.' The threat was all too clear.

He didn't need a crystal ball to know what the wizened little sergeant meant. Hastily he seized his wooden official pen and scribbled something on a message form. Hawkins looked at it, repeated it to himself and then to the younger NCO's surprise and relief, crumpled it up and swallowed it. Thickly, he said, 'Ta, mate. Appreciate it. Got to stick together, us lowly noncoms.' And with that he was gone, just as the telephone next door started to jingle urgently, leaving the other man slumped at his desk, looking very worried.

It was snowing again when Hawkins spurted over to the Packard. Lee had hidden it at the back of the Command car park, with its shattered windscreen close to the wall in an attempt to hide the giveaway sign of damage. For his part he was crouched down in the front, trying to avoid the snow drifting through the gap and shivering with the cold. Under other circumstances Hawkins would have laughed. Lee's face seemed to have turned a kind of sickly white with the cold. But not now. The situation was serious. Now time was ebbing away fast in a race between the big breakout, the US authorities catching up, and his own arrest by the British Army for desertion. As Hawkins would have put it: 'This ain't the time for ruddy larking around' – and he wouldn't have used the word 'larking'.

''Kay,' Lee said, his teeth chattering as he spoke, 'what's the deal?'

'You was right, sir. He's here – the Jerry – somewhere or other. HQ signals picked up a transmission a few hours ago. In morse, is my guess. I gather they jammed it right off because they couldn't locate the spot it was coming from. The signal was too weak and too short.'

'Shit!' Lee cursed. His face fell.

'But they got some of it. Two figures to be exact. Five and a pause and then six.'

'*Five and six*? What the hell kind of signal is that?'

'Search me, sir,' Hawkins said slowly and thoughtfully. 'But my guess is that it's got something to with Mr fucking Adolf—' He never finished. Up near the entrance to the nineteenth-century HQ building, a posse of redcaps in a jeep had skidded to a halt in a flurry of new snow. At the same time an officer, also a redcap, came hurrying out to meet them, buckling on his pistol belt and shouting orders, his breath fogging grey on the chill air. 'That's torn it, sir,' Hawkins moaned. 'I betcha we've been rumbled. That bloody Colonel Katz of yours—'

Lee didn't give him time to complete his sentence. 'Out!' he said. 'They'll have talked to that signals sergeant. They'll know we're around here somewhere.'

He didn't wait to give further explanations; they weren't necessary. Instead he opened the battered door, hoping and praying it wouldn't squeak too much, and dropped into the new snow. A moment later Hawkins did the same. He crouched there, waiting for orders, as the redcaps got out of their jeep and at the command of the officer started to spread out and, in the manner of their kind, started to check each vehicle routinely, although it was obvious that they all belonged to the British Army, and they were looking for an American one.

Lee considered. Should he surrender and tell the Limeys what he knew – that there was a dangerous agent loose somewhere in York, who had to be caught before he could cause a disaster? Would they believe him? He was sure, in the end, they would, despite what Colonel Katz would say and the unfortunate manslaughter of the big redneck military policeman at the crossroads. But by then it would be too late. The fugitive was already practising his signal, which would set off hundreds of thousands of able-bodied Krauts on the rampage. He couldn't afford to take that chance. Time was of the essence. He had to find the Kraut first. Then they could surrender and explain the events of the last few days.

'Are you game to make another run for it, Hawkins?' he hissed.

'You bet yer life, sir,' the other man replied loyally. 'If they catch me now I'm in the glasshouse in Aldershot to the frigging end of me natural days. And look at that!' Nosing its way through a platoon of ATS who were braving the driving snow and swinging their arms like guardsmen, an American sedan was slowly approaching the headquarters. 'Your bloody Colonel Katz is on to us, I swear.'

Instinctively Lee knew the Britisher was right. But this wasn't the time to bewail the fact the US Army had caught up with him already. It was time for action. He flashed a glance around the yard. The marching female soldiers barred the way out of the main gate temporarily. Besides, there'd be an armed sentry offside of the gate in the sentry box and further soldiers in the guardroom. That wasn't the way out. He swung his gaze round the walls. They were high and fringed with razor-sharp broken glass and wire.

Hawkins caught his look of frustration. He hissed, 'The barbed-wire hurdles, sir, next to the motor-pool petrol pumps.'

Lee looked in that direction, noting out of the corner of his eye that the first line of redcaps were getting ever closer. They had only a matter of minutes left. His face fell. The barbed-wire hurdles were about four foot high and packed with brand new wire, all deadly barbs that would take an age to work through. Hawkins cried, 'Never fear. You follow Old Hawk . . . I'll get yer through in a brace of shakes of a lamb's tail. Ready?'

'Ready,' Lee heard himself agree in a shaky, uncertain voice.

Hawkins waited no longer. In an instant he was up and running crazily through the driving snow at the hurdles. Lee followed, wondering if Hawkins had suddenly gone mad. But the old infantry sergeant knew what he was doing. As the redcaps raised the alarm on all sides and the ATS faltered and scattered as the MPs came charging through their immaculate formation, Hawkins flew forward and, without the slightest hesitation, flung himself at the wire, arms outstretched, impaled there, or so it seemed, like some latter-day Christ. But not for long. 'Climb up me, sir,' he gasped as Lee grew closer. 'Don't fuck about, sir . . . Run up me . . . I know what I'm doing.'

Lee hesitated no longer. Wincing at the thought of the pain his body weight must be giving the little Britisher, he scrambled up his spreadeagled body and dropped lightly over the other side. Hawkins was up in a flash. Everywhere the cruel barbs dug deeper into his flesh, making him yelp with pain. But it didn't stop the escapers. His uniform was ripped everywhere, the blood already oozing from a dozen tears, Hawkins was up and running almost immediately, as Lee crouched panting on the other side.

Hawkins flashed him a look. 'Don't stand there . . . like a spare prick at a wedding,' he gasped angrily.

'Yeah, but where—'

'Down to the river and then into the town . . . See that steeple,' he pointed through the flying snow at the vague outline of the Minster, 'That way . . . Come on . . . The town'll swallow us up.' Then, without waiting to see if the black officer was following, Hawkins set off running, arms working like pistons, head thrown back like a champion. Lee darted after him. Moments later the snow had swallowed them up and their pursuers were milling around in angry frustration, as if they wondered what to do next.

Now there were exactly twenty hours to the dawn of Christmas Eve, 1944 . . .

BOOK FOUR:

END RUN

'*God bless ye merry gentlemen . . . let nothing ye dismay*,' the old postman was crooning softly, as he crunched down the street over the frozen snow. '*For Christ Our Saviour has risen this Christmas Day . . .*'

The 'Little Doctor' awoke with a start. He half rose, then realising where he was, he snuggled momentarily back into the comforting warmth of the blanket-strewn sofa. In the next room the mad woman was snoring heavily; he supposed it had something to do with the amount of ether she had sniffed the previous evening. For it was the same sound that boozers make after a heavy drinking session.

He licked his dry lips and stared at the window. It was iced up in fantastic patterns of leaves and bows like he remembered from his youth when his mother used to turn up the green-tiled *kachelofen* and a blessed warmth had streamed through their little apartment, followed later by the smell of fresh coffee and the rolls that the baker's boy hung on the apartment door in a brown cloth bag every morning. He smiled fondly at the memory. It seemed like another world and it was too: one that he could never bring back.

Down at the bottom of Stonegate, where the medieval houses were still lived in, he could hear the elderly postman wishing people, 'Morning . . . Happy Christmas.' His voice sounded genuine enough, but perhaps he was only doing it to earn what the English called apparently, 'A Christmas Box'. Still, it was good to think that the postman really meant it – a little ray of hope in a dreary, war-weary world.

Shivering, he rose from his blankets, put on his outer clothes hastily and glanced through the door to her tiny bedroom. She had no sense of privacy, or shame for that matter. The enamel chamberpot beneath her bed was full of dark-brown liquid and she had thrown back her blankets to reveal her naked loins, that great black thatch and her fat mottled legs spread wide apart, as if she was already prepared for the night's sexual antics.

He looked away hastily. It wasn't a pleasant sight. The thought of having to 'impale' her, as she had put it, made him feel sick on an empty stomach. But there was nothing much to eat on the dirty littered table which served as the kitchen. '*Wie in der vedammte Judenschule!*' he cursed to himself and, tip-toeing into the lavatory so that he wouldn't wake her (he couldn't stand any of her crazy talk at this particular moment), he used the top of the cistern to wash himself from the bowl that still stood, greasy with soap and slick from the previous night, and then shaved. He felt a little better, but he was still hungry. But he ignored the noisy rumbling of his stomach.

Instead he crossed to the tiny mullioned window, rubbed it clear of the thin ice inside, and peered out at the snowy scene. The early morning street was empty. The postman had vanished and those householders who still lived in Stonegate had retreated swiftly indoors once more to enjoy whatever heat those miserably heated houses afforded. He shivered again. All the same, he thought the scene very pretty. All it needed was a couple of red robins to come swooping in to perch on the steep roof of the half-timbered building opposite to make it into one of those Christmas cards that the English delighted in.

A moment later two robins did exactly that and swooped to the ground to pick at the steaming horse apples left by the early morning milkman's horse. He smiled fleetingly. Now it really seemed Christmas.

In the other room, the mad woman's snores increased and became choked jumbles of noise. His smile vanished at the sound. Christmas wasn't going to be the season of goodwill and peace to all men after all. He turned and walked softly to the little bedroom. The mad woman was still asleep. But soon she would awake; he could see that. Already her fat fingers were

190

pawing at the great thatch of jet-black hair through which he could now glimpse the pale pink wet slit.

He looked down at her in disgust. She had been playing with herself earlier in the night. He had heard her bed squeaking frantically. How could any woman be so lacking in shame, he asked himself. She wasn't *that* mad; she must have known he would have heard.

He turned and dismissed the woman – for the time being. He'd deal with her later. Now he concerned himself with the transmission. It would have to be quick and a one-off transmission. Then he'd be off. He'd already planned the way he would go – local train to Pocklington to the east of York. Change there to the East Riding Bus Company as far as Beverley. Change again and take the local busline to Hull. There he'd go to ground in one of the foreign seamen's homes on the long bombed avenue that ran the length of the docks, especially those quays which dealt with wood imports, pit props and the like. There, he guessed, he'd find the neutral Swedish merchant seamen, who could be convinced to give him a passage to their home-land, thanks to the forged Yankee greenbacks, with which he had been plentifully supplied before he had left the Reich on that risky bombing raid.

The thought that he would soon be leaving this wretched cold country and taking 'a dive' in neutral Sweden pleased him. He'd done his duty to the German people and his poor dead parents. Now he was a free man at last. He glanced at his plump, so-German face in the flyblown mirror and winked. Softly, so that he didn't wake up the mad woman, he started to sing under his breath, '*God bless ye, merry gentlemen . . . let nothing ye dismay . . . For Christ, Our Saviour, has risen this Christmas Day . . .*'

'Here ye are, gentlemen,' the jolly old policeman in his open tunic, with the ribbons of the Old War on his breast, boomed happily as he opened the cell door and placed the tray in front of them with a flourish, as if he were a butler in some grand stately home. 'Breakfast, courtesy of the York Police Force.' He stepped back and beamed down at the two soldiers as if he expected praise for his efforts in the kitchen of the police canteen.

He got it. 'Well, I'll go to our house,' Sergeant Hawkins sat up and exclaimed, 'a real egg . . . a real fried egg!' He looked up and shook his tousled head at the beaming constable, as if he couldn't believe his own eyes. 'Wonders never cease! Not a bit o' powdered egg in sight . . . and fried bread done in bacon fat.' He licked his lips.

'And the char's real sarnt major's char,' the happy policeman chimed. 'A whole tin of Carnation Milk in the brew.'

'How can we thank you?' Lee said, taking his cue from Hawkins.

'Well, it is Christmas. And we like to do our little bit for our squaddies, even if you ain't exactly one of 'em, sir, begging yer pardon. But we was all in the Kate Karney in this station in the last show. We know what it's like. So the lads clubbed together with what bits and pieces they had left of their rations to give you a good scoff for your breakfast, at least.'

Lee's heart went out to the fat, red-faced cop. He couldn't see a bunch of American cops doing the same for two GIs who had turned up from nowhere and asked for a bed for the night. According to Hawkins this was standard operating procedure for a British Tommy if he missed his train or something like that – to ask to be put in a cell for the night till he could start again to wherever he was going. 'They know that the squaddie's not up to mischief – on the trot or something o' that sort – he wouldn't go to the nearest lock-up if he were, and it keeps him off the streets after the midnight curfew and saves them bothering themsens with checking his leave pass and the like.'

It had worked and taken the heat off. For they had spent a quiet night in the bare-walled nineteenth-century cells near the river, warm and snug under piles of grey woollen blankets. Now they were being treated to a splendid breakfast, complete with a fried egg – a rarity in wartime Britain, where, as Lee knew, the citizens cracked, 'One egg *per* person, *per* week, *per-haps*.' Realising that he hadn't eaten since early the day before, he tucked into the stodgy food, including the unfamiliar fried bread, with a hearty appetite. He even enjoyed the tea, so thick and rich with the canned milk that he could have stood a spoon upright in it.

Hawkins ate heartily under the warm gaze of the policeman, who in honour of Christmas was wearing a sprig of holly in his tunic buttonhole, but all the same he was not going to waste this chance of attempting to find their quarry. Apparently casually, as he nibbled his fried bread, the grease running down his chin, he asked, 'I suppose you have some Jerries on yer books here – I mean a big place in York must have had Jerries here even before the war, eh?'

The question didn't seem to surprise the bobby. He answered without hesitation, 'Ay, there used to be a lot of 'em earlier on – pork butchers and them that worked in the chocolate trade, Rowntrees and Terrys.' Hawkins cast a significant look at Lee at the mention of 'chocolate'. 'But most of them was interned in the last show and those who wasn't came in for a lot o' stick from the locals, window-breaking, terms of abuse and the like, especially after the Zeppelins bombed York in 1915. So they went after 1919.'

Hawkins speared a piece of the cops' bacon ration and pretended not to be overly interested. 'And now?'

'Them Jews,' the cop answered. 'Them Jerry and Austrian Jews who started coming in 1938. Most of them were in the clear – after war broke out. We checked them that was classified as enemy aliens, like. But them that was dangerous was sent to the Isle of Man when Old Winnie ordered 'collar the lot' back in 1940. Them that stayed here is a harmless bunch of folk, well, for foreigners that is.' He frowned.

Outside, some luckless inhabitant of the other cells was reluctantly sweeping away the snow, moaning to his guard, 'I know me rights . . . I'm not supposed to work like this,' to which the elderly guard growled, 'And yer'll know a bloody clip around the cakehole if you don't shut up an' get on with it.'

Lee noticed the frown. Swiftly, but without appearing to be too interested, he asked, 'Any trouble with these enemy aliens lately?'

'Funny you ask that, sir,' the policeman answered. 'But there was. We had a request to check out one of them Jewish ladies. She's a bit round the twist, like. You'd think she was a Nazi instead of a refugee. But I won't go into details. Anyhow, we was ordered last week by the Assistant Chief Constable hissen to have a look at her place in Stonegate – that's in the city centre – to see if she had company.'

Lee flashed a look at Hawkins.

'Company?' Hawkins took up the questioning, 'what kind of company?'

The bobby laughed heartily. 'Now Sarge, do yer think that the Assistant Chief Constable takes the likes of yours truly into his confidence?' He winked knowingly and lowered his voice. 'But me and the lads think it was something to do with spying . . .'

Freifrau von Stolzembourg farted. Next moment she wished she hadn't. The effort made a sharp pain shoot through her head. It was as if someone had jabbed a pointed stake into the back of her right eye. She moaned softly and felt sick.

Outside, Big Peter, which had wakened her, ceased booming (for which she was very glad) and she realised, as the fog in her ether-befuddled brain cleared, where she was and what day it was. At least she had the day off from the Quakers. After all, it was Christmas Eve. She gave a little sigh of relief. '*Gott sei dank*,' she croaked in German and reached for the glass of water she always kept handy for these occasions. She lifted it to her lips and took a greedy gulp. Nothing. For a long moment she was puzzled. Had she drunk the water already? But the glass seemed full still, as if it contained something. She looked down with her red-rimmed bleary eyes. The water in the glass was frozen solid. She cursed and then, pulling herself together, she staggered to the lavatory and directed a noisy stream of urine into the pan.

She didn't pull the chain – she never did. Instead she cried, 'Where are you?'

There was no answer.

She looked slightly puzzled, but she could rarely show her emotions or feelings now – she was too far gone. Her brain was virtually completely addled. She told herself he had gone to Borden's the grocer in Coney Street to get some non-rationed food, a loaf perhaps. Then she dismissed the missing agent and concentrated on trying to pull herself together in order to face the day that lay ahead, her mind slowly beginning to focus on the sexual pleasures of the late afternoon.

Up in the little hiding place he had made for himself between the low, timbered ceiling and the ancient roof tiles, the 'Little Doctor' watched her slow, shaky progress around the little flat below. Two nights while she had been sleeping off her ether-induced binge, he had worked on the wattle of the ceiling to make this hiding place. It was a provision he had felt he should make. A wise man always provided for every eventuality and, although he could hardly believe that anyone would find him here, it was better to be prepared. As the German phrase had it – quite truthfully – 'care is the mother of the china cabinet'.

Now he studied her from above through his peephole and wondered how – and above all *when* – he should do it. His plan was to alert Hamburg-Wentdorf that he was to send the signal to the camps just after sixteen hundred hours that afternoon. He had picked the time because he knew the English, unlike the Germans, would be celebrating Christmas Eve in their pubs and clubs.* Supervision of POWs would be at a minumum. Thereafter he'd transmit the Trojan Horse signal and the great operation could commence. Then he would be his own master and could – hopefully – disappear in the general confusion. But there was still the problem of the mad woman.

She could describe his appearance. She knew details of his life and with her assistance it would not take one of those cold-blooded, clever, aristocratic Englishmen in Intelligence long to make an educated guess what he had done after the alarm had been raised. So the woman had to go.

* The Germans celebrate the event at home with their families.

Down below, the mad woman was indulging herself in another of those disgusting habits of hers which he found so irritating. She was scratching her fat, dimpled buttocks as if her life depended on it. 'Great crap on the Christmas Tree,' he cursed to himself, 'must you always scratch like that? Makes me feel as if I'm damn well infested myself.' Of course, he knew the constant scratching was due to the ether. All the same, it was damn well unsettling.

He controlled his rage and concentrated on the murder of the unsuspecting fat cow below. He forced himself to think that particularly unpleasant piece through coldly and dispassionately. Under normal circumstances he would have used his training and his experience in the field to do the job as swiftly and as efficiently as possible – and with the least physical effort. After all, he wasn't a very strong man. He would have used his silenced pistol or the stiletto he kept strapped to his stockinged leg. But he knew he couldn't use those instruments of instant death in this case.

It would be too risky. In case anyone discovered the corpse before he was well clear of York that afternoon, he needed to make the murder appear to be a death from natural causes. Naturally, in the end, the police bulls would discover the truth, but by then he would be on the high seas heading for Sweden.

He frowned. She was mad, but also pretty hefty. Indeed, she was taller than he. Also, he had read that mad people sometimes possessed enormous strength when roused. That was the last thing he needed: a noisy battle in the centre of the city on a busy afternoon with a lunatic.

Below, the Jewish woman was now bent, still half naked despite the freezing cold, over her stained, rumpled bed making a half-hearted attempt to tidy it up. She was punching the pillow, which was yellow with the stains where she had vomited in her sleep during one of her ether binges. He wrinkled his nose up at the sight. How could she sleep with her face in a disgusting mess like that? But apparently she could.

Then it came to him and he forget the pillow immediately. Of course, she'd co-operate the whole way, especially if she'd been at the ether bottle beforehand, which he would ensure she had. He smiled for the first time that freezing morning. It would be as easy as falling off a log. His smile broadening as he realised he had solved his problem, he called silently to the unsuspecting woman below, '*Frohes Fest, Liebchen!*'*

'Betty's,' Hawkins breathed as they sought the address the friendly copper had given them (and a pack of Woodbines each, too. 'From the lads at the station. Happy Christmas. And get home safely'). 'Used to be a knocking shop back in 1940.'

Lee didn't know quite what a 'knocking shop' was but, to judge from the crowd of fresh-faced, excited Royal Canadian Air Force officers outside the cafe in the Mansion House square and their girls, all looking like B-girls, he could guess his little companion meant some sort of a 'cat house'. He shook his head in mock wonder. It seemed he learned something about the English every day.

He had come here believing England was something like the Mrs Minniver movie, all class distinctions, with thatched cottages and humble cottagers who knew their place and raised their caps to the gentry; and all of them soaked in tradition and slow-moving – far removed from typical Yankee get-up-and-go. But he had been wrong. Hawkins and the others had shown him that. They might be polite and careful of speech, but they were as smart in a crooked way as any New York wise guy. There were plenty in the States who could learn from ordinary Englishman like his wizen-faced companion . . . and then some.

Slowly they found their way to the entrance of the one-time tourist attraction, Stonegate, with Hawkins telling him his adventures in Betty's after Dunkirk, when he had posed as Captain the Hon. de Vere Hawkins, DSO and had so impressed the girls that 'I could have shagged me way home. In a way, sir, I was glad when I was posted to Egypt and could get a bit of a rest. The bints in Cairo were tame in comparison.' He smiled fondly at the memory.

* Happy Christmas, darling.

The old city was now beginning to come to life. A group of cheerful, dark-haired, Italian ex-POWs now that Italy was an ally classed as 'co-belligerents' – lazily sweeping away the snow. Excited schoolkids, eagerly tugging at their harassed mothers' hands, were urging them to the Coney Street shops in search, presumably, of what toys were still available. Outside the butchers, now decked out in holly and some home-made paper chains, a patient, orderly crowd of housewives waited for '*Offal today, Ration books B to H*', with the luckier ones boasting about the chickens they had managed to secure. Here and there skinny, undernourished kids wearing paper hats were warbling carols at the corners in the hope that someone might offer them a penny or two. It was, Lee told himself, not exactly a Norman Rockwell Christmas, with all the plenty of a rich booming wartime America, but at least it looked like Christmas.

Hawkins broke into his reverie. He pointed to the middle of the street near the sign advertising the Starre Inn, which had apparently been built over 300 years before, presumably a one-time tourist attraction to judge by the faded gold of the board's lettering. 'Should be about here, if that bobby was right, sir.'

Lee nodded his understanding. He eyed the shop frontage and two half-timbered houses on either side. They were, it seemed, as empty as the shop. No smoke emerged from the Tudor chimney, a sure sign that an English house was unoccupied. Yet his keen gaze noted that someone had attempted to remove a circle of frost from an upper window in the house to the right. That seemed to indicate that someone had been in the place as recently as this morning. 'House on the right,' he whispered out of the side of his mouth . . . and keep walking, Hawkins,' he added a warning. 'Just in case the bugger's watching us.'

'Got it, sir.'

Slowly the two of them continued down the little street, dodging a group of schoolboys with crosskeys on their dark-red caps, snowballing each other and crying out in the excited manner of kids in snow. Lee smiled momentarily. How nice to be a kid like that and not know what life was to bring. Pity one couldn't stay a kid for ever.

Hawkins dodged a snowball and said dourly, 'Kids have no respect these days. Fancy throwing a snowball at a senior member of His Majesty's Forces! Wouldn't have done it when I was a—' He broke off abruptly and hissed in an urgent whisper. 'Ten o'clock, sir. Get a gander. Looks like trouble to me, sir.'

A moment later, Lee agreed with him. Two burly soldiers were coming their way, striding through the shoppers in a purposeful, masterly manner and there was no mistaking who they were. Officers in the US Military Police! Lee didn't need a crystal ball to know either why they were in this provincial northern town where there were no US troops stationed and, as far as he knew, there had never been any: they were searching for him. Colonel Katz was going to have his revenge before he went forth to do battle. He was going to pay the 'black bastard' back.

'What we gonna do, sir?' Hawkins asked swiftly. 'They're coming this way. They'll see us soon – you, I mean.'

Lee almost laughed. Of course, for a change, Hawkins, the white guy, was going to be the 'invisible man', as he always thought of the Negro in the US Army. He, among all these whites, was all too visible. But in the event he didn't laugh; the situation was too serious. He had to find a way out.

A moment later he had it, for better or worse. 'Listen,' he snapped urgently, 'I'm gonna take a powder for the time being. You scout out that place,' he indicated the house. 'You've got a picture of the German dame. See if you can get on her tail. She'll lead you to the Kraut, I'm sure.'

'Sir. And you?'

Lee indicated the tall, grey structure outlined against the hard blue winter sky at the end of the one-time tourist trap. 'There. I'll double down one of those lanes. It's a big place, that church.'

Swiftly Hawkins nodded his agreement and said, 'It is.'

'They'll have a job finding me in it,' Lee continued. He flashed a glance at his watch. 'Give 'em an hour to go away and I'll meet you in, say, half an hour after that. 'Kay?'

''Kay, sir . . . and watch yer back.'

But Lee had no time for an answer. The two MPs had quickened their pace, their big feet crunching the frozen snow and slush. They'd spotted his black face. It was the only one around. They were heading straight in his direction. 'So long,' he cried. Drawing a deep breath, Lee swung himself into the little winding lane to his right, which stank of cat urine, and vanished . . .

'Hello,' he said with false cheerfulness as he came through the door with a loaf under his arm, his face glowing as if he had been in the biting crisp air outside for a long time, instead of a mere five minutes.

She turned slowly. She still wasn't fully dressed. But then again, he told himself, she never was except when she went to work. At the other times she was in a state of permanent confusion. One day they'd find her wandering the streets, totally naked like so many other demented women, who seemed to like to take off their clothes for some reason he couldn't fathom. But then, he told himself, as she looked at him puzzled, as if she couldn't quite make out who he was, there would not be 'one day'. This was going to be her last one on this earth.

He shivered dramatically. 'I'd give my right arm for a hot drink,' he declared, 'especially one with an alcoholic kick in it.'

'It's early.'

'You could have something yourself. After all it *is* Christmas Eve.'

'I suppose I could,' she said, showing some interest now at the thought of the ether, just as he thought she would. People like her would sacrifice their own mother, even their kids, for their particular drug. Anyone who wanted to ruin people, the whole human race, only needed to hook them on some particular, easily available drug, and they would be done for. The Führer had got it wrong. Instead of military might in his bid for world power, he should have employed some cheap and effective narcotic. All the Churchills, Roosevelts, Stalins on the globe wouldn't have been able to stop him then.

Half an hour later she was reeling, hardly able to focus her eyes correctly, giggling and laughing foolishly, as he tempted her into sniffing more until he had her in the right state for what he knew he must do – and do soon. He pretended to drink the wine she had stolen for him, but she really didn't care whether he did or not, she was totally concerned with her own pleasures and what was to come. And for some damned reason he couldn't fathom she kept calling him 'Hardt', whoever he was.

By now, seemingly totally unaware that the place was freezing, she was slumped opposite him at the rickety table, flaunting her heavy, hanging breasts, occasionally lifting one of them playfully and pretending to kiss the fat, purple nipple. He supposed she thought that would excite him; in reality those great puddings of hers repelled him. Still, he knew what he had to do. Every now and again he would reach over and attempt to grab one of her breasts, as if seized by an overwhelming passion, crying, 'My God, I just can't keep my hands off you, wench!' to which she would reply, jerking her body out of reach, 'Show a little Prussian discipline, *please*, sir. Wait until I give the order.' Thereupon he would pretend to sulk like some frustrated youth out on his first sexual adventure in the back of a barn and she would add laughingly, 'Never fear, *mein Herr*, you will have the pleasure of my body – soon.'

He barely concealed his shudder at the mere thought.

So the time passed leadenly. Outside, the bells were chiming somewhere. A man went by below, probably already slightly drunk, bawling a Christmas carol in a tuneless bass. A kid began crying, 'You oughtn't to have pushed the ice down me neck, Ticker Kenny. I'll tell me mum on you . . . It ain't fair.' His answer was a snigger and a wet raspberry. A long way off, only barely audible, to the east of the old city the air-raid sirens began to sound their dread warning. The 'Little Doctor' didn't hear. For now the woman was completely gone, laughing her head off at something told her by those crazy inner voices with which she was now conversing, stumbling over her words, her tongue snaking in and out of her loose wet lips, as if it were too big for her mouth.

He conditioned himself for what was soon to come. He knew now he could do the job once he'd got her on to the bed. But he had to get her that far and he knew, too, that there was only one way to do so – he'd have to broach the subject he dreaded most. Indeed, he felt sick and nauseated at the very thought of doing so. He licked his dry lips and, when he spoke, his voice was parched and hoarse as if he had not drunk for a long time. 'I think . . . it's time that we did—' he indicated the rumpled filthy bed and its yellow vomit-stained pillows with a jerk of his head.

She flapped a pudgy hand at him like some young village innocent. 'You naughty man,' she said thickly, foam lingering in the corners of her slack, degenerate mouth, 'you're like the rest . . . Only one thing in yer heads.' She made an obscene gesture with her thumb and forefingers. '*Nur ficken im kopf!*'

Sickened as he was, he played her dirty game. 'No, not in the head,' he said, grabbing the front of his pants suggestively, 'but in the trousers!'

She laughed uproariously and nearly fell from her chair. 'All right then, if you must, you dirty dog.' She rose with difficulty. He jumped to his feet, apparently greatly concerned and caught her ample bulk. 'Be careful, my little cheetah,' he said, 'I don't want you, my beloved, to hurt yourself.' He loathed himself as he said the words.

She chucked him under the chin playfully – and it hurt – saying, 'Well, there's one part, I promise you, that won't be hurt. Ha, ha.'

She collapsed on the bed and, for a moment, he hoped she had passed out. But that wasn't to be. With a grunt she turned, raised herself and pulled off her skirt. 'The knickers, I shall give you the pleasure,' she said in a voice muffled where she pressed her mouth into the dirty blanket. 'One moment.' With another grunt, she tugged away one of the filthy, disgusting pillows and, squirming mightily, inserted it under her abdomen. 'The knickers,' she said in a voice that was almost gone. 'The rest is yours.' She wiggled those tremendous black-clad buttocks in what he assumed she thought was a seductive manner . . . 'The knickers,' she said again in that fading, drugged voice. 'All . . . all . . . yours.' Then she was gone, snorting mightily. For a long moment he stared down at her, sprawled out, bottom raised absurdly into the air. 'Pig,' he muttered bitterly. 'Pigs in shit, indulging in piggery.' Slowly, very slowly, he started to reach for the other pillow.

Lee felt he had to tiptoe. Somewhere in that great expanse of gothic gloom which seemed to mingle with the December haze an organ was playing softly. It could have been Bach. He wasn't sure. But he did know that he was in a place of peace and rest at last; though the curiously unreal blue figure of Christ on the cross, with the drops of red, which were his blood, dripping down his greased, stone face reminded him of violence and war.

Yet Lee, moving almost noiselessly down the aisle with the yellow candles flickering in the breeze, felt a sense of compassion coming from that stone figure. His gaze ran along the frieze – Jesus sinking down beneath the weight of the cross, to which his persecutors were soon going to nail him, as if he were some defeated warrior brought low by the sword strokes of the victors. Although these figures of Jesus represented a white man, he felt a sense of identity. He, too, was in that same position. He knew, with the clarity of a vision, there was no real hope for him. He had to follow that path of doom that had been ordained for him, on account of his skin colour, at birth. There was no escape for him and it had to end in death, his death.

But, as despondent and desperate as Lee's thoughts at that moment might have seemed to some, he himself felt a sense of elation, a kind of joyous elation, at the knowledge that he was coming to the end of the trail which had led him, the son of Southern ex-sharecroppers, to Harvard and the Sorbonne and a commission in the Army of the United States, however bigoted that Army was. It gave him a sense of achievement and hope for the future. Not for his own (he knew now he would never live that long), but for that of those his colour who would follow. Malloy, his old CO at Verdun, had been right.

But even if it did take fifty years, as the tough Chicago ex-cop had predicted, it would *happen*: that was the important thing.

He stopped short and smiled to himself. It was almost like one of those sickly sentimental Hollywood films, perhaps starring Bing Crosby as the lovely Irish priest Father O'Corney. But what seemed an almost heavenly choir was singing in the gloom at the far end of the great grey Gothic nave. The music was beautiful. It soared up to the vaulted roof, drowning out even the wail of the air-raid sirens as they started to cross the city from east to west.

Up ahead in the gloom he heard an official voice call, 'Everyone out of the cathedral, please. An air raid will soon be in progress. Everyone out!'

Lee stopped short, as if puzzled, his reverie abruptly forgotten. A gaggle of little boys in red robes with white lace surplices came sweeping by him out of nowhere. They were the choir of the great church, he guessed. Abruptly the organ ceased playing.

An old man in a dark-blue uniform like that of an English bobby came panting after them, waving his hands as if he were shooing a collection of squawking hens. He spotted Lee standing there a little helplessly in the side aisle. The black face obviously puzzled him for a moment. Then he called, 'Sir . . . sir, you must come out now and follow me to the air-raid shelter in the Zouche Chapel.'

It was then he saw him. A little man in nondescript civilian clothes of an English cut. He looked mild-mannered, even avuncular, in his glasses and with his plump red face. He might well have been some lower-class clerk, enjoying his Christmas Eve away from the noise and smoke of the pubs to which his fellows in the office had gone to celebrate the feast day. But he wasn't. Despite the different clothes and the gold-rimmed glasses, Lee recognised him immediately. He gasped with surprise. There was no mistaking this strange apparition which had suddenly appeared in this provincial English church. It was the same man whom he had spotted in the night-club-cum-brothel in Cherbourg an instant before Marie-Claire had been killed and he wounded. It was his man, he knew that instinctively. It was the Kraut agent!

Lee did not have time to overcome his shock and react there and then. Before he could do anything about it, women came streaming out of the side chapel, dedicated to some long-dead Elizabethan notable, and before he could stop himself, he was swept outside with them into the snowy afternoon . . .

The 'Little Doctor' was quicker off the mark than the American. As that familiar put-put – sounding very much like the noise that an ancient two-stroke motorbike engine might make – came closer and closer, he ducked down behind the chancel. The mob of frightened women in their pre-war hats and headscarves, urged on by the cathedral policeman, streamed into the forecourt, while he crouched there, realising that Skorzeny's bold aerial attack had come right on time; the whole place was his, as the first flying bomb came skidding across the city, red flame jetting from its exhaust. For the time being, at least . . .

Despite the odds of weather, enemy radar, and flak ships off the north-eastern coast, protecting the great ports of Hull and Newcastle, the German operation was turning out to be a tremendous success.

The *Kampfgeschwader* of sixteen planes, mostly Heinkels, was not particularly well trained or experienced, save for the three flight commanders and the officer in charge. But they had managed the long flight from their snowbound bases in Norway without mishap. Once they had cleared German airspace, the twin-engined converted bombers, with their heavy loads, had sunk to almost wave-top height. Mile after mile they had risked life and limb, skimming the white-tipped, grey waters, each crew member knowing that the slightest miscalculation and they would plummet beneath the waves. Then, if the arctic cold didn't get them, the sea would.

But the daring gamble had worked. They had flown right across the North Sea, way below the British radar detectors, until, within sight of the white cliffs of Flamborough Head, they had started to climb in order to gain the height they needed to be able to launch their deadly weight.

Now the pilots and air-gunners, scanning the grey murky skies, were on tenterhooks. For they knew they were already appearing on the green-glowing screens of the enemy radar and the surprised Tommy operators (whom they hoped hadn't expected an attack on this day of 'peace and goodwill to all men') would already be calling the local fighter fields, crying 'Bandits. . . . bandits . . . SCRAMBLE . . . *FOR GOD'S SAKE – S C R A M B L E . . .* !'

Yet even in this moment of greatest tension some of them smiled to themselves at the surprise coming to the British fighter pilots. For all of them, so far away from London and its special air-raid problems, would never have seen 'bandits' like this before.

They hadn't. The British defenders were caught completely and totally by surprise, as the first pilots began reporting their sightings to Driffield, Linton, Bridlington and all the other East Yorkshire bases. 'They're firing frigging buzz-bombs!' they yelled down into their intercom masks. 'The Jerry buggers are launching V-1s everywhere . . .'

They were. For, as Northern England prepared for a jolly night in pubs, clubs and dance halls (as long as the special beer rations lasted), the flying bombs, which had been devasting the British capital ever since the summer, were heading westwards across Lincolnshire and Yorkshire by the score. This terrible type of new warfare had reached the North at last.*

Slowly and carefully, the 'Little Doctor' came out from behind the lectern with its great polished brass eagle and peered about in the bare grey nave. To the West of York there came a muffled thud. Even the cathedral shook momentarily. It was the first of the V-1s, packed with a ton of high explosive, hitting the ground and detonating. But he was alone. He sighed.

---

* In fact, this Christmas Eve attack was the first recorded one in the history of aerial warfare. Long forgotten, this early cruise-missile type of assault heralded the start of modern air combat.

The mad woman was dead. He thought he had heard some-one at the door in the very same instant that he had slightly relaxed his grasp on the pillow ten seconds after she had given her last compulsive sob, her naked right leg jerking upwards like that of a dead chicken. He had not panicked. She was dead, but he had reasserted the pressure, counting off ten seconds. Then he had released his hold on the pillow with which he had suffocated her. This time even the leg had not twitched. She was finally dead, the great dirty cow, but there was definitely a sound coming from below, as if someone was trying to force the medieval door.

He had not panicked. He had been prepared for even that eventuality. The 'stubble-hoppers' of the German infantry called it 'mouse-holing.' In street fighting, the veterans didn't pass from house to house outside on the street where they were vulnerable to an enemy's fire. Instead they worked their way forward down a row of dwellings by breaking open the interior walls with their entrenching tools, or better, moving from loft to loft.

He had done the same, crawling through the dust of centuries from ancient house to house, until finally he had dropped into a backyard at the very end of Stonegate, some 50 yards from where the dead woman now lay naked and choked, and had fled with his case into the great church just before the sirens had commenced sounding their warning.

Now, alone in that vast space, he retrieved the case with the wireless transmitter and stepped into the aisle. Opposite him on the board there was the notification, '*David, 19th Psalm*'. Idly he looked at it, as he unclipped the case's catches and prepared for the long ascent of the central tower. It read: '*How long wilt thou forget me, O Lord? For ever? How long shall mine enemy be exalted over me? Consider and hear me, O Lord my God. Lighten mine eyes lest I sleep the sleep of death.*'

He stopped. He had read enough. Speaking aloud in the manner of lonely men, he said, 'No enemy will be exalted over me this day, O Lord.' His voice was full of confident cynicism. 'No sir!' he grunted as he took the weight of the case, and then he started to climb the endless steps which led to the rooftop of the great church. Operation Trojan Horse had entered its ultimate phase . . .

'*Oh, my God in Heaven!*' the sergeant in the tin helmet stencilled with the word 'POLICE' cried, 'What a mess!' He gasped and grabbed at his collar as if he might choke or be sick at any moment.

Behind him, Hawkins, who had called him from Betty's, experienced the same nauseating sensation. The tip of a room stank and the body lying spreadeagled on the bed gave off an even worse odour. Since her death, she had evacuated her bowels and the stench was overpowering. He swallowed hard and tried not to see her and the yellow stinking mess. Instead, his gaze searched the room for the killer. For the little NCO knew the man couldn't have escaped through the door, the only exit. He'd been there all the while, even, he realised now, as the murder itself was being carried out.

Gingerly the sergeant touched the body, as the police photographer pushed through the door with his box camera. 'Still pretty warm,' he concluded, snatching his hand away quickly as if he might catch something. 'So whoever did it can't be far away.'

'He didn't come through the door, Sarge,' Hawkins said, 'because I was there all the time.'

'So where is he then?'

The photographer looked up from focusing his camera on the grotesque figure sprawled out on the soiled bed. 'Perhaps he's that "Invisible man". I saw in the flicks at the *Regal* last week. Took off his bandages and he disappeared—'

'Shut up and get on with it, you big, stupid lummox,' the police sergeant ordered. 'You've seen too many pictures as it is.' He turned to Hawkins and looked down at him, as if he were seeing the NCO for the first time. 'Now then, what were you doing here in the first place? Seems a bit odd to me. You being at this—' He stopped short. The other man wasn't listening. Instead he was staring upwards at the ceiling of the little living-room-cum-kitchen. 'What d'yer see?'

'That hole . . . that's the way he got out without me seeing him.' Hawkins snapped, 'Come on, don't stand there like a frigging spare penis. Gimme a leg-up and yer truncheon as well. He might still be up there.'

But Sergeant Hawkins had no need of the policeman's polished, leaded truncheon. As he emerged, covered with dust and smelling of bat droppings at the far end of the row, the crop-haired woman with the severe features, who for some reason he couldn't fathom was tying down the heavy breasts of another female in a petticoat with a thick scarf, said, completely nonplussed, 'He got out into the yard. He went that way.' She indicated the passage that led to the west door of the Minster. 'Through yon ginnel.' And as if she encountered a sergeant of infantry appearing from nowhere every day of the week, she went on pulling the scarf ever tighter, telling the other woman, 'Don't kick up such a fuss, Cynthia. You know that we don't like women with big breasts. It's so unmanly.'

Sergeant Hawkins fled.

In front of him the cathedral was outlined a stark melodramatic black by the sudden cherry-red flame of yet another V-1 exploding in the distance. Fifty yards away, Lee dodged the officious Cathedral policeman and ran back towards it in the very same direction . . .

The 'Little Doctor' gasped painfully. A sharp pain was stabbing his side. He felt he couldn't take another step. But he knew he had to. He had to reach the open roof, high above the ground, in order to send his two signals beyond the confines of the Vale of York. The air came through his lungs like the sound of cracked leather bellows as he made the effort. The case with the radio seemed to weigh a ton and it took him a conscious effort of sheer, naked will power to raise his legs to take each of the winding steps, smoothed by nearly a thousand years of devout feet ascending them.

The V-1s were exploding ever further away now. It seemed the surviving flying bombs were heading for other unsuspecting targets further west, and there wasn't a Tommy fighter in sight.

They had caught the English by complete surprise. The thought pleased him. He felt the last surge of patriotism and hoped that Operation Trojan Horse would come as an equal surprise for the English. 'Thereafter, old house,' he told himself happily, 'you can retire gracefully from total war – for good.' Despite the tremendous effort of climbing those last steps, he felt a sense of happiness and smiled. The whole bloody business had seemed to take so long and he had had so many obstacles in its execution, but now it was about to end. In success! Then he could come to a semblance of attention, raise his right hand to his forelock and report – to whom exactly he didn't quite know – '*V-Mann 2722 meldet sich ab. Bitte abtreten zu durfen.*'* That would be a fitting military ending to his long career in the *Abwehr*.

He reached the top, the open parapet, and nearly dropped the case with the precious radio; his body was trembling so much with the effort of climbing so many hundred steps. With hands that shook like leaves, he opened the heavy case. Now, on that narrow platform with the icy wind howling about his ears and York spread out in the growing darkness below, he ran the thin wire aerial from the set to the flagpole, where during the day the flag of St George fluttered bravely. He tied it in a quick knot, trying to control his trembling fingers.

Carefully, for it was slippery on the worn flags of the parapet, he returned to the radio and, crouching there, enjoying what shelter from the wind the raised parapet afforded, he prepared to transmit to that lonely turn-of-the-century mansion just outside Hamburg. In five minutes it would be all over and he would be a free man, relieved of the burden of the war, his past life, even history too, he thought. He could live his remaining years in uncluttered obscurity, pleasantly occupied with the minor linguistic riddle of how in high German the medial double 'ss' became 't' in the low German dialects, including English. Despite the freezing cold, the tension, his virtual exhaustion at the long climb, he smiled at the thought.

* 'Agent 2722 reports his departure. Request permission to withdraw.' *Transl.*

That was a life worth fighting for. He controlled his breathing and, slipping on his headphones, he started to tap out the *Abwehr* call-sign . . .

In the same instant the the Home Guard rocket battery opened fire from the same York racecourse where Hardt von Hartenstein had once been imprisoned before his seduction of the Jewish woman. With a tremendous earth-shaking crack, the multiple rockets shot into the darkening sky. The gunners hadn't a chance in hell of hitting the last of the flying bombs speeding westwards now. But the elderly retreads from the Great War and the youngsters who had not been called up yet had waited a long time to see real action. Now they went to work with a will.

The sudden barrage caught Sergeant Hawkins completely by surprise as he sprinted up the cathedral steps behind Lee. He hesitated in mid-stride as the heavens blazed in red fury. Then he put his steel-shod ammunition boot down once more. Suddenly, surprisingly, his foot went from beneath him. Wildly he grabbed for the rail. His hand missed it. He went down with a crash. For a moment the wind was knocked out of him. He pulled himself together. 'Fuck this for a tale,' he gasped and tried to drag himself up with the aid of the rail. An electric stab of red-hot pain shot through his left foot and ankle. He yelped and dropped to the ground once more, gasping for breath with the shock of that sudden agony. 'Cor, stone the ferking ducks!' he moaned, staring up at the great stone wall of the cathedral towering up above him. 'What a ferking time to break me ankle!'

Washington Lee now knew exactly what he had to do. It was clear to him that his quarry had picked the great church because he needed the height to transmit safely from the valley in which York lay. It was also clear that the place inside the cathedral where he would get the height he needed was the steeple. As he stared through the grey gloom, broken only by the noisy electric-red flashes of the rockets exploding, he could see the narrow arched door, heavy with ancient studs, that led to the steeple's winding steps. He didn't hesitate. Although he guessed the agent would be armed and would be prepared to use his weapon, he wasn't afraid. Indeed the black officer, his face intense, even predatory, was dying to get to grips with his adversary. It had all taken too long and he guessed his military career (at least in a combat role) was ruined now whatever happened. Now he wanted revenge. He moved to the door and opened it.

A chill wind blew down the long stairs. But even its sound and that of the intermittent roar of the rocket batteries a mile or so away couldn't quite cut out the noise of high-speed morse. His guess had been correct. The agent was indeed up on the parapet far above sending his fatal message. Washington Lee drew a deep breath, just as the 'Little Doctor' had done minutes before, and commenced the winding ascent.

Time seemed interminable. Just when he thought he had turned the last bend, with the passage getting ever colder the higher he got, he found there was another flight of worn steps in front of him. Under his breath he cursed angrily and continued.

Up above, the 'Little Doctor', his face a bright red with the biting cold, signed off and, far away in Germany, the unknown operator signaled in morse, '*H und B*.'* He allowed himself a little smile. For him there would certainly be 'happy landings'. He couldn't say the same for the unknown operator over 500 miles away. But he and his fellow Germans, indeed Germany itself, no longer mattered. In a matter of seconds he would be making his separate peace with the Western Allies.

He took his hand from the morse key. He shook it hard to revive the circulation. His hand felt like a block of ice. To his south, the rocket batteries thundered once more. Like a flight of angry red hornets the missiles hissed into the grey sky. Uselessly. He grinned. All war was purposeless. It solved nothing. Still, he told himself, he had made his promise on the bodies of his dead parents and once, in another age, he had given his

* *Hals und Beinbruch*, roughly 'happy landings'.

sacred oath of loyalty to the Führer of the vaunted 'Thousand Year Reich,' which he guessed wouldn't last another year. Now he would use his name as the last signal to those young men behind barbed wire to break out of their cages all over the British Isles to create the murder, mayhem and general destruction that had been planned so long before. Two numbers. 'Five' and 'six'. The numbers of the Führer's own name – *Adolf Hitler*'.

He put his hand on the key once more in the same instant that a voice said in understandable but accented German, '*Lass' das nach!*'

Totally shocked, he did exactly what the voice had ordered. He stopped. Next moment he swung round. Facing him was a tall, lean man in US uniform, his black face lathered with sweat and gleaming, his dark eyes full of controlled rage. '*You!*' he gasped.

'Yes,' Lee said carefully, watching the man crouched there over the transmitter with the utmost care. He knew he was dealing with a man who had wriggled out of situations like this time and time again. He couldn't be too careful. 'Now just take your hands away from that set and place them behind your neck . . . nice and easy.'

'Yes . . . yes,' the 'Little Doctor' responded hurriedly in English, as if he was prepared to do anything to appease this black angel of death. 'I won't do anything wrong . . . Please believe me.'

'I believe you,' Lee said drily. 'Just do as I say. OK?'

The German nodded, as if he were too afraid or shocked to speak now. Slowly, very slowly, he started to comply with Lee's command. His face revealing only that he seemed to be scared out of his wits, he raised his hands from the set. Inside, his brain was racing electrically. There was a knife in his sock. But the lean, tough negro would jump him long before he reached it. But there was the other weapon. Could he? Dare he? With infinite slowness, not taking his gaze off the American for an instant, he did as he was commanded, willing himself an opportunity to grab the weapon before it was too late. For he knew he couldn't tackle the American physically. Besides, it wasn't his style. If he was going to kill, it would have to be that way. Abruptly he broke out in a sweat, despite the cold. He was afraid, really afraid, for the first time in his life. If he didn't succeed in the next few seconds, he'd end up on a rope. The English hanged traitors and convicted spies. For one terrible moment, he imagined that sudden drop, the hemp rope tightening about his fat neck, cutting into the soft flesh, his urine soiling his trousers, tied at the ankles, fighting for breath, the life being choked out of him.

The last burst of the rocket battery at the Knavesmire caught both of them by surprise. Lee caught the full violent flash in his eyes. He blinked momentarily and staggered back. The 'Little Doctor' didn't hesitate. He pulled the little .22 pistol out by the string attached to his neck where it was held down the small of his back so that a cursory body check would never find it and fired in that very same instant.

At that range he couldn't miss. Lee screamed shrilly. The impact lifted him clean off his feet. A great red star of blood welled up instantly in the front of his shirt as he slammed against the parapet and hung there, knees sagging, breath coming in short, shocked gasps, his eyes threatening to close the very next second – and for good.

The 'Little Doctor' hesitated. Should be continue? Should he send and run? Or should he blast the dying negro into eternity and run for it immediately?

Lee didn't give him a chance to consider much further. By an effort of sheer naked will power, feeling his life force stream out of him as he did so, he raised himself. Slowly, one bloody hand stretched out in front of him like a blind man feeling his way, he staggered towards the man holding the gun.

The 'Little Doctor' gazed at him in horror, '*Nein*,' he shrieked hysterically. '*NEIN!*'

Lee continued.

Hardly knowing he was doing so, he pressed the trigger once again. Another bullet slammed into Lee's poor, broken body. The whack of steel hitting soft flesh was clearly audible above the roar of the rocket batteries. Lee staggered violently. His right arm fell abruptly to his side, blood jetting from the great jagged wound in a bright red arc. Still he continued that terrible progress.

The 'Little Doctor' stared at him in horror. 'Please,' he pleaded in English, 'let me go . . . Oh, please.' By now the tears of self-pity were streaming down his face.

But Lee was beyond hearing. He knew he was dying. Yet his brain was working with astonishing clarity and sense of purpose. They were both outcasts – he the Negro; the other, a German and a spy. They *had* to die. No one had need of such outsiders. 'Die . . . die,' he mumbled, the blood frothing at his lips . . . '*Die* . . .'

'*No!*' the 'Little Doctor' screamed high and hysterical like a woman. He pressed the trigger once more. Nothing happened. He did so again in a frenzy of fumbling. Again nothing. He had a stoppage. With all his remaining strength he flung the useless little gun at the dying avenger. Lee easily avoided it and then his hands were around the other man's throat and they were staggering towards the edge of the parapet, with the German screaming, eyes popping out of his head like those of a man demented and Lee, dying on his feet, squeezing his hands tighter and tighter until they were over and falling.

The scream seemed to go on for ever and then they lay there in the dirty snow of the gutter, still locked in that embrace of death like two star-crossed lovers joined thus for all time, with Sergeant Hawkins staring at them in absolute utter disbelief, the tears streaming down his contorted, wizened face . . .

OPERATION TROJAN HORSE WAS OVER.

AUTHOR'S NOTE

Although Operation Trojan Horse failed, there were escapes from German POW camps all over the United Kingdom in the remaining five months of the Second World War. Desperate, fanatical, bored, sex-starved German POWs escaped singly and in scores from POW camps reaching across the country from Scotland to South Wales.

Most of the escapers were soon recaptured; a few got away, with, in a couple of cases, the Germans reaching their own country eventually (one of the escapers decided he didn't like ruined post-war Germany and actually returned, asking politely if the camp authorities would let him in again. They obliged).

Another, a Herr Teske, let out on parole at the end of the 1940s, was actually forgotten by both the British and the new West German authorities. For years he petitioned both for repatriation. His request was ignored. In the end Herr Teske, the last German POW at large in Britain, decided to live out his days in Milton Keynes.

Sergeant Hawkins? Despite the fact he was over-age for front-line service, the little regular volunteered for active service in early 1945. That year the British Army needed 'bodies' urgently. A blind eye was turned to the fact that he was at least twenty years older than his fellow infantry. He lasted a week in combat. He was killed at the crossing of the Rhine in late March 1945. And there he rests, ironically enough in the soil of that alien country which he hated so much. The fact says something about life, but I don't really know what . . .

Leo Kessler, Bleialf, Germany

217